Pandemonium in 2012

LEE CROSS

Pandemonium in 2012

Virginia City Publishing
P. O. Box 51389
Sparks, NV 89435

Copyright © 2008
Leland W. Cross

For permissions, or serializations, condensations, adaptations, or for our catalog of other publications, write the Publisher at the address above.

This novel is a work of fiction. Any references to real people, events, establishments, organizations, or locales are intended only to give the fiction a sense of reality and authenticity. Other names, characters, places, and incidents portrayed herein are either the product of the author's imagination or are used fictitiously.

ISBN: 0-978-7596-2-1
ISBN: 978-0-9787596-2-9

Cover Design: George Foster
Interior Design: Desktop Miracles, Inc.

Printed in the United States of America

Publisher's Cataloging-in-Publication
(Prepared by The Donohue Group, Inc.)

Cross, Lee (Leland W.)
    Pandemonium in 2012 / Lee Cross.
      p. ; cm.
    ISBN-13: 978-0-9787596-2-9
    ISBN-10: 0-9787596-2-1
    1. United States—Politics and government—2001– —Fiction.
2. Presidents—United States—Fiction. 3. Twenty-first century—Forecasts.
4. Adventure fiction. 5. Political satire. I. Title. II. Title: Pandemonium in two thousand twelve III. Title: Pandemonium in two thousand and twelve
PS3603.R67 P36   2008

                                     813/.6

INTRODUCTION

How can I best introduce this political satire? Is it fiction, prophecy, how about literary insanity? As a work of fiction, this story might come closer to reality than any of us would want. You may see an allegory here. Cassandra was a daughter of Priam, King of Troy. She was also a priestess to Apollo, but she angered him. In response, he gave her the gift of prophecy. Everything she prophesied would come true. But there was a dark side to Apollo's gift; no one would believe her. This work is not designed solely for diversion, but also to promote critical thinking.

Almost everything within these pages actually has a true or potential parallel in these troubled times. Many of the more outrageous aspects of this book are totally factual, though locations, names and dates may have been altered. Except for past presidents and a few other world figures whom I deem unworthy of camouflaging their identities, any casual resemblance to a living person is purely coincidental. It is the hope of this author that the content of this novel remains just a good rip roaring yarn. If not, we should have listened to Cassandra.

Lee Cross

I, Martin Raggio, lived through it. If only Illyana were still by my side, life would have meaning. But life doesn't make many promises. I guess I just have to take what it offers up. Almost there now, I can see it across the canyon straight ahead. I can relax in Virginia City; maybe even forget for a few hours. No; I'll never do that. At least we erected stones for George and the others. And Jim Scott sent me an email; he received my memoirs. I was the last of the surviving Patriots to write them. Someday, long after we're gone, maybe someone will even publish it. I don't care. Every day I only live for what lies around the next corner.

The cold wind in my hair feels good. This powerful Harley under me is begging for speed. A few more turns in the road and I'm there. What's that ahead? That idiot passed on the curve; he's heading for me . . .

———

It was thirty years after the death of Martin Raggio. Most of the leaves had fallen and the air was crisp on this November day in 2046. Snow would be coming soon. The Moran family was celebrating Thanksgiving on their farm in central Ohio. They congregated around the dinner table, standing and holding hands as they bowed their heads. The father invoked the blessing, "Heavenly Father, we give thanks for the food thou hast placed before us. We thank thee for each of us here today. Bless this food that it may give nourishment to our bodies. May thou bless and keep us all in thy kindness and eternal love."

All answered, "Amen."

After dinner, the father walked into the living room and sat down in his favorite chair. Seven year old Renee ran up to him and held out her open palm. "Look, Daddy; what I got! Aunt Emily gave it to me."

Dave Moran smiled as he took the shiny new half dollar from his daughter's hand. "Yes, honey! I've seen a few of these. They put President Nancy Colton's image on these new ones!"

"Who is Nancy Colton, Daddy?"

"She was one of our greatest presidents, honey. She led us during the reorganization after the great pandemonium in 2012. Her administration brought the rebirth of our country. Unrestrained prosperity and peace returned."

"What's a pandemonium, Daddy?"

"It was a horrible time in our country's history, honey. As a nation, we almost ceased to exist. If not for Ramsey, we wouldn't be sitting here today."

"Who was Ramsey, Daddy?"

"He liked to style himself as just an ordinary man, Renee. Oh, but he was so much more than that! His inspiration saved our republic. Then, when all seemed lost, other men rose to the task and took up the fight."

By now his ten year old son Scott had joined them. "Daddy, Grandma told me we live in a democracy."

The father sighed. "Yes, Scott! They used to teach that when she went to school. You live in a republic, son. Because of people like Ramsey and Colton, our great republic was saved back in the pandemonium of 2012."

"What happened in 2012, Daddy?" asked Renee.

"Come up here and sit in my lap, sweetie. This is going to be a long story."

A Taste of Evil

From the cluster of men standing in the background, Manuel stared in horrified silence as he watched the man strapped on the gurney shriek and beg for mercy. Death was something he had lived with since the age of fourteen when he had killed his first man. But never had he witnessed anything like this, as the poor creature lying there lost all bodily functions on each end and begged for death. Showing any emotion or sympathy was a sign of weakness and Manuel had to choke down the nausea in his stomach as he watched the spectacle before him.

The mustachioed man in the immaculate three-piece suit walked over to the helpless man and looked down, gloating. Suddenly slapping the prostrate figure, he muttered, "*Hijo de puta*." Bending over the quivering body, he spat into the man's empty eye sockets. As he did the tattoo of the snake on the back of his neck became visible to Manuel. *Culebra* straightened his body and casually turned his head toward him. His lip curled up slightly. He sensed the other man's discomfort. "See Manuel, that's how we do it."

Manuel nodded in recognition. "Si, Culebra, as all pigs should die!"

"It pleases you then?" asked the other man toying with him.

"*Seguro que si!*"

"Good, then I shall expect you to watch the rest." As soon as this was said, another of Manuel's men cupped his mouth and ran for the door. Laughter followed the man's retreating steps.

Manuel forced a smile as he tried to play the game. "But I arranged for our flight to leave this afternoon. We must go soon, and be in New Orleans by evening. My nephew is there now and arranges for the boat."

Culebra turned his gaze to the well dressed man standing next to Manuel. "All is made ready, Mahmoud?"

"I have a diplomatic passport." He tapped the locked briefcase handcuffed to his arm. "The Yankees will think I am there for the international trade conference."

Turning his attention back to the other man, "Manuel?"

"Si, Culebra?"

"My man, guard him well!"

"He shall be as safe as a baby in his mother's arms."

"And of the shipment; I want to hear this again."

"Our people will take care of this. Two days from now the waterproof bales will be dropped from the yacht eighty kilometers off the coast of Louisiana. They will be tied together; none will be lost. The waiting shrimp boat will pick them up in its net. And the boat will return to port before dawn next morning. The cargo will be covered by a thin layer of shrimp and ice. Trucks will be at the warehouse waiting. It will be safely delivered to your people in Kansas City by late evening."

"This much is crucial, Manuel. There can be no mistakes with this delivery."

"Si, Culebra!"

"You know, Manuel; the American Coast Guard will have that yacht on radar every second of its voyage. The shrimp boat too!"

"*De veras, Culebra. No importa!* All will happen at night. The two boats will never come within a kilometer of each other."

"Very thoughtful!" the well dressed man replied. After regarding Manuel for several seconds, he again responded, "Well, then go! As they say here in Colombia, *Vaya con Dios!*" This brought laughter from the man's inner circle.

Manuel uttered the necessary niceties of respect before turning and leaving the room, followed by his man Raul and Culebra's messenger. He walked up the steps of the cellar and into the hot Colombian air outside. Manuel's eyes squinted under the bright sun. He remembered the horror he felt from the moment that wretched remnant of a man was strapped on the gurney. The scene he had witnessed played over in his mind. He muttered under his breath, *"Madre de Dios, Madre de Dios, salvenos!"* As Manuel's entourage drove away, he stared into the empty road ahead, feeling he had lost his soul.

Inside, Culebra turned his eyes back to the man on the gurney, "This game bores me."

"Do we kill him now?" asked one of his lieutenants.

"No, I hate cops. Undercover cops posing as one of us I hate the most. He dies slow. Use the vise and flatten each of his fingers one by one. Then let *El Cortador* finish him with his knife! That should take some time. I go now."

All but two left the cellar as the man on the gurney cried, *"Merced? Gracia de Dios!"* His unheard cries continued in the hidden silence of the cellar until he was no more.

———

The drop and subsequent drug pick up off the coast of Louisiana had gone smoothly. Manuel was in the pilot house of the shrimp boat as it plied its way toward Bayou Dularge. The air was thick with cigarette smoke as the boat captain neared the channel opening at Bay Caillou. He looked to Manuel's nephew. "I get my money when we dock. Yes?"

Casting back an arrogant glance, Julio responded in a denigrating tone. "Get us there; don't ask me again."

Julio's men narrowed their eyes at the Cajun fisherman. Their intent was clear, no more questions! Realizing these were dangerous men, the fisherman concentrated on steering the boat toward the bay's entrance five miles distant. The waves became choppy as a brisk wind and rain kicked up the Gulf waters around them.

Manuel was troubled. Pretending sea sickness, he left the cabin. As the boat rocked from side to side, he held on to the net's boom and gazed into the murk surrounding them. He opened his shirt and pulled out the crucifix hanging about his neck, gently rubbing it as he looked into the rain. He was soon joined by his old friend, Raul, who came and stood silently beside him. Raul said nothing, though he could feel his capo's mood. "Raul?"

"Si, Manuel?"

"I am troubled in my soul."

"I know, Manuel. I can see this in your face."

"This Culebra, a man such as he leaves only a taste of evil in my mouth. Look at us; what we do for money! Is all in life money, Raul?"

"I hate him too, Manuel."

"You know about this man, this Culebra?"

"No, Manuel."

"It's not just drugs with him. He hurts people in other ways. Do you believe in the devil, Raul?"

"Si."

"This Culebra, he is not one of us. He is a Turk. Do you know that?"

"No, Manuel."

"He takes his orders from another bad man, one named

Ahmajinedad. I believe he serves the devil. I have been a bad man too, Raul. But I will not serve the devil. Are you with me?"

"*Si, Patron.* What will you do with that man who came with us from Colombia?"

"I killed him already and hid his briefcase in the storage locker in Metairie. If anything happens to me, call Mark Obledo. He is FBI; you remember him?"

"Si, Manuel!"

Manuel reached into his coat and pulled out his Glock. "Raul, there is a phosphorus grenade in my travel bag. *Mira,* it is there by that winch. Take it out. Go to the engine room and place it on the fuel tank. Pull the pin and get out of there. This boat will not go to shore; it must burn and all these men must die."

"Your nephew too, Patron?"

"I kill him first."

Dawn had barely broken as the crab boat sped down Bayou Dularge. The sultry, yet still cool south Louisiana air filled their lungs as they anticipated today's catch. Joe's flat bottom boat was coming up on his first crab buoy seven miles beyond the boat launch at Theriot. Coming into view as they rounded a bend, the first one bobbed softly in the water, its distinct colors painted in the red and yellow pattern belonging to him. Positioning himself on the starboard side, he watched with satisfaction as the bow rake hooked the buoy and scooped up the crab pot attached to its line. The forward motion of the boat dragged it to the surface. With a skill born of twenty years experience, his heavily muscled arms pulled the cage into the boat, where he emptied it into the receiving box. Deftly opening the bait well, he filled it up with catfish heads; closed, sealed, and tossed the cage overboard, carefully, so that the bait well was on the downward side. Otherwise, he would be feeding the crabs for free. From start to finish, this process had taken less than a minute and would be repeated three hundred times today. No sooner was this done than the rake scooped up the second pot.

Jenny, his wife of twenty-five years rapidly sorted the crabs as he dumped them inside. Males were separated from females and any five inches or less across were thrown back. Like so many well-fed Cajun females, she was still attractive though beginning to sport a round belly. Her brown eyes, accented by the red scarf tied around her head, seemed to smile as her hands screened the catch. Lightly browned from working in the sun, her skin was still smooth and supple. Joe tossed her a momentary glance, fully appreciative of her full-breasted figure. Three hundred years of continuous habitation had perfectly adapted their race to this clime.

The Frious were happy today. Marie would be coming home from college day after tomorrow. Joe and Jenny would prepare a big crab boil and invite all the kinfolk and friends. Though they didn't realize it, they were content. The tragedy of losing their son T-Bob in a car accident five years ago had subsided. Life in south Louisiana was replete with good food, plenty of drink, music and close family relationships. A world within a world, Cajun culture remained distinct, an ethnic group unabsorbed by greater America. The Friou's main concern was lying to the tax man, who couldn't understand how they could afford a brand new Fork truck on an $8,000 a year declared income.

Passing the stand of oil drilling platforms stored off to the east, Joe wove his boat past the oyster luggers in Caillou Lake. By now the sun was high. Joe yelled to his wife. "Jen, the sky, she is blue blue, a good day!" Jenny smiled back at him. Within minutes they would be in the Gulf of Mexico. Turning sharply to port at the bend beyond navigation buoy number two, Joe followed the coastline until passing into Gulf waters at the entrance of Grand Caillou Dularge. Opening the boat at full throttle in Caillou Bay, he headed in the general direction of Cocodrie where more crabs waited in nearby bayous. Three miles further lay the entrance to Turtle Bayou where more oyster pots waited. Jenny blushed as Joe pointed to a group of dolphins engaged in group sex in the open water. "Jenny, look there; see! They make the *gogo.*"

A former school teacher herself, Jenny was better educated than one would expect. "Oh, *Sha* (cher);" she answered, "Don't you know, only dolphins and humans do it just for fun."

"*May no.* Is it so?"

Jenny smiled. "You wish you were one of them; there in the water too? *May ya?*

A sly smirk came over his face. "Jen; no! They're just fun to watch."

The rising breeze blew his thick mane of dark hair downwind as he made a sharp turn to port side by the navigation buoy. The Frious enjoyed the rushing air over the next mile in silence. Suddenly Jenny spoke to him in a reprimanding style. "Joe, You don't stay late at Franks' today. We must go shopping for Marie's homecoming Saturday."

"Sha, you make too much worry over this."

Within minutes, the boat's bow entered Turtle Bayou. Here, Joe cut its speed to deal with its meandering curves. The Friou's boat barely entered the waterway as Joe noticed something unusual on the nearby mud bank. Pointing to the prone figure he yelled, "Jenny! Ga (look)! A man!"

Maneuvering his boat up to the bank, Joe threw the anchor on it and stepped into ankle deep water and up to the marshy surface. "Wait here, Jen!"

The man was laying prone, dead still, his lower legs protruding into the Gulf waters. Nearby, almost hidden by the tall swamp grass, was a flat waterproof bale secured to a pair of floats. Joe knelt and gently rolled the man over. The horribly burned man slowly opened his eyes and attempted to move his lips. "Galee," muttered Joe in shock at the man's appearance. "What happened? What's you name?"

"Raul," he replied.

"Jenny, call the pleece; this man, he's bad hurt!"

"Sha, it doesn't work. I forgot to charge it!"

"Me, Ah got to get this man some help." As Joe gently scooped him up, the injured man tried to speak. Joe leaned his ear to pick up the faint sound as he carried the man to his boat. Wading outward he passed him into the boat where Jenny received him with her firm grip. Pulling himself on board, Joe gathered up the anchor and turned the boat back toward Theriot. It was the closest place to get emergency medical care. Slowing only long enough to hail another boat, he quickly explained the situation and they called for an ambulance to meet them. Demanding all his motor could give, Joe skimmed by the navigation buoys at maximum speed. Raul was dead before they reached Theriot.

Joe reported finding him at the mouth of Turtle Bayou. His mind was elsewhere; the biggest part of the day's fishing had been wasted. He almost forgot to report the bale lying near Raul. When the police retrieved it later, it contained five million dollars in street value of the highest quality cocaine. He relayed the dead man's last words, "Briefcase in Metairie; Mark Obledo."

The authorities quickly associated Raul's death with the missing shrimp boat. He had been seen at the dock earlier where it was moored. The police quickly concluded that a tragic accident had aborted a major drug delivery. After a few days' search, the Coast Guard attributed the sinking to a fire at sea with no survivors.

RAMSEY

It was early on a crisp winter day in February, 2011. Ramsey felt good. Cinching tight the Windsor knot in his tartan styled tie, he looked at his reflection in the bathroom mirror. Marveling at the strange meanderings of fate that brought him here, he sighed, flipped off the light switch and walked out of the bathroom. Pausing at the front door, Stuart said goodbye to his housekeeper and took the lustrous leather briefcase she handed him. Lost in thought, he never heard the door as it closed softly behind him. It was a short walk from his newly purchased condo in Arlington to the garage. Within minutes, his bright red Dodge Ram truck was speeding toward the U.S. House of Representatives. The flowing mural of the American Flag spanning the length on each side of his truck delighted most passers by. Equally, in this bastion of liberality, it horrified others.

Bored from listening to a local news pundit, he switched off the radio and thought out loud. "And I wanted this? I'm just another geek in this Washington freak show. If I were back home, I'd be fishing." With a sudden burst, the sky opened and the city was deluged with icy rain from the dark clouds above. Undeterred by this challenging downpour, Ramsey sped forward. "Well, as we say in Georgia, this is real frog choker."

This was the beginning of a new term. The House was equally divided, 217 Democrats to 217 Republicans. And there was Ramsey. After winning the mid-term congressional election in 2010 from a rural district in North Georgia, he was the only third party delegate in Congress. Approached by friends a year before the election, he made it clear; politics was not for him. Nor was either major party! Uninterested in the beginning, he allowed himself to be wooed. Ego played a hand; Stuart Ramsey accepted the challenge.

The Republicans had barely recovered in the mid-term election following the Bush debacle. The first woman president, Kipper Rodwell, had been elected just two years before in 2008. The national debt was twenty-five trillion. Inflation was eleven per cent, and unemployment was eight. It was almost two years after Kipper came to power, when she finally kept her promise to end the war. Troops had been withdrawn from Afghanistan and Iraq. She promised massive aid to deflect Muslim wrath as fundamentalist Islamic Republics now stretched from Pakistan to Syria. Vast increases in social spending and entitlement programs over two years had nearly bankrupted the U.S. This cost the Democrats numerous House seats in the 2010 election. Now, Osama Bin Laden traveled openly throughout the Muslim world. There were at least fifty-five million illegal immigrants in the United States and the U.S. had not been this polarized since 1860.

The atmosphere in the House was partisan. No one was backing down. This floor fight had gone on for days. The House was without a speaker; the work of the nation was paralyzed.

Entering the chamber, Ramsey paused and studied the mass of overinflated egos sprawling in view before taking his seat. He silently reflected. "How many times? I can't remember! Each side has approached me to break this tie. Sweetheart offers! The committee of my choice! Yes; and how many veiled promises? How many unmistakable innuendos of good times with those obliging ladies? I'm probably the most sought after man in Washington. After only a few days here, I'm sick of it. When this term is over, they can shove it. This ol' boy has a long standing date with the catfish in his lake."

But there was another side to Ramsey. He wasted no time becoming acquainted, as his new colleagues, from both sides found him likeable. He remained laconic on major issues which psychologically disarmed many of them. Few outside of North Georgia knew his politics or philosophy; few in Georgia knew either. Spreading his charm like butter on warm bread, Stuart Ramsey was embraced. A natural leader, he could read people and win them over. Even his ex-wife Sharon told him long ago, "Stuart, when you want to, you can charm a snake out of its skin."

The limousine headed up Pennsylvania Avenue toward the House of Representatives. Senior Republican Don Barton broke the silence with his colleague, Representative Domenick, as they neared the stop. "Fred, this could go bad. Rick Lawson may die; colon cancer is taking him down fast. If he does, the Dems got it. Holding on to the House means everything! If we lose it, with Kipper in the White House and the Senate still under their thumbs, we're in trouble. She along with her brain-dead zombies will have this country by the balls for another two years. And if they do, quite frankly, I have my doubts if America or the Republican Party will ever recover."

"What about this Ramsey character, Don? Hell, he's from a conservative part of Georgia. Why can't we get him off the pot?"

"He's a strange bird, Fred. I don't understand him. Whatever his game, he's the *Lone Ranger*. There's never going to be a Constitution Party. Running for office must have been an ego trip for him. And enough locals just happened to like him."

"The rat bought his election. He knew what he was doing."

"What do you mean, Fred?"

"He was nobody, a nothing. Just an ordinary working man! Then, he won that big lottery a few years ago, almost 350 million dollars. The whole enchilada, all by himself. He parlayed it into billions making lucky investments and then moved to Georgia."

"You mean he's not from Georgia?"

"Hell no, he's from Nevada."

"I didn't think Nevada had a lottery?"

"It doesn't, Don; he was on vacation and bought that ticket in Sturgis, South Dakota, at that big motorcycle rally."

"The hell you say! What did he do there in Nevada?"

"Just a working man, a miner, in a large goldmine near some little town in the middle of nowhere, called Winnemucca."

"Fred, that means he was likely a union man; so he's probably anti-business."

"I don't know, Don. The work ethic in Nevada is a little better than in most places."

"Well, some of that gold dust must have enchanted his fingertips. Look at him now. But that doesn't solve our problem. We've got to win this guy over before Lawson dies."

Barton's cell phone began ringing as the limo pulled along the curb. Both men sat there while he answered the call. His face darkened; then he closed the phone and put it away. "Fred, that was Lawson. The doctor gave him less than a week to live. He'll come to the House this morning. He is going to support us as long as he can."

"Don, this is serious. Maybe we can control this Ramsey. Suppose we throw our support behind him for Speaker of the House; maybe he'll back us too."

"Ridiculous; whoever heard of a first-term Representative becoming Speaker of the House?"

"What's the alternative? You know that pinko liberal, Muller, from California will get it if Lawson dies."

Barton fell silent as he mentally digested his colleague's words. "Let's talk to our people!"

It was late that afternoon when the House reconvened. Though stunned by the offer, Ramsey accepted the Republican overture. Beyond his understanding, he had been caught up in the flow of history, and now had a date with destiny. Ramsey reassured them of his conservative credentials. They promised to back him for Speaker. When the vote came down, it was Ramsey 218, Muller 217.

That same afternoon, the new Speaker took his position with the half-hearted applause of his colleagues. At seven o'clock in the evening, Lawson was taken to the hospital. He died before midnight.

The headlines from next morning's edition of *The New York Times* read:

REPUBLICANS ENGINEER COUP IN THE HOUSE
Washington, D.C.

Republican strategists in the House take control through a surrogate. Reacting to the adverse health of Rick Lawson, a floor vote puts independent, self-styled Constitution Party delegate Stuart Ramsey in as the new Speaker of the House. Democrats cry foul. Ramsey has no experience or credentials for the job they say. Southern governor already appoints a Republican replacement for Lawson.

CULEBRA

Bashan, known as Culebra to his Colombian associates, was in a murderous mood. Two days earlier a call came from New Orleans. The shipment was lost at sea and his courier was missing.

Pounding on the door, the young girl screamed. "*Ayudeme* (Help me)? *El Turco va a matar mi hermano* (The Turk is going to kill my brother)!"

The men outside glanced at each other in silence. An open bottle of rum stood upright on the table between them. One filled up his glass, then his companion's. They continued playing cards, ignoring the girl's pleas.

She stopped pounding and ran back to the man leaning over her brother, trying repeatedly to grab his arm. He casually flipped her away as one would a troublesome bug. "Let him go; I beg you!" she screamed. Then she crumpled on her knees beside the two and begged the large man for mercy.

Bashan's arms were beginning to feel good. They had finally loosened up and his tension was released after dealing dozens of blows to the unconscious boy beneath him. The boy looked like a stray cat might after being ripped apart by the junk yard dog. Bashan considered using the boy one more time but in his unconscious state the limp body would have to be held up. And this is something Bashan did not have patience for. He stared with satisfaction at the boy's unrecognizable features. Then he placed his massive left hand upon the bloody pulp that used to be a fourteen year old boy's face, pressed two fingers against his eyes and spoke to the girl. "Will you do anything for me?"

"Anything, Patron!" she nervously answered as she trembled in horror beside him.

Bashan released the boy, stood up and walked over to a small table where he stopped and stared at his own naked body in a mirror on the wall. He motioned for the girl to attend him. She hurriedly came and he pointed to the bottle of lotion upon the table. She reached for it; but her trembling fingers almost knocked it over. Recovering it as fast as she could, the frightened girl poured the lotion on her hands and rubbed it all over the man's body, kneading it into his skin as much as her small hands would permit. He casually picked up a reefer lying on the table and lit it with satisfaction. In spite of the bad news, this had been a fun afternoon. "Now!" said Bashan after his rub down. He reclined on a low couch and pointed to his private parts. The girl kneeled there and gave him one last bit of satisfaction.

This had been one of the better times. At least once a month his sexual tastes demanded that he use both a young boy and girl. His men had found this fourteen year old set of fraternal twins in the streets of Cartagena. Over the last twenty-four hours Bashan had used them unspeakably in many ways. Only a half hour earlier while mounting the girl he had cruelly twisted and tortured her flesh as she lay beneath him. Her hideous cries of agony brought her brother running to her aid. This was the desired result from the torture. As Bashan hoped, the boy had grabbed him. After which, Bashan turned his attention to him for the highlight of his blood lust.

Finally growing bored with the game, Bashan stood up and grabbed the girl by her hair. Dragging her over to the door, he yelled to his men to unbolt it. In hardly more than a heartbeat the door burst open from the other side. "You want this girl?"

"Si, Culebra!" they both answered eagerly. Bashan flung the girl by her hair to the floor. "Will they be leaving soon?" asked one of the men.

"No! Her pig of a brother put his hands on me."

The man nodded. Whatever satisfaction he and his associate would derive from the trembling girl would have to be taken soon.

Bashan backed into the room and the other man closed the door, careful not to lock it this time. The boy moaned once while still in an unconscious state. Bashan walked to the table, picked up a pocket knife and opened it. He casually approached the unconscious boy and sank to one knee. Holding the youth's forehead with his left hand, he plunged the knife into the boy's jugular vein and circumscribed a cut around the boy's throat to the jugular on the other side. It brought him much pleasure to watch blood squirt from these arteries. After wiping his knife upon the corpse, Bashan stood up.

He dressed; and then lit another reefer before leaving the room. The afternoon's adventure almost was forgotten as Bashan walked outside to look around, lost in thought. He was troubled. These unspeakable, infidel sons of bitch dogs had lost everything; the shipment, and his courier was missing. How could these Kafirs lose two hundred million dollars worth of cocaine? Now he must explain this to his superiors. Something had to be done. But what?

Suddenly approached by one of his men who held a cell phone out to him, Bashan took it without speaking. "What's that you say? My courier is dead. Manuel's man, Raul, was picked up by a fisherman. But you don't know who has the briefcase. You find out who this fisherman is. I fly to Louisiana tonight."

The fifty-gallon pot was already boiling as Joe added the last ingredient, the crab. Timing it just right to avoid overcooking any ingredient, he covered the concoction and waited. Savory Cajun vapors soon emanated and spread from the pot all throughout the mix of tables and chairs spread out from the front of the Friou doublewide near Des Allemands. The camaraderie was lively. The younger men played horseshoes while the womenfolk sat around large tables and gossiped. The younger children impatiently waited their turn to climb a slide and tumble into an above ground pool. Everyone was having a good time.

Joe walked over to the cooler and pulled out a beer. He noticed old Louie sitting alone in the corner of the group. Louie's wife had long passed away. He was a relic from another age. Joe paused, then went inside the trailer and returned with a bottle of cognac. Joe poured Louie a tall shot. At eighty-five, Louie was his family's oldest friend. Louie and Joe's own deceased grandfather were among the last of the old generation to use French as their first language.

Louie greeted him. "*Comment allez vous.*"

Though Joe was exposed to the old tongue when very young, he remembered little, only using it in social situations such as this. Yet, he responded in kind which he knew old Louie would like. Louie was best friends with Joe's grandparents, his *mamou* and *papou*. The old man often reminisced about the old days. Speaking in English, Louie again retold the story about the day Joe's grandparents got married. They all lived in a village on a shrimping platform by the sea. No priest was available to marry them. Joe's grandparents jumped over a broom stick together to seal their marriage vows. After learning of this later, the church almost excommunicated the pair. The story produced a good laugh. Everyone loved it. Joe glanced at his watch; the crab boil was almost ready.

The Friou's anxiety melted as the long wait for Marie's arrival ended. Her boyfriend's Lexus turned into the driveway and came to a halt. Eagerly, everyone gathered by it. Beautiful, chocolate-eyed Marie gracefully slid out of the passenger seat into Joe's waiting arms. Squeezing as he picked her up, he turned in a full circle. "Y'all finally come home to you daddy."

Jenny was next, then everyone else took turns hugging and complimenting the girl. Her boyfriend stood smiling in the distance, silently enjoying Marie's adoration. She broke away long enough to take him by the hand. "Everyone, this is Alan Prudhomme. Alan is from Shreveport. He's studying to be a doctor." She took him on a round of introductions beginning with her Dad.

After shaking Alan's hand, Joe left him and went over to the boiling pot. He pulled out a piece of crab meat and sampled it. Nodding in satisfaction, "We gonna eat!" he announced.

Everyone found a place at the tables as the crab boil was spread before them. Sacks of seasoned onions and potatoes were spread on the table before them and emptied. Sausage, crabs, and carrots, it was all there as dozens of hands eagerly sought their share of the bounty. "It make my mouth feel good" was heard all around the table.

By late night, the crowd had dwindled. A few women sipped coffee or wine and chatted. The remaining circle of men played *Booray*. Old Louie was winning and enjoying every minute of it. Beer cans and liquor bottles adorned the table. The men progressively became louder.

Joe lost another hand. "Ah go booray," he announced, throwing in his cards. Looking at his watch, Joe realized he must be on the bayou within four hours. Getting even two hours of sleep was impossible. "Work, she comes early." He stood up; Jenny followed him inside the modular home. They walked past Alan asleep on the couch. Marie was fast asleep in her room. The Frious knew these youngsters probably had a sleeping arrangement of their own. But it wouldn't take place here. Jenny let Marie know in advance that she and Alan would not make any gogo in the house.

It was 2:00 A.M. as the Frious finished their breakfast coffee. As Joe headed outside to hitch up the boat trailer, Alan woke up. "Y'all go back to sleep," said Joe.

"Yes, sir!"

The knock came at the door as Alan and Marie sat drinking their breakfast coffee. "I'll answer it," said Marie cheerfully. Effortlessly, she glided to the front door. Still in her robe, a smiling Marie opened it to the cluster of strange men.

"Is this the home of Mr. Friou?" said the powerful looking, well-dressed man with a foreign accent.

"Yes, it is. My Daddy is working now. He's a crab fisherman and leaves early. Who should I tell him came by?"

"My name is Bashan. I will come inside."

"Oh Mr. Bashan, I can't let you do that. Daddy will be home at,"—she began.

JIM

Jim Scott pushed away the sheaf of papers on his desk, relaxing long enough to clear his head. Through the window from the third floor in the FBI building in New Orleans, he could see the lake in shades of blue and green. Darkening skies suddenly released a downpour over Lake Ponchartrain. It would soon be upon them; he was pleased. Maybe it would obscure the ugly sight of those FEMA trailers. University students were still being housed in them years after Katrina wasted this area. Flood ravaged houses were still visible off to his right.

The phone on his desk rang. Picking it up, he pressed it to his ear. "Hello."

"Jim, let's go to work!"

"Is that you, Mark?"

"In the flesh."

"It's good to hear from you. Are you in Washington?"

"No. I arrive in New Orleans about eleven this morning. I'm on special assignment."

"What's up, buddy?"

"I'm tracking down a lead on a Colombian drug lord."

"What's it all about, Mark?"

"Remember that guy from the fishing boat down in Terrebonne? The one that died of burns?"

"I've got a memo on my desk now about it. The Sheriff of Terrebonne Parish wants any information we have on this man. We know his name was Raul. The daughter of the fisherman who found him, and her boyfriend were murdered in his home near Des Allemands a couple days later. Do you have anything on this?"

"Yeah, the body was identified. His name was indeed Raul and he belonged to a drug cartel operated by Manuel Cordoba. I knew Manuel. Guess he figured he owed me a favor; once I tipped him off when his son was going to be hit. Earlier that day I got a call from him. Said he had information for me, a briefcase hidden away. He promised to deliver it the next day. Well, I was interested! Figured he wanted to get even with a rival. That fisherman who found him told the cops that Raul said 'briefcase in Metairie, Mark Obledo' before dying. Now, Manuel's missing. Word on the street has it he's dead."

"So what? These gangs are always pissing each other off.

He's probably sleeping with the fishes. Isn't that what they call it?"

Mark smiled. "The Italian mob puts it like that! These Colombian types are a little more vicious. Anyway, I reported the call to my supervisor. When Raul mentioned me by name, the Director himself put me in charge. I'm supposed to find that briefcase. Strange, I figure your field office should have handled this with me along to assist. Anyway, I asked for you personally. The big man said OK. Well, I'll arrive on the next plane from D.C."

"Has a message been sent to my supervisor here?"

"If not, it will before I get there. I learned long ago to use every resource. Now, you're assigned to me. Besides, it's a chance for us to get together. Anyway, I put two and two together. Raul was Manuel's top man. He was dead, Manuel was missing and Raul mentioned Metairie and the briefcase before dying. I figured they used a storage unit in Metairie for the goods. I remember some of Manuel's aliases. We're going out there this afternoon."

"You know you're going to need a search warrant if you come up with anything?"

"Figured you could handle that detail for me."

"I can. Let's have lunch first. I'll be at the airport at eleven sharp."

"Good! I'm partial to Brennans."

"We can do that. See you then!"

Jim checked his answering machine. Liz had tried to call. He pushed the redial button. Waiting patiently, his ex-wife finally answered the phone.

"Jim, is it you?"

"Hi, Liz. What's up?"

You're taking the kids tomorrow! Can you pick them up early? I want to leave for Baton Rouge before breakfast."

"Liz, you can just as easily drop them by my place."

"Come on, Jim. Be nice about it. That will take away thirty minutes from my travel time. Jeff and I want to get an early start in the morning."

"I wouldn't want to delay you and your potential new-ex from going to Baton Rouge, especially over such a minor detail as the kids."

"Jim, don't be a son-of-a-bitch. My life is my own and how I live it is none of your business."

"Why don't you marry this dude and then really get off my back?"

"Oh, but darling, you pay so well and always on time."

"And what time would you be wanting this little favor, my dear?"

"Say seven sharp!"

"Liz, I'll be there when I'm there."

Jim hung up as she unleashed a series of colorful invectives into his ear. Opening a desk drawer, he pulled out their old marriage photo that used to lie on his desk. As he looked at it, Jim marveled at her uncommon good looks from days long gone. He remembered all the lies they used to believe in when both uttered their wedding vows. Imagine; she used to teach Sunday school and visit the sick with other ladies from the church.

Reminiscing silently, he mumbled, "You dumb son of bitch. She's right. You brought this on. You had that affair four years ago. The gal was kind enough to share her VD; and you passed it on to Liz. Counseling didn't work for her. She took up drinking and running around after recovering from the infection and that hysterectomy. Then we called it quits!" Jim held her photo next to their children's pictures. He compared her fine lines to theirs. "It's easy to see why the kids are so good looking," he said aloud.

———————

It was a quarter after ten; Jim grabbed his coat and headed for the door. True to Mark Obledo's wish, Jim was assigned to him. One of the office secretaries, Betty, looked up as he passed by.

"Going to lunch, Mr. Scott?"

"Probably gone for the day, Betty. Please don't call me unless it's really important. I've been reassigned. I'm working with an agent sent down from Washington. My cell phone is on if you really need me."

Leaving the elevator, Jim inserted his card into the receptacle and walked through the private door of the FBI Field Headquarters. He took a deep breath, enjoying the moment.

The cloudburst earlier had freshened the air. Minutes later, he drove the Chrysler out of the garage onto Leon C. Simon Boulevard and turned toward the Louis Armstrong New Orleans International Airport.

Mark was waiting by the curb as the Chrysler purposefully pulled over and stopped by him. Jim popped open the trunk for his colleague. Mark stowed his gear; closed it, and went to the passenger door, easing inside. They shook hands.

"How's Lupe and the kids?"

"Fine. She's finally got the house fixed up; her dream home. A five bedroom all brick house in Fairfax County. We got four acres. You gotta come see us soon."

"I'd like too, Mark. Someday! I'm pretty tied down at the moment."

"Is your divorce from Liz final?"

"Yeah, over a year ago."

"So, you been seeing anybody?"

Jim laughed. "I have a girl if that's what you mean. She takes good care of me!"

"Not the one who got you in all that trouble?"

"Naw; Christ no. Here, look at this," Jim said as he pulled out a photo.

"Nice packaging!" replied Mark.

"Her name's Elaine. Now for Brennans! Hang on to your hat."

That afternoon Mark and Jim analyzed the contents of the briefcase found in the storage unit under the name of Alfredo Menendez. Along with this were found two million dollars in cash, hundreds of pounds of cocaine, and several fully automatic firearms. Next morning, the New Orleans' *Times Picayune* would report this as a major drug bust and coup against organized crime by the FBI.

Back in Jim's office, both men sat at his desk and examined papers from the briefcase. "I can't make much of this stuff," said Jim, throwing a page down.

"I can read the Spanish; but this one is in Arabic script. It could even be Farsi," answered Mark.

"What's Farsi?"

"Iranian! This network reaches deep into the Middle East. This is more than drugs. Here are lists of names; contacts. Looks like these boy scouts have a hidden agenda. These drugs are meant to finance projects. Manuel's family somehow got tied in with this operation, no doubt motivated by money. I got a hunch; I don't think Manuel liked these people. He was probably in too deep and got killed. This paper for example!" Mark held up a sheet. "It contains a set of instructions for this guy named Mahmoud to distribute money among influence peddlers in Washington. I recognize some of these names: lawyers, politicians, businessmen, foreign nationals. Some are linked to the Rodwell administration. These drugs were headed for Kansas City. That must be the main hub. Hey, look at this figure on this sheet. It's a snake. And some of this stuff refers to Culebra."

"What's that?" asked Jim.

"Culebra is Spanish for snake," Mark answered. "He may be the same guy called Bashan on other papers here."

"Well, that almost finishes it on our end. I was hoping this one would last a little longer. Have you booked a return flight?" asked Jim.

"I will soon. Jim, go see that fisherman. What's his name – Friou?"

"Done!"

At that moment, the secretary came in. "The DEA is here, Mr. Scott."

"We've been expecting their arrival; send them in," he answered.

Marie's body was held by the coroner for a week pending investigation into the homicide. Both she and Alan had been horribly mutilated by blade and fire. Semen from four men was found inside her. The Frious, who found their bodies that same afternoon were cleared of any suspicion. Forensic evidence proved the intruders were looking for something. The inside of their modular home had been ripped apart. To protect them from further harm, the police released the details of Raul's death, emphasizing that the briefcase had been found in a storage unit in Metairie and was now in possession of the FBI.

Jim and Elaine were sharing a candlelight dinner at the Bombay Club in the French Quarter on Conti Street. The vibration in his pocket signaled a call was waiting on his cell phone. With no intention of answering it, he decided to at least see who was calling. In the dim light he saw that it was Mark Obledo. "I better take this one, honey," he said to Elaine. "I'll be right back." He flipped it open as he stood up and walked to a quieter corner. "Mark, you're interfering with my dinner. And my love life!"

"Sorry, buddy. I gotta few things to say. I'll try and make it quick. Remember those DNA samples from that Friou girl? The one who was murdered along with her boyfriend last week?"

"Yeah; what do you have on it?"

"The information was sent to Interpol. They found a match in their files in Lyon, France. One of those semen samples belonged to a Turk who was heavily engaged in the drug trade years ago in France until the heat got to be too much for him. His name is Bashan Bashan. He's a real bad apple, implicated in at least a dozen murders. He spent two years in prison in France. During this time he reconnected with his fundamentalist Islamic teachings. When he was a teenager, his grandfather sent him to a Wahhabi school in Yemen. Sometime after he was released from prison he became involved with Al Qaeda. Then he disappeared for a few years. When he resurfaced he was living in Colombia under a different name. He infiltrated and took over one of the drug cartels. And it looks like he may have converted most of them to Islam. They're the baddest, meanest bunch in South America. He's known in the business as Culebra."

"What do you know about the murder of the Friou girl?"

"It has to be over that damn briefcase. This son-of-a-bitch Bashan—Culebra sent an emissary to influence certain interests in this country. Listen, I may be in trouble over this. The Director wasn't happy when he found out I looked at some of that material."

"What's it all about?"

"I read more of it after we parted. Soon after Rodwell was elected, she quickly scaled down military operations and we lost that war in Iraq. The Middle East fell into Fundamentalist Islamic control all the way from Pakistan to Lebanon. You know that much already. Then certain business interests in Europe and America began taking it in on the chin. It looks like a lot of these are linked to the rich and powerful associated with a group sometimes called the Bilderbergers."

"Whoa, Mark. Stop right there before my steak gets any colder. Is this some conspiracy theory crap you're laying on me?"

"I don't know anything about conspiracies. But I do know a lot of influential people want to keep doing business in the Middle East. And these ragheads still want Western investment capital and technology. Some of the names on that list are high-powered lobbyists, congressmen and magnates who want to keep business as usual. And some of 'em have secrets, like using cocaine. This messenger was instructed to keep a lot of them happy. He was also directed to steer the profits from sales to certain people. If that list fell into the wrong hands it could upset a lot of plans. This new Director, he's a Rodwell appointee too. Well, guess what?"

"It's your dime!"

"The list I brought in disappeared. And during her first two years in office a lot more of these Muslim types were hired by the Bureau under her diversity program. I talked to a friend of mine, Professor Kohn, at Georgetown University. He used to work part-time as a translator for the Bureau. Then he got disgusted and quit. He tells me there's an Islamic mole in the Bureau. I may know too much. But I have a word for you."

"What?"

"Caution! Don't tell anybody in the agency you know anything about that briefcase. You never saw its contents. I never discussed anything with you. I didn't make this call. Fair?"

"Thanks, Mark. Hey, you be careful. I'll talk to you soon."

"Adios, Amigo. Don't keep that steak or your girlfriend waiting any longer."

———

The wind swept the falling rain into Joe's face as he stood looking down on his daughter's grave. He didn't care. Just minutes before, his cheeks had been deluged with tears. The funeral procession including his wife Jenny was long gone. The rain now pummeled the multitude of flowers around her final resting place under the cruel February sky in south Louisiana.

He sank to his knees and clawed at the fresh dirt of his daughter's grave. Raising two fistfuls to his forehead, he slowly released them as he spoke. "Marie, come out of that cold, cold ground! Marie, why this happened? Sha, you daddy's gonna miss you. We come together someday. Then we pass a good time. Just like before!"

Resigned to his loss, Joe stood back up and finally turned his soaked and frigid body toward his pickup truck parked by the gravel road of the Catholic Cemetery in rural Terrebonne Parish.

Standing there, waiting respectfully was Jim Scott. He spoke as Joe came within hearing distance, "Mr. Friou?"

KIPPER

Pressing the phone to her ear, Athena recognized the voice speaking in English. It was that American woman.

"May I speak to George?"

Athena felt a wave of revulsion as she replied. "Just a moment." She carried the phone out of the main cabin onto the stern of the yacht; and handed it to her father, George Tauros. "For you, Papa," she said in Greek.

Replying in Greek, he asked, "Who is it, child?"

"The Bitch!" replied Athena in English, loud enough to be heard on the phone.

Tauros scowled at his daughter as he took it from her. Athena returned inside the cabin leaving him alone.

"Is it you, Kipper darling? I've missed you. Can you join me on the island for a few days?"

"I'd love to George. But you know how busy I am; don't you? Someone has to run this country."

Though President Kipper Rodwell was married to George Tauros, they seldom saw each other. It was no particular hardship. He had his share of girlfriends in Greece, Paris and New York. So did she. They had married years before and Tauros financed her bid for the presidency. He was one of the world's five richest men. Tauros was born in Greece in 1940 but became a naturalized U.S. Citizen in 1961. By 2010, he had bought up most of the island he was born on. This was Kipper's first marriage. She had no children, and kept her last name. She could swing both ways. Those rare liaisons with Tauros were fun for her too. He placed no undo demands on their marriage and was content to be close to the source of power. His international profits had also soared twenty per cent in these first two years of Kipper's Presidency. There had been allegations of misconduct, but nothing serious could stick. Kipper was the darling of the entire world liberal press.

Athena was intensely jealous. She was one of Tauros' many children by past wives and concubines. It wasn't her father's affection for Kipper that bothered her. Athena had known about his philandering ever since she was a child. Kipper would be a rival for her father's money. Tauros was seventy-one and Athena stood in line to become the world's richest woman. Only Kipper stood in her way. She had been Tauros' favorite before he married Kipper.

"Is there some problem, darling?" asked Tauros.

"It's that bastard Ramsey, the new Speaker of the House."

"Oh yes; him! I've heard he's hard to work with."

"That's not the half of it, George. Nothing gets through committee. I've got a lot of important legislation to move. Our people might as well be trying to shove these bills through the eye of a needle. And worse! He's organized enough support to press for repeal of the Fairness Act. Other right-wingers are taking up his cause on this one. They even approached me about pardoning the felony convictions of Russ Shaumbaugh and Ike Ravage. I will not bend to this kind of pressure!"

"Who is this Ramsey, my darling? A Fascist?"

"Just another right-winger; it didn't take him long to come out of the closet. Can we do something, George?"

"Don't I always fix things for you, my darling?"

"Can you do this, George?"

"My love, I control half the free world's news. I own Reynard News International."

"Yes, George darling, I know; that French company. What will you do?"

"Through Reynard International, I bought out one of the big three American television companies. That was just a couple of years ago. I know you remember."

"Yes, George; I know."

"Reynard News International is now number one. Our

programming has even drawn some of Fox TV's audience back from the cable networks. We're the prime movers of public opinion. It's easy keeping Americans happy. We dish them up Monday night football; pretty commentators showing lots of leg, sitcoms and political satires. I call the shots; Reynard News International does the rest."

"Where are you going with this, George?"

"To start with, I'll have Gilbert O'Mallie invite this Ramsey to appear on Straight Talk. Gill will destroy him in front of the whole country. Before long every Republican constituency in the country will be pressuring their congressman to dump him as Speaker. Then, we'll get something on him and finish the bastard off."

"How do you know you can get something on him, George?"

"Kipper, my darling, I can get something on anybody. Nobody has a halo. We all have skeletons in the attic."

"I see perfectly; dig up the bad stuff in his past."

"I don't worry about reporting the news, my darling; I create it."

"George, I knew I could depend on you. By the way, on Wednesday I'm going to Beirut for a Middle East conference starting Friday. That Palestinian-Israeli thing you know. Why don't you meet me there?"

"I look forward to that, my love; the Pegasus can sail there in only two days. We'll have fun. It's been too long, Kipper, my darling."

"I know, George! Have you missed me?"

"I never cared for any woman as much as I do you, Kipper."

"I look forward to seeing you too, darling. Love and kisses, I've got to go now; bye."

"Goodbye, my darling; I love you." Tauros turned off the phone.

A pretty dark-haired girl emerged from the Aegean water onto the stern of the Pegasus. The sun glistened off the water droplets from her tanned skin as the red bikini left little to the imagination.

Tauros motioned her to him. Pulling her into his lap, he said in Greek. "I never cared for any woman as much as I do you, Artemisia."

Kipper continued holding the receiver as she dialed Sandy. Before her election to the House of Representatives, Sandy had been a top level ACLU attorney in New York. They met years before when Kipper was running for Senator. Sandy quit her law firm, and diligently worked for her election. This enabled her to ride Kipper's wave of success into public office too. They became close friends, closer than either dared talk about. With the recent mid-term election, Sandy won her fourth term.

She answered, "Hello."

"It's Kipper here, darling."

"I almost gave up on you. I'm getting ready to leave for New York and make a long weekend of it."

"No, Sandy. You're staying in Washington."

After a brief pause, Sandy replied in a serious tone, "Is there a crisis?"

"No; Sandy! I've got a special job for you."

She chuckled. "So you won't need my services as a lawyer?"

"That's right, darling. You have a special future in the Rodwell administration."

"What then? A cabinet post? I don't want to give up my elected office for that!"

"Vice President!" replied Kipper. After saying this, a loud intake of breath became audible to her.

Surprised; Sandy responded in a loud voice, "What about Villalobos?"

"He's dying. A bad heart, and I can hardly wait! You already know why we put him on the ticket."

"Yes, Kipper; we needed a Hispanic moderate to round out the ticket. He solidified that base for us in the big election back in '08. That put us over the top after the disaffected redneck coalition fell apart. Bushy Baby left us sitting pretty when he went down the tubes. Will Villalobos last long?"

"He had a triple bypass. Three of his four valves are almost closed."

"Let's celebrate! I'll join you tonight!"

"No, Sandy! There have already been rumors. I must think of my position. The only place you'll see me is in church."

"Oh Kipper, the only churches I ever saw you in were black and that was at election time."

"Yes, dear; but each time was worth a hundred thousand votes to me. But I am taking you to Beirut with me this week."

"What am I going to do there?"

"You'll go as an observer on a special fact finding mission. I'm going to put you in the public eye. It will increase your profile and I can represent you as knowledgeable on international affairs. Be ready when the time comes. I must go now."

———

President Rodwell's secretary interrupted the conference with an emergency call. "Madame President, I think you need to take this!"

Irritated, Kipper took the phone. "This is President Rodwell."

"Madame President, you have an emergency call from Walter Reed Hospital concerning the Vice President," said the government operator. "Shall I connect you?"

"Yes, I will take this call; standby." Before she resumed the call; Kipper cupped her hand over the receiver and spoke to the assembly. "Ladies and Gentlemen, one moment please. This could be important. Go ahead," she said to the operator.

"Connecting."

"President Rodwell?"

"Speaking! Who is this?"

"Sorry to bother you, Madame President. This is Dr. Levinson at Walter Reed Hospital."

"What can I do for you, Dr. Levinson?"

"Madame President, it's about Vice President Villalobos; he had a severe stroke and was brought here twenty minutes ago. I thought you would want to know immediately."

Kipper suppressed a smile. "Oh, that is awful. Please keep me informed of any change? Will you do that for me, Dr. Levinson?"

"Yes, Madame President."

"How bad is he really?"

"We immediately put him on life support, Madame President. It's aggravated because he has a bad heart. Vice President Villalobos had a triple bypass earlier this month."

"Yes, I know, Doctor! Thank you for everything, goodbye."

"Goodbye, Madame President."

Kipper rose from her desk. "Ladies and Gentlemen, I have some very sad news," she said with a solemn tone. "Our beloved Vice President Villalobos is hospitalized at Walter Reed with a massive stroke. Let us observe a moment of silence for him."

The next morning, the headlines of *The New York Times* read:

VICE PRESIDENT GRAVELY ILL

Washington, D.C.

Vice President Villalobos suffered a massive stroke, yesterday at 6:45 A.M. He was immediately hospitalized at Walter Reed. Doctors say he will probably not be able to resume his duties. President Rodwell is distressed, says she relies heavily on Villalobos for advice.

It was Wednesday morning, two days before the Middle East conference in Beirut. President Rodwell was conducting a press conference in the West Wing prior to leaving for Beirut. She unexpectedly introduced Sandy, who smiled and silently watched Kipper as the mainstream press doted on her words. Forty minutes later the press conference concluded with the dignitaries of the Rodwell delegation standing for a group photo.

After the meeting, Kipper took her aside privately. "Sandy, your time is almost here. I hope you're packed and ready for this evening."

"I am. Is there any more news on Villalobos?"

"He appears stabilized for the moment, but his right side is completely paralyzed. I think he may resign soon. Don't be impatient; we have to play the game. Give him some time to recover. Don't worry darling, Villalobos is history. When I nominate you for his job, remember to act surprised. Until then, I have another job for you."

"What do you want from me now?"

"You're going to help me defuse this Mid-East crisis."

"How can I do that? When we get there, I'll be on a fact finding mission."

"Not any longer, darling. Your profile is going through the ceiling. I'm appointing you as my special ambassador to the Palestinians. After we conclude this business, you will swing through Western Europe and meet some influential men."

"Will I be in Beirut long?"

"No, darling; just briefly! My husband, George, is meeting me there. I want you to join us on his yacht."

"Oh, Kipper! I can't stand that Greek. He's already made a pass at me. He'll screw anything in skirts. Why do you put up with him?"

Kipper laughed. "Boys will be boys! Besides, George is very useful to me. Lighten up, Sandy."

"Men! They're only good for one thing, Kipper; sperm donors. And most of them are no good for that. They spend nine months trying to get out of us and most of their adult life trying to get back in."

"Control your passion, darling. You must be Ms. Congeniality. I know you can do it when you try. In a world largely dominated by men, we still have to win them over. Put on your best smile and be ready to go to work. When you talk to those Palestinians, remember to wear a head scarf and be deferential."

"What am I supposed to do with those people? They're uncivilized!"

"Don't be racist, darling. Those damned Israelis ran most of them out of the West Bank. The Palestinians have rights too. Why can't all of these people just get along?"

"You already know why, Kipper. Two years of renewed violence by Hamas killed more than three thousand Israelis just in the last year. That nerve gas attack in Tel Aviv last month was the last straw."

"Nevertheless, darling, you are going to help me calm them down before the whole Mid-East blows up in our faces. I will deal with the Israelis directly. You promise Hamas the U.S. will take in hundreds of thousands of displaced Palestinians.

And we'll pledge more money to rebuild their settlements."

"Kipper, it's rumored that Osama Bin Laden is going to Palestine and lead them himself."

"He wouldn't dare! We might have missed him. The Israelis wouldn't be so careless. Anyway, I'll see you this evening! Goodbye now, darling."

That evening, Air Force One waited on the tarmac at Andrews Air Force Base as President Rodwell's limousine drove up. Kipper called out to Sandy who was standing at the bottom of the ramp. Soon the entire delegation arrived. After numerous hugs and well wishes, the entourage boarded the plane.

It was an unusually hot day in late May of 2011. The new Palestinian refugee camps outside of Beirut were overflowing. Emergency food aid from the United Nations and the U.S. barely sufficed to feed all of these refugees. A right wing government had swept into office in Jerusalem. The 1,500 deaths from the nerve gas attack in Tel Aviv had been compared to the Nazi Death Camps. Reminiscent of the holocaust, these new hard-liners publicly stated—never again! The West Bank was becoming depopulated as Israeli troops rounded up Palestinians by the tens of thousands, transporting them north in heavily guarded bus convoys to the Lebanese border. Thousands more fled on foot. Refusing to accept this deluge of humanity, the Jordanians had sealed their border. As the Israeli Parliament considered permanent annexation of the

West Bank, an emergency session of the U.N. convened. Threats of jihad resounded from Pakistan across the Middle East and into North Africa.

Kipper and Sandy, along with U.N. and Lebanese dignitaries, observed the scene from the Blackhawk helicopter flying low and slow over the refugee camp. Escorted by two Apache gunships, President Rodwell expressed her displeasure at the appalling conditions below. The U.N. sponsored conference in Beirut later today was critical. She had to get it right; Kipper must defuse this crisis. She planned to be especially firm with the Israelis. After all, weren't they acting like Nazis too?

Muhammad al Akmed sat in silence, swatting the flies buzzing around his head when he heard the helicopter approaching. Though only sixteen, he was already a soldier in Hamas. During his flight from Palestine, he had picked up an RPG–7 from a fallen comrade. It was wrapped in a blanket by his side. Muhammad saw the American helicopter and immediately knew what he wanted. Within minutes he would be in paradise, and become a martyr. Soon, his people would revere his name. Uncovering the launcher, he quickly raised it to his shoulder. Taking careful aim as he led his target, Muhammad fired. The Blackhawk with its stellar assemblage had a date with destiny.

"What's that?" said Lt. Colonel Travis to his co-pilot in the Apache gunship. "Is that man holding a weapon? Open fire." It was too late; the RPG rocket found its target and exploded. The Blackhawk crashed onto the refugee camp below, quickly deluged in flames from its exploding fuel tank. Immediately, the escorting gunships began pouring fire into the crowded camp. Dozens of Palestinians were killed and wounded. Muhammad's severed head lay on top of a dead fifteen-year old boy nearby.

Within minutes, news of the disaster flashed from communication satellites above, as the world waited for news of President Rodwell. It was not long in coming. There were no survivors from the crash of the Blackhawk. President Rodwell and other members of the U.N. delegation were dead.

In Washington, both Houses of Congress were called into emergency session. The Democrats called for a special election. Speaker of the House Ramsey couldn't assume the Presidency as long as Villalobos was alive. The discussion was heated. At five o'clock EST, the issue was settled, as word arrived at the House assemblage from Walter Reed Hospital. Vice President Villalobos had just died. At nine o'clock that same evening, the Chief Justice of the Supreme Court swore in the new President of the United States. In the midst of a solemn congregation, Stuart Ramsey pressed his right hand on the same Bible that George Washington had sworn his oath upon over two hundred years before. The event was televised to a shocked world.

The press went wild over the next few days, comparing Kipper Rodwell to Lincoln, Roosevelt, Princess Diana, Mother Teresa and Kennedy. Talk show hosts were already referring to Ramsey as a caretaker for the next two years. Cries from the liberal intelligentsia derided him for being only a high school graduate. The Hollywood crowd derogatorily called him that "redneck." Ramsey was bandied in the press as "democracy's ultimate mistake" in a flawed process of succession. Special interest groups called for his resignation in favor of the more capable and experienced next in line, the President of the Senate, Democratic Senator Edmund Canaday.

The morning after Ramsey's inauguration, Jim Scott took a few minutes to read the headlines of the *Times Picayune*. The events of the previous day were the talk of the office. There was no end to speculation. He was secretly pleased after reading the brief biography of Stuart Ramsey presented in the paper.

NANCY

The tall, attractive, blonde was admitted into the Oval Office. At forty-two, she could easily have passed for a woman in her early thirties. She glided across the room with the smooth, confident motion of a jungle cat. Ramsey rose and walked around his desk to greet her. As she stopped in front of him, her smile widened while she extended her right arm full length.

Taking her outstretched hand with his right, he warmly pressed his left hand upon hers. "Thank you so much for coming, Nancy. I really appreciate your prompt response to this request."

"Thank God you're not one of those hand kissers," she replied. "I get a belly-full of them, always so eager to approach me."

He laughed, motioning for her to sit down, "Have you guessed why I sent for you?"

Nancy Colton was a self-made woman, an ex-lawyer, writer and part-time commentator, superbly confident, and the ultimate enemy of George Orwell's Newthink. To mainstream liberals she was the devil incarnate. "I figure you intend to offer me a job."

"That's why I always liked you, Nancy; you're smarter than any man I ever met."

"So, President Ramsey, what's it going to be? Your press secretary?"

"Try again; and call me Stuart."

"Wow, I am flattered, a cabinet post then? Maybe a Federal Judge," she teased.

"No."

"Well; let's see! What will it be then, Stuart?"

"I want you to be my mistress. What else? I filled up the hot tub just before you arrived, and the champagne is on ice." They both laughed.

"Wow, this house hasn't had action this good since Bill lived here," she answered.

"Seriously, Nancy; I want to nominate you for Vice President."

Stunned, she sat silent looking at him before replying. "I didn't think you could surprise me quite this much! There's not going to be anything dull about your administration, even if it only lasts for these next two years."

"Two years, Nancy; if they don't impeach me first. How about it?"

"Do you think the old boys club of the Republican Party will go along with you? You must already know the Democrats hate me!"

"They think I'm just their puppet, Nancy. I can already feel the tug from their strings. Yes, they plan to control me all right. You should see their wish list of appointments." Grasping a folder on his desk, Ramsey tossed it in front of her. "Here, see for yourself. I'm stupid; don't you know? I don't even have a college degree."

Nancy sat in awe before responding. "I think you are going to educate this whole country, and very soon. If you nominate me for VP, I will take the job if you can pull this off. I have my doubts. What makes you think you can? And why did you choose me?"

"I read everything you ever wrote. Some of it twice! You don't just have brains; you have courage and principle. And besides, you're a hell of lot prettier than Kipper was." This brought another round of laughter. "I am quite serious about this, Nancy; you're not going to be some cosmetic job for my administration. I need your help. I want good people around me, smart people, only the very best. Over the years you've met more influential people than I probably ever will. I only have these last few weeks of political experience. I don't want to botch this job. You must help me choose wisely; you'll be part of the decision-making process. I do have one great big advantage over all of my predecessors in this office. Know what that is?"

"I'm on pins and needles waiting for you to tell me," she replied.

"I don't owe anybody. No one helped me get where I am. I'm the biggest goddamn accident in history since fire was discovered. These entrenched power brokers, well frankly, they can all go to hell! And, take their list of appointees with them!"

"I am curious, Stuart. The rumor around Washington is that you bought your seat in Congress. I don't believe it. Will you tell me the truth of it?"

"I've heard that rumor too, Nancy. Years ago, I got lucky and came into some money. You probably know about that lottery?"

"Everybody does."

"Well, I invested wisely; became a billionaire many times over. I love Nevada, and still own property there. But every man has his dream. Mine was owning hundreds of acres covered with trees and pasture with a stream and a lake too. I was tired of those cold winters in Northern Nevada. Naturally, I turned to the sunny South. Acreage was more affordable down there, and I found just what I wanted in Georgia. Then came that long drought years ago. Do you remember that one, Nancy?"

"Yes; it was horrible! Thousands almost lost their farms. It took them years to make a comeback."

"That's right! My new neighbors in north Georgia and adjoining parts of South Carolina were affected. These hard working farmers stood to lose everything. I had more money than I could ever spend. My own origins are pretty humble. I remembered where I came from, and for that matter where I might have to go back to someday. I loaned over a billion dollars, interest free to these folks. Most already paid me back. I wasn't looking for a ticket to Washington; but I made friends and saved more than a few livelihoods. They must have figured I cared enough to represent them in Congress. The local party bosses weren't very happy that I chose to run as a Constitutionalist. I won't be a hack for either major party."

"You're the right man for the job, Stuart. Why did you keep us waiting so long?"

"Nancy, here's what I want."

"Whoa, Stuart! You already told me what you want. Doesn't the girl still get the champagne and hot tub?"

"Nancy, I . . . !"

She took an inviting step toward him. "You were sincere, I hope. I must believe in my President."

"But I was only . . . I can't say no to a lady. Come here!" He embraced her lithe body and she planted a moist kiss on his lips.

"This is the stuff legends are made of, Mr. President. I don't mind being part of yours."

They spent the day together. The shock wave of Colton's nomination hit Washington that same afternoon. Later that week, Gilbert O'Mallie invited President Ramsey to appear on his show, Straight Talk. He accepted.

The savvier of his new colleagues cautioned Ramsey about taking up the challenge. Gilbert O'Mallie had broken the careers of many influential people. Undeterred, he accepted it with gusto!

The front page of next day's edition of *The New York Times* read:

RAMSEY NOMINATES
RIGHT WING WRITER FOR VP

Washington, D.C.

Republicans visibly upset over President's Ramsey's choice for second spot. Rumor has it that the nomination won't fly. Democrats aghast at Ramsey's ultra-right wing pick. Filibuster threatened unless Colton's nomination is withdrawn.

President Ramsey's thoughts dwelled on this afternoon's upcoming meeting. "Let the games begin," he thought. "Soon these bastards will arrive." His apprehension increased as he watched the approaching stream of cars circle the Rose Garden from a window in the Oval Office. A sudden knock and the friendly voice of a Secret Service man informed him of their arrival.

He smiled as he thought of the coming struggle. The blood hounds were here and hungry for the fox. Ramsey answered, "Escort them into the Roosevelt Room, Mike! I'll be with them momentarily."

"Yes, sir; Mr. President," the man replied before leaving.

Ramsey paused, taking several deep breaths before joining them. All of those present rose out of respect, many of them wearing plastic smiles as he walked into the Roosevelt Room. How many of these people would prove unswerving, he could only guess. But the defensive barriers blocking those ramparts in their minds would have to be surmounted. One thought haunted him. Could he do it? No; this was not enough. Ramsey knew he must prevail.

The most influential of both houses were invited today. The room was filled to capacity with the leaders of each party. Extra seating had been provided in the modest sized room. Some of these politicians wielded influence far beyond their elected positions, a fact which Stuart had seriously weighed in advance. Here in the West Wing, he had more control. There wouldn't be as many to win over. In face to face situations, Ramsey's personality had always been his strongest asset. As he made a circuit around the room, he warmly greeted each one.

His tone of conciliation became apparent as Ramsey began his pitch. "Ladies and Gentlemen, it may seem irregular to have such an informal meeting here; and I appreciate your attendance. I confess, I am overawed by these walls surrounding us where so many men greater than I have tread. Just think, Jackson, Lincoln, TR, Wilson, Roosevelt, Kennedy, Reagan and our own dear departed Kipper Rodwell graced this room. I am a man whom history has thrust within a temporary vacuum of greatness; and I know what my mission must be. And that, my friends and colleagues, is to provide an orderly transition between duly elected presidents. Most of you have already expressed doubts as to my choice for a Vice Presidential nomination. But consider, didn't Kipper herself set the precedent. Women make up over fifty per of the American population. Can I let politics alone influence my decision? Oh, I know what you all must be thinking. Ms. Colton is a right-winger. But please think of her as the balancing weight bringing the arm of the scale back even. She will help me unify our government. No longer will conservatives feel like the unwanted product of an ill-conceived union. Didn't the scale tip far in the other direction when President Rodwell occupied this office?"

For Senator Canaday, this was an opportunity, as he suddenly interrupted. "Mr. President, there are at least three dozen women in the House and Senate whose credentials far exceed that of Ms. Colton. We need solid professionalism in the person who is going to be one heartbeat away from that chair you're sitting in right now."

"Please, I don't make a habit of interrupting you, Senator. Did that same concern apply when many of you supported me for Speaker, not so long ago? My heart is healthy; I can assure you. Ms. Colton is further away from my job than you realize. We've had too much partisanship in Washington lately. Let's have a détente. This is a big job. I can't do it without you." He scanned their faces for a sign. It was there. The reasonableness of his tone was relaxing their defenses. The time was now; he would spring the trap.

"We need to move on. There are cabinet positions to fill; judges to appoint and a host of lower level positions. For these, I need recommendations. Non-partisanship must be the rule, with neither party alienated. Otherwise I must depend upon whichever party fills the void. I don't want to exclude either of you. All of America's elected representatives must share their guidance with me. Should I steer this helm of state alone? Demonstrate your leadership. Show the way. Help me? This is what I'm asking for. But, we must have a Vice President, someone whom I trust."

The assembled legislators slowly took the bait. His silver tongue wooed them into a sense of security. Though he made no promises, all were certain that this President would be non-confrontational. Each man and woman there came to the same conclusion, the one he had guided them to; Ramsey would let them run the show. His non-partisan stance was breaking down their defenses. The wheels of their imaginations turned as power seemed within reach for those quick to act. Each listener now calculated his party's share of the prize. The President skillfully read their expressions. He was winning them over.

Amid private murmurings, each politician made it clear that

Nancy Colton would have to answer comprehensive questioning in front of the Senate. A handful, including Canaday himself expressed doubt that she would prove worthy of their vote. But the seed had been planted in enough minds. As his pitch came to an end, Ramsey iced the cake. Telling them he wanted to make some key appointments soon, he asked for recommendations. Neither party wanted to be left out of this. Neither could allow the other to become dominant.

The end game played out to his satisfaction. Nancy would face a grilling over the Senatorial coals but she would be well coached in advance.

Both liberal and conservative news pundits had already buried Nancy Colton's candidacy. Their shock was unfathomable when she was approved later that week. Ramsey's supporters were able to override even Canaday's carefully orchestrated opposition. *The New York Times* and liberal intelligentsia cried *sellout*. Her ascension to office was heralded as another miracle. It soon would join the mystique of what would come to be called the *Ramsey magic*.

Late on the evening following their triumph, Stuart and Nancy would share a few hours savoring their victory. This followed the press releases, photo ops and reception after she was sworn in. They sat across from each other at a small table in the White House sharing wine and cake.

Nancy smiled with a twinkle in her eye as Stuart raised a

glass of wine and toasted her. "Madame Vice President," he said. "My Madame Vice President!"

She leaned forward, resting her chin on interlaced hands and stared dreamily into his eyes. The pool of desire she saw in them was unmistakable.

"My President," she responded. "No, I think you must be Aladdin. That's it! Aladdin with the magic lamp! It wasn't enough to cast your spell on me; you have enchanted a whole nation."

"Let's forget the rest tonight, Nancy. There's just you and me, here in our own world."

"It's strange, darling," she said. This was the first time she ever called him darling. "I never wanted to marry. But I feel like I'm yours. Finish your cake, darling; we have more important things to do."

"Take it in your hand; raise it to my mouth," Stuart replied.

Nancy tilted her head slightly. "Why?"

"It will taste better if you touch it."

"That's so sweet. But I don't think I want to wait that long."

"Who needs cake? I can think of something far better." He pushed himself away from the table, extending his right arm to her. "Nancy?"

She rose and melted into his arms. He crushed her body into his and buried her head in his chest. Suddenly she thrust her face upward. He smothered her lips with a lingering kiss.

Their tongues greedily sought out each other's. She mumbled, "You wooed me; you won me; now take me!"

Stuart pulled back and swung Nancy off her feet and into his arms. She giggled and kicked off her shoes, nestling her head against his cheek as he carried her. Their mutual satisfaction would not be long in coming!

———

Secret Service agents knew Nancy stayed that night. It wasn't the last time. With words unsaid, all could guess why. Mum was the word with them. With utmost discretion, they protected the President's reputation as well as his life, even after the rumors began to circulate.

———

The Democrats pushed for a rollover of all the Rodwell appointees, especially in the cabinet. Their choice of judicial nominees, all with ACLU connections soon found its way to Ramsey's desk. The Republicans submitted their own wish list of oil and financial moguls that would have made the elder Bush envious.

After Nancy's confirmation, Ramsey personally thanked Congress for its support. Almost as promptly, he trashed their proposed nominations of brain dead zombies. There were exceptions. Some of these came from conscientious legislators, men and women of character and principle.

Then came the Ramsey bombshell! No members of the Council of Foreign Relations, Trilateral Commission or

Bilderbergers would receive any appointment in his administration. The House and Senate retaliated. None of his nominees got through committee. The pace of business in Washington flowed like molasses in winter.

Except for the most essential services, including the Department of Defense, Treasury and Post Office, most departments of the government were shut down. Ramsey fired hundreds of Rodwell appointees. Many other career bureaucrats were put on paid administrative leave.

Large headlines on the front page of *The New York Times* read:

RAMSEY BULLIES CONGRESS, SHUTS DOWN CABINET
Washington, D.C.

International contact is put on hold as vacancy in the Department of State goes unfilled. Rancor is rampant in Congress as President Ramsey refuses to compromise on appointments. Ramsey maintains his right to choose, says he has the right to pick men and women he can work with. Senator Daphne Feinberg from Oregon calls Ramsey "bull headed." Senator Canaday of Maine calls the Ramsey Administration, "regression into nineteenth century mentality."

MARTY

The air was sweet. The sun had just dropped below the horizon. A cold breeze wafted in my face as the sleek riverboat plied against the current. Sounds of jazz came from the piano inside the bar. The couple next to me left the railing and walked inside toward the music. As they pulled away my side vision captured the lithe form standing alone. We turned our heads toward each other at the same moment. Her long pretty hair hung below her shoulders. She flashed me a haunting smile.

My eyes held hers while I considered the next move. God! How could anything look so good? Glacier blue eyes vividly contrasted with her dark hair. Creamy skin reminded me of Snow White. This girl probably doesn't speak English;

but Marty, I thought; you've got nothing to lose. Slowly I approached as her eyes held mine. "Hi! Pretty night, isn't it?"

The curl in her enchanting smile increased as she replied. "You are an American?"

"Yes! We show up everywhere; don't we? What's your name?"

"Illyana Petrovna." she said, offering me her hand.

"I'm Martin Raggio. What's a pretty girl like you doing all alone on a Russian riverboat?"

"I have never had a vacation until now, Mr. Raggio. I want to grab something from life while I'm still young."

"I understand that, Illyana; I feel the same. You speak English so well!"

"I studied English and French at Moscow University. When I was young, I wanted to become an interpreter and travel. I had to quit when Natasha was born."

"You're married then?"

"No! Mr. Raggio. I was never married."

"Why don't you call me Marty; then I can let my guard down."

"As you say, Marty." The girl reached into her purse and pulled out a pack of cigarettes. She fumbled, but couldn't find her matches. "Excuse me please, do you have a light? I forgot my matches. They must be in my cabin."

"I don't smoke, Illyana. We can get some in the bar. May I buy you a drink?"

"Thank you, Marty. That sounds like fun."

We walked inside. There were two vacant seats at the piano bar and we quickly covered the intervening distance taking them. The girl sat at my left. A cocktail waitress came and Illyana asked for a glass of red wine. I ordered a scotch on the rocks and some matches. We made small talk until the waitress returned. Silently, I struck a match and raised it to her waiting cigarette.

Her shoulders heaved slightly as she gratefully breathed in that first long draught of smoke. She blinked once before speaking. "You are on holiday, Marty?"

Her pretty eyes seemed to penetrate my mind, as she waited for me to reply. I wondered what kind of life she led. "I guess you could say that."

"You are a businessman, maybe?"

"No, Illyana. It's more like your first question."

She exhaled again, silently regarding my answer, before putting her cigarette in the ashtray.

"You see, Illyana; this is more like one last act of financial independence before I return to the reality of life back in the 'States."

"I always thought that reality of life in America was very good. Is it the exception for you, Marty?"

I didn't feel like lying to this girl. I would probably never see her again. "No; not so very much, Illyana. With me it's escapism. I always dreamed of traveling around the world. And then a stroke of bad luck motivated me to make it happen. I said to myself, Marty, you've always done it the other guy's way. Do something for yourself this time. So, I've got this little card in my pocket, American Express you see. And I'm going to live my dream before financial ruin catches up with me."

Illyana put her wine glass down, her body vibrating as she laughed. "You are a pirate then?"

I laughed too. "I like that, Illyana. Yes; I guess I'm hijacking American Express."

"They don't put you in jail for that in America?"

"No, they think of other, more creative ways to ruin your life. But with me that would happen anyway. So, I'm going to have a little fun first. It's sort of like a payoff to me from me for being me. I guess so anyway. I never thought it out deeper than that."

"You make me laugh. So what was so bad that happened to Marty?"

"Oh, nothing much, I just lost my job after nineteen years. I have to start over. And, I owe everybody in town. I don't want to think about me; let's talk about you."

"What is there to say? I am a woman."

"I've noticed!"

"When I was in my second year at the university, Natasha was born. I had to live with my mother in her little apartment and take any work I could get. These last years, I started my own business. Now I make my own money."

"Where is Natasha's father?"

"I don't know," she said as she reached for her cigarette. "I haven't seen him since before she was born."

"How old is Natasha?"

"She is twelve."

I could see she was trying to read my mind.

"And I am thirty-two."

"Illyana, it is noisy in here. Let's walk."

She nodded and reached for her purse. We went outside onto the main deck. Making our way to the bow, we leaned over the railing. Here we laughed as the spray and wind chilled our faces. Russian evenings were still cold in late May, but neither of us cared. Invigorated, I took her hand and we strolled endlessly around the deck, unaware of the hours passing so quickly.

The evening rolled on. Sounds of music still emanated from the bar. Though her warm grip responded willingly to my touch, I knew she must be getting cold. I took her back inside and offered to buy her a drink.

Illyana looked at her watch. "I am tired, Marty. I must go to my cabin now."

My hopes were running high. "I'll walk you there." We stopped by her cabin door and she said goodnight. I gently pulled her into me.

Her willing lips lingered on mine. Then she gently pushed me away. "I must go inside now, Marty; alone."

"Can we have breakfast together, Illyana?"

"All right, come to my cabin at nine."

My cabin wasn't far away. But I didn't remember walking there. All I could think of was—Illyana. Her smile and lovely face haunted me until I finally drifted off to sleep.

The first light of the day warmed my eyes. I rolled out of bed. Through the porthole of my cabin I could see barges and other river craft pass by. The *Novikov Priboy* was a large inland water passenger ship. I boarded her yesterday morning in St. Petersburg for one leg of the Waterway of the Tsars River Cruise. Major Russian cities were well-linked by water through an interconnecting series of canals, rivers and lakes. One could travel from the Baltic Sea all the way to Moscow. This was our destination. We would cover it in six days.

My ticket was waiting in Moscow for the Trans-Siberian Railway to Vladivostok. This last part was a flight of fancy for me. Almost my entire adult working career was spent as a railroad man. And for most of that, I was as an engineer. The journey from Moscow to Vladivostok by rail would take another ten days.

Losing my job meant that financial ruin would come within a month. I wasn't going to wait placidly for its arrival. With gusto I sought escapism. An old girl friend, Kristin, helped me plan this marathon of madness. Until now my life lacked direction. My childless marriage to Janet ended five years ago. Then I went through a chain of live-in girl friends. Most of them were recycles from someone else's bad experiments in life. After many years, I became emotionally hollow.

Then I met Illyana. From that first night, she became my constant companion. She responded warmly to my attention and her affection seemed genuine. But she always stopped short at the failsafe point. She had everything a man could desire in a woman, most of all class. Our days were spent sightseeing. Evenings, we dined and danced. Before we got to Moscow, I knew that train ride across Siberia would not take place.

I took a room at the Sheraton Moscow. We saw each other every day. With her, duty came first. But she saved her free time for me. The flame which was kindled that first night continued to grow. Illyana became everything.

She lived with her mother and daughter Natasha. Over the years, she scrimped and saved to start a fledgling business. She was a graphics artist and designed greeting cards. After the enterprise gained momentum, she moved her family into a better apartment. Natasha always had nice clothes and Illyana's mother was well cared for.

Her feelings toward me were like a slow blooming flower. She had never allowed romance to interfere with her goals. Her experience with men was limited, a fact for which I was grateful.

It was my last day in Moscow. Tomorrow on Sunday, I would fly back to Reno. My trip around the world was permanently cancelled. What did matter was Illyana. Financial ruin couldn't be my future; I wouldn't allow it. A way must be found to salvage my career. Hoping we could spend my last afternoon together, I was waiting in the bistro when she arrived. Soon after our coffee was served, she apologized. Illyana must return and fill an order. It was no surprise; she often worked six days a week.

I realized our time was precious. We had never consummated, which only served to enhance her mystery and deepen my longing. Rampant with desire, I wanted her in the flesh. She couldn't remain just my vision of a goddess. Illyana must be mine.

I begged her to stay. "Illyana, a few moments more? I was going to ask later; but, I can't wait. Will you marry me? You know how I feel. I love you!"

Her eyes held me in a trance. That perpetual smile widened, concealing her true thoughts. Raising her hand, she ran her fingers though my mane of hair. "I do care for you, Marty!"

I took her flawless hand into my palm, gently stroking it with my other. It felt like silk and looked like fine cream. Raising her hand to my lips, I kissed it. My God, I thought; it must have taken ten thousand generations to produce this perfection. "I can be good for you, Illyana."

"Marty, you must know by now that I have strong feelings for you. But no, Marty, not right away. I have to think."

"What's the matter, Illyana? Don't you know that I love you?"

"I know that. I think I have known it since that first night on the boat. Darling, I have only gone backwards one time in my life. It will never happen to me again. What little I have didn't come easy. I put Natasha first, and my mother needs me too."

"I had a good job. I'll get it back and work hard. We can all live together. Reno is beautiful. Life is good in Nevada. You made it possible, Illyana. You brought me back; now I care what happens too."

"I am Russian, Marty. That is enough for me, at least for now."

"Illyana, please don't tell me this is so."

"It is for now; we just met. Marty?"

"Yes, my love?"

"Don't give up! It's easy to love you. I need time."

Strangely, before we left the bistro, Illyana said she would come to my hotel later that evening. And I must wait for her there. Our last night together was already planned. We would go to a ballet, and then have a late supper afterward. I had never been to a ballet. Illyana sold me on the idea days ago.

It was still early when I answered the knock at my room door. She walked inside and stood looking at me in silence. "I'll be ready in a few more seconds, Illyana. I'll get you a glass of wine." I pointed to an easy chair. "Here, sit down while you wait." Before she could speak, I dashed to the bar, quickly returning with the wine. I held it out to her.

"No, darling!" she replied.

"OK, I'll just get my coat and tie; then, we can leave early."

"No, Marty! You won't need them. Tonight, darling, I am your ballet." She put down her purse. Slowly unfastening her dress, her eyes spoke to me as her enchanting smile held me captive; that same enchanting smile I had grown to love so much.

———

I had a one hour layover at JFK Airport, waiting for my return flight to Reno. Chatter was lively in the corridors. President Rodwell's sudden death yesterday was on everybody's lips, Villalobos too. Dozens wept unabashedly. No less stunned than the others, I decided to buy a newspaper. There was a bookstore in the waiting area. I walked there.

Once inside, I watched the overhead news monitor. The commentator spoke at length. A relatively unknown Nevadan had ascended to the presidency. "Few events in history have produced accidents such this," he said. "President Ramsey will be giving his first press conference ten minutes from now."

After paying for a copy of *The New York Times*, I stood there waiting under the news monitor. A crowd of people gathered as we all waited for the new president to speak. Soon a tall, bronzed, lean, broad shouldered man stepped up to the podium. Did he look like a president? I wondered. No, more like a marshal out of the Old West. Maybe even a gunfighter! He was solid, sincere and confident. I was overjoyed. As far as I could see, the country had only gone to hell under Rodwell. And then he spoke. I knew then; this was my president. I felt he was speaking to me personally. Every one of his words counted. Ramsey inspired confidence. A couple liberal types, one looked like a swish, openly disparaged him. I couldn't take it any longer. "Why the hell don't you shut up and let him talk," I yelled.

One of them, wearing a lip ring, got in my face. I could have put him away in forty seconds. But the challenge wasn't worth spending that night in a New York jail. I had to get home and put my crumbling economic house in order. I wanted Illyana.

Returning to the waiting area, I sat down and unfolded the newspaper. The article contained a brief biography of

Stuart Ramsey. Wide-eyed, I read through it twice. Wow,
I thought. Here is a common man, like me. From Nevada
too! This is worth saving, a nice memento. I separated the
relevant parts of the paper and tossed the rest away.

———

In Reno, I tried to get my old job back. I contacted my old
union griever, Bud Albright.

He promised to make the calls. The answer wasn't long
in coming. "No dice, Marty. You had a level five offense. You
went through a ten mile an hour slow order at sixty. You'll be
off at least a year if you get back at all."

"You tried. So long, Bud."

"Take care of yourself, Marty."

———

I had one card left to play. One winter when railroad work
was slow, I hired out for a non-union construction outfit in
California. They taught me how to operate heavy equipment.
That was eighteen years ago. Would I remember anything?
I checked with operating engineer's local in Reno. The news
wasn't good. I would have to go through a five year apprentice
program with them. Five years was too long.

Why not work for myself? I needed equipment. But I
would have to get the start-up money. I quickly learned there
was no source of capital for an out of work railroad man with
no assets. But I was not totally without resources. My dad died
when I ten and my maiden Aunt Irene, the school teacher, was

always there for me. I was afraid at first to approach her. She had been stiffed out of money by relatives before. Embracing me, she was eager to assist. Aunt Irene claimed I was like her own child. I now had a $25,000 stake.

I began putting my life back in order. Working out a repayment schedule with my creditors, including American Express, I salvaged my credit. From an equipment leasing company I acquired a fifteen ton Caterpillar bulldozer with an old semi and low-boy trailer to haul it. After a few days practice, I was able to give a decent account of myself. I beat the bushes about Northern Nevada looking for work. This wasn't so easy; nobody knew me. At first all I got were small jobs. I put my furniture in storage and slept in the semi. I quit drinking, showered in truck stops and ate frugally.

It was early July, 2011. I was drinking coffee at a truck stop in Winnemucca. Almost given to despair, I had just been turned down after trying to sub-contract to one of the mines. I was politely told they were union. Some phone company field supervisors were sitting nearby, discussing their predicament. I overheard their conversation. A landslide had isolated their transmitters on a steep mountain peak nearby. The microwave relay tower was down. They lacked in-house resources to reach it. Other hauling contractors were playing a high-dollar game with them. Even the possibility of using helicopters was being considered. Here was my chance. Though it was dark, I offered my immediate services that same night. I displayed confidence and they went for it.

It was dangerous. I could have slid off that damn mountain and died that same night. Indeed, I came close to it. But my luck held. I dragged their equipment to the relay tower. Within thirty days I got my check in the mail, one thousand dollars for that first afternoon's work. I gained a reputation as the guy who could get anything anywhere. Weather or lack of roads didn't stop me. The worse outdoor conditions became, the better the money. It wasn't long before more was coming in than going out.

Business was booming everywhere. The Rodwell depression-recession had disappeared. Ramsey's tariff policies encouraged entrepreneurs to risk business capital in America. With its favorable tax structure and pro-business policy, Nevada was among the first states to benefit. There was no shortage of work. I was making more money than I ever dreamed possible. My railroad career became ancient history. I would never go back to it.

THE BORDER

With his sleeves rolled up, coat and tie off, President Ramsey leaned over a map showing the border with Mexico. Silence followed shock as they listened to his declaration. Secretly this assemblage of admirals and generals resented having a former Marine Corporal as their Commander in Chief, even if Ramsey had received the Bronze Star with Combat V and was wounded in Vietnam.

"Gentlemen, let us proceed." As Ramsey began speaking, he looked at each officer individually, holding momentary eye contact before moving to the next. "By this time tomorrow, the first stages of deployment will be taking place. Gentlemen, we are going to seal our southern border. Illegal immigration from that source has ended as of this meeting.

Bear in mind we may have to do the same on the Canadian border. It's possible these unauthorized entries may shift and come from that direction."

He was questioned about the legality of taking this action. Congress had not been consulted and the courts may overrule it.

"I've carefully thought this over. I am the Commander in Chief. Our country's security rests with me. The statutes are on the books. I'm just going to enforce the law. The Border Patrol can't do the job. There are not enough of them; I don't think there ever were. We are dealing with an invasion. It may be benign in some respects, but it is nevertheless an invasion by persons who don't respect our laws. Tonight, I am going to address the American Public in a live broadcast. I will declare martial law along the U.S.-Mexican border within distances from one-half to three miles in various locations. Law enforcement officers within the counties included in this zone will be empowered to arrest and detain illegal aliens. If Congress or the courts take issue, the law will have to change. Until then I'll enforce this one."

One general suggested Ramsey might face impeachment.

"I appreciate your concern," replied Ramsey. "It was a risky move in 1776 when a handful of men put their signatures on the Declaration of Independence. They defied the strongest military power of Earth, risking everything. Failure to them meant a hangman's noose. I don't put myself in their class. It's still a shock to me that I occupy this office; but I'm going to do my job. I don't have much regard for the way my predecessors did theirs. I may have to go to jail. That may be, yes; but history will be the judge."

Silent until now, the Chairman of the Joint Chiefs of Staff spoke. "President Ramsey, how do you propose to begin?"

"A fair question. I propose to move elements of the 4th Mechanized Infantry Division from Fort Hood toward the Southern Rio Grande along the Texas-Mexican border. Equally, we'll call up reserve elements of the 7th Infantry in conjunction with the 24th Infantry of the National Guard, both of which are currently headquartered at Fort Riley, Kansas. These will cover the upper Rio Grande in Texas and the border along New Mexico. To patrol from this juncture to the Pacific Ocean, we will move those troops of the 4th Infantry stationed at Fort Carson and activate the 40th National Guard Infantry Division from California."

Among the assembled officers, respect for their new Commander grew. One thing was certain; Ramsey was not afraid to lead.

It was seven that evening. All major networks broadcast the speech live from the Press Briefing Room in the White House. The nation listened in shock as viewers watched sixty million TV sets. In homes, businesses and bars, America listened to President Ramsey's declaration of martial law along the Southern border. After his announcement, Ramsey took questions from the press.

An attractive young reporter from the *Chicago Daily Sun*

asked, "Mr. President, what will you do if Congress and the Supreme Court forbid this move?"

"Thank you, ma'am. I knew this question was coming. Federal Law will be enforced unless it's formally changed."

A reporter from *The New York Times* raised his hand. Ramsey acknowledged him. "President Ramsey, it's pretty clear that this is directed against Hispanics, do you also plan to stop illegal immigrants from European Countries?"

"Thank you for the question, sir. I solemnly pledge to arrest and detain all of those ten million blond-hair, blue-eyed Swedes who are sneaking in too." A wave of laughter followed.

A young Hispanic reporter from San Antonio was next. "President Ramsey, a lot of people could get hurt. Why are you subjecting our troops to this? The immigrants might throw rocks at them."

"Thank you, sir. The zone is martial law. Ordinary protections under the Constitution are suspended where it is in effect. Rocks kill! If disaffected illegals throw them, I have already given the order; troops are authorized to use deadly force. Our soldiers will not become targets."

Unbelieving glances passed back and forth among the reporters.

A young, female Chinese-American from the *San Francisco Chronicle* raised her hand. Ramsey pointed to her. "Yes, ma'am? You there!"

"President Ramsey, what gives you the right to authorize the murder of innocent people and defy the courts? You weren't elected as president of this country anyway."

Ramsey smiled before answering. "Ma'am, ordering the troops to defend themselves from potentially lethal attacks is not murder. Enforcing laws is not defying the courts. As far as not being elected, that statement is somewhat subjective. Our forefathers determined the method of succession in unusual circumstances; so if I wasn't directly elected, those who were determined the process which brought me here."

The press conference ended at eight that evening. Ramsey retired for the night. Talk show hosts and news commentators were having a field day.

Next morning, the front page of *The New York Times* read:

RAMSEY VOWS TO STOP ILLEGAL IMMIGRATION
Washington, D.C.

In his nationwide telecast yesterday evening, President Ramsey announced a unilateral declaration of martial law along the U.S. / Mexico border. Ramsey declares he will defy the courts. Lawmakers are taking up this issue in Washington. Hispanic organizations nationwide call for a strike. Senator Canaday of Maine calls Ramsey racist, vows to overturn this move in the Senate. President of Mexico threatens to recall the Mexican Ambassador, says this will not be tolerated. The Rainbow Coalition and other civil rights groups vow solidarity with Hispanics. The Supreme Court has immediately taken up consideration of the issue.

On page sixteen of *The New York Times* a few lines read: Overnight Gallup Poll shows 68 per cent of Americans approve of President Ramsey's decision. Some African-American leaders also approve. They cite unfair competition in the job market from low-paid illegals.

Nancy smiled as Stuart reviewed headlines from major national newspapers. "Nancy, you're smiling like the cat that ate the bird."

"Stuart, I told you this would happen. May I be perfectly honest with you?"

"That's the only way I ever want it from you, Nancy."

"They are going to fry your balls in oil." She grinned at his startled expression.

Stuart bellowed with laughter from her unexpected vulgarity. "So, if I get impeached, I can go home and fish on my private lake. Then you can deal with these bastards on your own."

"Oh no, I wouldn't want to miss having you in that seat for the remainder of this term. I haven't had this much fun since I had my first orgasm. How are you going to handle that first Federal Judge who rules this move is unconstitutional?"

"This wasn't an impromptu decision, Nancy. I took certain steps beforehand. The Attorney General is submitting a Constitutional challenge to its legality as we speak. The judge is on our team; he will rule in our favor. A friendly Appeals Court will quickly back him up. This muddies the water for the opposition. Now we can take on the Supreme Court directly."

"They won't like it on the hill, Stuart. We can expect Hispanics to strike nationwide. Businesses will shut down, especially restaurants, hotels and services industries. We're going to see big demonstrations."

"Should I cave in? Maybe if I crawl the liberals will start loving me!"

"Stuart, your bacon is already cooked with those people. They wouldn't accept a recommendation for you from the Archangel Gabriel, even if they believed in God. So what's next with this immigration war you've started? This is not the end of it. They're not going to idly sit by while you dry up their major source of new Democrats."

"That's right, Nancy. Very soon, we'll require all hospitals, schools, welfare agencies, employers and public housing projects to turn in a list of illegals they have serviced, hired or cared for. Then, I order them picked up. If they haven't already dropped a kid on American soil, they get a one-way ticket back where they came from."

"You're not realistic Stuart, how can a handful of agents round up these illegals?"

"There were two presidents before me, Hoover during the Depression and Eisenhower in the '50s, who did just that. Between them both, millions of illegals were deported. Those were during times of economic crisis too. Hoover and Eisenhower wanted to protect American jobs. It's far more serious now. It comes down to life and death. Terrorists and drug dealers have almost unlimited access to our country."

"That doesn't solve the immediate problem, Stuart. The police won't round them up. What will you do?"

"Except for the lawful entry points, I'm shifting the Border Patrol into the cities, while the military guards the border. These agents will raid workplaces, restaurants and maintain a permanent presence at hospitals across this entire land. Restrictions and additions will be added to welfare requirements."

"It won't fly, Stuart. After they make an arrest, these people are entitled to an immigration hearing. No way in hell can the courts handle these numbers. They won't even try. Statistics have proven that very few will even show up for their hearings. They just move on to another location, assume another identity, and become lost in the multitude. And there's no way to detain those millions of them; beds and space just aren't available."

"We'll deport them as soon as we legally can. We'll be one step ahead, constantly busting their employers. When they get really hungry, we'll see some head south. As far as detention goes, a brave Sheriff in Arizona, Joe Arpaio showed us how, tent cities!"

"Are you going to let any return later?"

"I'm willing to work with Congress, if they enter legally with a work permit. We must know who is here and be able to screen out criminals. They're not going to bring their dependents or be entitled to unemployment, disability, or social security. If they fill American jobs, they'll pay American taxes. When they want to see their families, they can return home. If they get too sick, they go back to whatever third-world paradise they came from. That way we take the sting off of our social services."

"Now you're that heartless ogre to the liberals. Even some fundamentalist Christian groups are joining them."

"For every enemy I've made, I've also gained a new friend. I might even come off better in numbers with the latter."

"Stuart, your administration will be remembered. Everyone will either love you or love to hate you."

President Ramsey soon implemented phase two of his plan. Now, municipal and county law enforcement agencies would have to detain illegals pending extradition. The Border Patrol Chief complained. He was a leftover Rodwell appointee. Los Angeles, Denver, Chicago and Detroit refused to comply. Ramsey vowed to bring Federal charges against all City mayors, councilmen and police chiefs who snubbed enforcement of Federal law.

The border issue was taken up by the Supreme Court. By a vote of 6 to 3 they ruled Ramsey's actions were illegal. He accused the High Court of overstepping its authority, and refused to comply. The border tightened. Hardly any illegals were getting in; tens of thousands were being deported every week.

The showdown came. Ramsey faced impeachment. Canaday and Feinberg drafted a compromise offering to drop these proceedings if he would honor the Supreme Court's decision.

Remembering General McAuliffe's reply to the Germans at the Battle of Bastogne, he sent a sack of nuts to each of them.

⸻

The Secret Service Man opened the door of the Presidential Limousine. Ducking into the back seat, Ramsey smiled at him and joked. "Thanks Henderson, did you bring a set of handcuffs for the return trip?"

"Mr. President, please don't say that. We're on your side." Ramsey was well liked by these men guarding him.

There was no applause as his arrival was announced in the Senate. Respectfully, all stood up. With a pat smile he sat in the place prepared for him. The proprieties were soon observed and the questioning began.

All eyes and cameras were on the President. Senator Canaday was the first speaker. "President Ramsey," he said arrogantly, "Do you know why you're here?"

Ramsey laughed, "I heard a rumor I was going to be impeached." Some laughter followed.

Canaday scowled. "President Ramsey, before you ascended to your high office, this country had a rule of law. It was usually respected by your predecessors. And I hope it will be restored in our democracy at the end of this impeachment hearing. Do you understand me, Mr. President?"

"No, Senator Canaday, I don't. I have adamantly demanded that the rule of law be practiced. That includes all laws, Senator Canaday; even a few that I personally don't care for.

Oh, and just in case you don't know it, Senator, you don't live in a democracy. This is still a republic."

"President Ramsey, my Canaday ancestors fought in the Revolutionary War to create this country. I know what a democracy is."

"Senator Canaday, there is no mention of the word democracy in either the Constitution or the Declaration of Independence. The word was never used to describe our government until Woodrow Wilson became President. Our ancestors knew the difference between a republic and a democracy. Perhaps you should learn that difference also."

"Maybe I was never as well-educated as you, Mr. President; though I did go beyond high school and I graduated from Harvard."

"Yes, I heard. And after you were expelled for cheating, your daddy had to pay big money to get you back in."

Canaday fumed. "President Ramsey, it is clear that you are a racist and this new border policy is designed to discriminate against Hispanics. Who will you victimize next, Mr. President? Women? Do you plan to put cameras in the bedrooms and abortion clinics?"

"Senator Canaday, American women are safer with me as President than they would be riding in a car with you." Several in the room laughed.

"President Ramsey, are you showing contempt for Congress?"

"No, Senator; I'm trying very hard to conceal it."

Now there were ugly murmurs. Canaday's face turned red. His round of questioning ended.

He was followed by Senator Daphne Feinberg of Oregon. "President Ramsey?"

"Yes, Senator Feinberg?"

"I know you never had the benefit of higher education, and perhaps that's part of the problem here. Do you understand that the high courts of the land, including the Federal District Courts and ultimately our Supreme Court exist to interpret the laws? Do you understand that, Mr. President?"

"Senator Feinberg, please don't concern yourself with my education. I've read hundreds, maybe thousands of books in the fifty odd years since I reached the age of reason. Most of this was non-fiction. As far as the courts interpreting the laws, I have no problem with this. But, I made it clear in the beginning, that any Federal Law on the books would be enforced. I also made it clear to those elected to both houses; repeal any law you don't like. I would respect your decision. Congress legislates, not the president. But, 2 plus 2 always equals 4. No court is going to tell me that it equals 3 or 5. We are a sovereign independent country with borders. There are laws telling us who can be here and who can't. Illegal immigration is against the law. I'll uphold the Constitution of the United States as I swore to do, not very long ago. I may have to go the jail. That may be! Until then, I'll do my duty."

"Mr. President, these immigrants are needed. America is desperate for their labor."

"Your statement is staggering, Senator Feinberg. Fifty-five

million babies have been murdered by abortion within these last fifty years. And you say that America had no place for them. Remarkable isn't it, their places have been taken by fifty-five million illegal aliens within those same fifty years."

"Abortion is not the issue, Mr. President. Besides, it is a good thing. Millions of girls have been saved from unwanted pregnancies."

"Perhaps you're right. Maybe I don't get it. If abortion is such a good thing, why don't we make it retroactive and start right here in this chamber," said Ramsey as he looked at Canaday. A wave of laughter rolled throughout the room. Canaday's bloated, alcoholic face turned crimson.

Feinberg was incensed; she raised her voice. "Do you also plan to rescind the Nineteenth Amendment and take away a woman's right to vote?"

Senator Duane Mallard rose and left the chamber. He cast Senator Sandy Chambers a glance. Chambers took the hint and followed. Outside Mallard spoke. "Sandy, this man has integrity. He's right!"

"Maybe Duane, but there is nothing we can do. This is a feeding frenzy. You know it. We can't save him."

"Sandy, I've been sick of the high court's dictatorial power for a long time. Remember that Supreme Court Justice back in the fifties? Remember what he said, 'The law is what we say it is.'"

"Yes, Duane; we were both young lawyers then. There's a colossal amount of arrogance there. They believe it's their mandate to bring social change. For fifty years, controlling the border has only been talk. This man does something about it.

Overnight Duane! He just does it; others only talk. It's just like he said, the laws are on the books."

"Screw Canaday and Feinberg, Sandy! Let's derail this crucifixion."

"I'm with you."

The Senate recessed for two hours. Senators Mallard and Chambers organized a group of predominately Southern, Midwestern and Western Senators. Twenty-five in all opposed impeachment. But Canaday could easily get the two-thirds he needed. They would filibuster.

During that same interval, there was another meeting among a distressed few. Ugly rumors were coming from home. In states where recall elections were allowed, petitions were being gathered. Two of these recalls had already acquired the requisite number of signatures. Now these Senators would face the voter's wrath.

The Gallup Poll showed an overall approval rating of 55% for Ramsey. The economy had been improving since his rise to the office. On the immigration issue, his approval rating was 73%. Overall, 22% of Republicans and 13% of Democrats had already reregistered in the new Constitution Party. And in some places, this was as high as 42% among all voters. Already, new Constitution Party candidates were throwing their hats into the ring for the next election.

"Ladies and gentlemen, this Ramsey is going to wreck our party," said Jason McCann. "Everything we recovered in the mid-term election is going to be lost."

Senator Lisa Cole replied, "Jason, the Democrats are being

hurt too. People where I'm from support his border policy. He stands up to the courts. He's also popular in the Southwest, your part of the country."

Senator Ted Corrigan began speaking in his distinctive drawl. "Colleagues, please think about this. If not for Ramsey exercising his veto, we'd have been swamped with more Democrat taxes. There are 61 Democrats in the Senate. Why give Canaday what he wants? Who's our biggest adversary, him or Ramsey? Most folks in my state are siding with the President on this border issue too. Let's remember who we are, politicians. Ramsey is riding a tide of popularity; let's ride it with him."

They all reflected on Corrigan's observation. That afternoon, McCann's group made an alliance with Mallard and Chambers. Together, they had enough votes to block impeachment. Canaday was approached to bring the matter to an early vote. The numbers were in just before five. Impeachment failed by seven votes. Canaday bellowed; he felt betrayed by his colleagues. Feinberg was devastated. The Supreme Court was unnerved. Andrew Jackson was the last President to defy their power.

Parties ranged far and wide. America had a new hero. Hundreds of thousands of bets changed hands. Bar room pools were paid up. The odds against Ramsey surviving impeachment had been 5 to 1. A few major book makers didn't share in the tumultuous joy that evening.

The new Attorney General, Carl Remini, staged a victory party. The two were already conferring when Nancy arrived in the large room. A band played soft jazz in the corner as waiters darted through the crowd with cocktail trays. She walked into the throng, paused, looking for Stuart. Their eyes met. Tactfully, she sought escape from the throng now swamping her for attention. She skillfully detached herself and glided toward him. Her long, elegant, black evening gown gleamed, highlighted by the reflection of brilliant stones around her neck. Knock-down, drop-dead gorgeous, she mesmerized the crowd as it followed her movement across the floor. She stopped in front of Stuart. At that moment, everyone present could see their mutual attraction. For these two, no one else existed as they shared this silent moment.

The band switched to a slow waltz. Stuart took Nancy by the hand and led her to the dance floor. Remini was grateful. He hoped their non-professional relationship would be overlooked by the crowd. He was wrong; wagging tongues were already at work. Lively applause followed them as the President and Nancy stepped onto the dance floor. Slowly, they were joined by other couples.

The party lasted late in the evening. But it ended early for Stuart and Nancy. Next morning, she awoke in his arms.

THE RAMSEY MAGIC

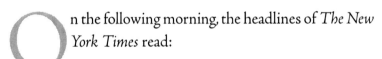

O n the following morning, the headlines of *The New York Times* read:

RAMSEY SURVIVES IMPEACHMENT
Washington, D.C.

In the first real test of his power, President Ramsey survived impeachment by seven votes in the Senate. Senator Canaday accuses Republicans of forming a cabal. Civil Rights Groups say Ramsey is disgraced; they call for him to resign. Senator Feinberg calls Ramsey incompetent, compares him to Harding and declares the future of American Democracy is at stake. Six Supreme Court Justices say Ramsey is setting a dangerous precedent.

That same morning, the President called a conference among his advisors.

"Stuart, isn't it a little too soon after this impeachment thing for you to drop another bombshell?" asked Nancy. "Oh, I forgot; you have the Ramsey Magic."

"Nancy, I remember reading the words of General Ulysses Grant. They were, 'Attack, attack, attack!' And I remember General Robert E. Lee's words too, 'Duty is the sublimest word in the English Language.' We'll do both; attack constantly, always performing our duty. The opposition will be off balance and always on the defensive. What about this, Carl; are you ready?"

"President Ramsey, tomorrow morning we'll file a Federal suit against the State of New York."

"I know your people have been working hard, Carl. Can we prosecute this successfully?"

"President Ramsey, our information is comprehensive and compelling."

"Did New York really ban the private ownership of handguns for ethnic reasons?"

"It's true. This stems from the Sullivan Act of 1911. It was originally directed against immigrants of Southern-European heritage. It makes it almost impossible to obtain a concealable firearm. Though not a total ban, it serves the same purpose through bureaucratic abuse. It was instituted for reasons of ethnicity, one of the most blatant examples of discrimination in this country. It denies equal protection under the law. Even Senator Carl Shrecker was granted a permit; and he's one of the strongest advocates of gun control. For everyone else! This law is taken for granted just because it's been around so long. But do you think we have the moral imperative to do this?"

"Let's not forget the words of the greatest American, George Washington: 'A free people ... ought to be armed.' These New Yorkers will get back their rights. Pass my thanks to your people, Carl. Go get them!"

Two days later, the headlines of *The New York Times* read:

RAMSEY SAYS GUNS ARE GOOD, SUES NEW YORK

Washington, D.C.

ACLU warns of increased carnage on the streets if President Ramsey successfully overturns New York's long standing ban on handguns. The State vows to fight. Women's Groups complain for the safety of their families. Civil Rights Groups say more minorities will be murdered in the streets. Senator Feinberg calls Ramsey the ultimate redneck.

———

It was 8:00 P.M. EST when Gilbert O'Mallie greeted President Ramsey on his popular show Straight Talk. "Welcome to Straight Talk, President Ramsey."

"It's a pleasure to be with you and America this evening, Mr. O'Mallie."

"Call me Gill!" said O'Mallie with a smile. He began by hitting the president on a personal issue. "Mr. President, this Ramsey

Magic is a new phenomenon in American politics. Tonight you can tell America more about yourself and your plans for America. But before you do, can you comment on those rumors about overnight female visits in the White House. I won't mention any names; but what do you say to this?"

"I say nothing about it, Mr. O'Mallie. It's cheap gossip. A lady's private life is none of your business. I am an unmarried man. I have been for many years. But I didn't become a monk and I don't intend to. If I have an opportunity for feminine companionship, it stays between her and me. I'll say no more."

"But, Mr. President, really, the White House shouldn't be used as a brothel."

"It never will be, Mr. O'Mallie; but it's my lawful residence. Would you suggest I rent a motel room instead?"

O'Mallie was overjoyed by this response. Silently he was already spending the bonus promised by George Tauros. "Mr. President, whatever happened to Free Trade? Business is up in arms over these new tariffs."

"Do you know what Free Trade is, Mr. O'Mallie?"

"Tell me your version, President Ramsey."

"Free trade means we export American jobs and factories overseas. Corporations can avoid taxes and deny American workers a decent wage. Then, we import cheap goods made by underpaid workers without collecting any revenue on them. The American worker loses his job, probably his house and maybe his family. His community is denied the taxes levied on his income and property. These corporations escape paying local property taxes too. To fuel their growing industries, China competes with us for imported oil, driving up its price. This imposes another hardship on our people. America sinks further into debt. National security is affected. Free trade, along with its cousins, foreign aid and pork barrel spending, have combined to drive this country hopelessly in the red. Try running your household like this! Send your job overseas, buy more than you sell and then tell me how well it works for you! That, Mr. O'Mallie, is my understanding of Free Trade."

A shocked America watched this live interview from tens of millions of TV sets. That evening, the country met its President.

Horrified liberals and conservative apologists were all quick to respond. Next morning, scores of celebrities, journalists and politicians were televised across the land calling for his resignation, and even impeachment. The ACLU went on immediate alert; their consensus: Ramsey had to go!

But there was another America listening, one that approved of his message. Here was a man of the people!

From her office in the West Wing, Nancy Colton worked tirelessly devising strategy. Today was special. She was having a private lunch with Stuart. She only called him this in private. The Washington rumor mill was in full swing. Her overnight stays had become rare. It was uncertain how their affection would be received by the American people. Stuart was willing to be open.

Nancy advised caution. "The press will paint my appointment as a pay off for being your girl friend."

Both savored these moments together. Their lunch was shared in quiet intimacy. Stuart broke the silence. "None of my appointments will be given an up or down vote. Both parties have decided there will be no philosophical shift during my watch. I'll just have to accept this."

Nancy responded, "Defeat isn't your style, Stuart. Don't change now! I have a plan to blindside them. Do you remember what you told me that first day in your office?"

"Barely, I remember what happened afterward much better!"

She blushed. "Enough of that! You asked me to help you. You wanted to make good appointments. While you've been running around sticking out your chin for everyone to take a sock at, I've been doing my homework. The list of your best men and women is ready."

"They'll get treated like the rest."

"Not this time, my dear," she replied. In a few days, both Houses will take their summer break. During their absence you're going to make hundreds of recess appointments. They will occupy those positions for one year. The record was set during the Reagan years at 243. You'll make over 600."

"Can I get away with it?"

"Yes; and you can repeat it once more while you're still in office. We must keep this in confidence. If Congress suspects, they might not adjourn. We can't even let the prospective candidates know. I will send feelers to them through third parties. When the right moment comes, you slam dunk the ball. Then it's over!"

"What will they say at this?"

"They'll rant, rave, and scream. But you never cared before; I don't think you'll start now."

"You know me pretty well, Nancy!"

"What do you think of my plan?"

"Marvelous! I can't wait to get started. Did you forget anything?"

"Just one thing!"

"What's that?"

"Do you remember what you just said just now? You know me pretty well; do you remember saying that to me? I know you do!"

"Yes."

"I'm still working on that. Today we can work on physiology; maybe another time I'll want to probe your mind."

"Nancy, is this leading where I think it is?"

"Uh huh!"

———

Richard Taylor, former accounts supervisor at Franklin Liberty Bank finished cleaning out his desk. His job had just gone overseas. The President of Franklin Liberty Bank in New York explained it this way; "Rick, we can get six people in India for what we pay you here. We will become more efficient. You can take advantage of this too. Look at it as an opportunity to improve yourself."

For years, Richard Taylor had parroted this same line to others as they were handed their pink slips. Now the bird of prey had come into his home. It didn't feel good. Rick paused along Madison Avenue long enough to pick up a copy of *The New York Times*. Ramsey was being attacked again.

Rick paid his money and took the paper. There was a major article on page one entitled Ramseynomics. The President proposed penalizing banks and corporations engaged in outsourcing white collar American jobs overseas. The evening that Rick Taylor watched him on Straight Talk, he perceived the President as being naïve on economics.

Numerous captains of industry and banking offered their professional assessment of his plan. They lambasted this attack on free trade. Moguls of the left who cared nothing for business vocally supported their position.

Free Trade had just cost Rick his job; Ramsey wanted to save it. The switch in his brain flipped. "America can use this Ramsey magic. I believe in him."

———

It was mid-evening in Reno, Nevada. I was waiting impatiently inside the Reno-Tahoe International Airport. Illyana would be arriving in twenty minutes; I could hardly wait. To pass the time I reached for the copy of the *Reno Gazette Journal* lying on the chair next to me. I scanned the front page.

Turning to the editorial page, I saw a derogatory cartoon showing Nancy Colton explaining to a barefoot Ramsey how to spell illegal alien. It had a footnote with him apologizing for barely getting through high school. Why do I read this rag? I don't care what they think about him. At least he tries to be a President for America, not just another American President. Besides, he's got that Ramsey magic.

It was October. I had four months of unrestrained prosperity behind me. This enabled Illyana and me to advance our wedding date. Natasha and her mother were coming too. We would be married at the Holy Royal Martyrs of Russia Orthodox Church in Reno. Illyana wanted to honor her mother's request. We would have a traditional Orthodox wedding. I was Catholic, but this didn't matter.

———

Under Senator Canaday's prodding, the Senate was called into an emergency session. This was followed by another in the House. These followed Ramsey's pardons for recently imprisoned news commentators, including Russ Shaumbaugh and Ike Ravage. These persons were sentenced to a Federal Penitentiary for terms of three to five years for violating the Fairness Act. This was Kipper Rodwell's project. It was pushed through Congress before the mid-term election that brought Ramsey to Washington.

They were prosecuted for denying coverage of liberal views on their programs. Thus in the written decision of one

Supreme Court Judge, they had denied the First Amendment rights of opposing views over publicly owned airwaves.

Ramsey did not seek recommendations or reviews, bypassing the regular parole process. He waived the rule that petitioners must wait five years. Indeed, these men and women didn't apply at all. There was talk of a second impeachment. Congress demanded an explanation.

"A moot point," Ramsey observed. "The Constitution gives the President power to pardon Federal offenses. It doesn't impose restrictions on this power. The five year waiting period is an internal Justice Department rule. It's nothing more than a guideline and doesn't limit my constitutional authority. These people were wrongly convicted. They always invited opposing points of view from the left. Let the self-proclaimed legal experts haggle and whine. I exercised my Constitutional rights. I stand by my decision!"

Senator Canaday responded in a televised interview. "This President does not have the right to nullify law. There is a prescribed method whereby pardons are considered. It is Ramsey's duty to wait five years and take those Justice Department recommendations into consideration. This unelected President is on record as stating that he will automatically pardon any further violations of this law. He is practicing executive nullification of law."

The backlash against Congress was phenomenal. The unpopular Fairness Act had virtually destroyed talk radio. This had been a major goal of Kipper Rodwell. The law's existence depended upon the radical wing of the Democratic Party controlling both Congress and the Executive branch.

Ramsey's strategy worked. Public pressure added weight to his pardons. Congress wisely repealed the law. And the Supreme Court backed down. The Ramsey magic was still working.

THE FAR EAST EXPLODES

It was just after twenty-four hundred hours. Lt. Nolan was the duty officer standing watch on the bridge of the American ship. Alarmed by the maneuvering of five North Korean warships, he called the Commander. Fast asleep in his cabin, the Skipper soon joined him on the bridge. He quickly determined this was an intimidation game and only sent a rudimentary report to CINCPAC. After all, they were far from the North Korean coast, in international waters.

As dawn's first light illuminated the horizon, North Korean destroyers closed on them from both sides. Shells from rapid-fire guns raked the superstructure of the American ship. The senior North Korean Captain demanded that the U.S. Commander bring his ship to a halt. Almost unarmed, having a mixed crew of men and women, both Navy and civilian, the Skipper surrendered.

President Ramsey met with the Joint Chiefs of Staff, Secretaries of State and Defense, Vice President and Heads of the CIA and NSA at the Pentagon. This was serious beyond imagination, reminiscent of the capture of the USS Pueblo in 1968. North Korean destroyers and gunboats had attacked, boarded and captured the USNS Observation Island, a missile range instrumentation ship (T-AGM 23), a part of the Military Sealift Command. It was operating thirty-eight nautical miles off the North Korean Coast in international waters. The ship was there to monitor the missile testing activity of the North Korean regime.

Kim Jong-il demanded immediate resumption of U.S. oil shipments to North Korea. These were permanently suspended by Ramsey's executive order. The North Koreans were caught cheating on the 2007 nuclear accords. Their allotment had been increased to 125,000 metric tons per month by the Rodwell administration. North Korea openly tested a hydrogen bomb last month. This violated the treaty hammered out between them and the Bush Administration. The North Korean leader threatened war if the oil shipments were not immediately resumed.

Ramsey took a hard stance immediately after Kim Jong-il broke the treaty. He announced the United States would no longer subsidize the North Korean economy. "North Korea will have to make its socialist paradise work without aid from the American People." Ramsey also called Kim Jong-il that "pig of a Third World parasite."

With a grim face, the Secretary of State relayed a message from the Chinese Ambassador. The U.S. was warned about taking any military action against North Korea. This was followed by Admiral Craighead's glum account of the ship's capture. Sensitive equipment and codes were taken with it. This disaster was compounded by the fact that the Navy had been reduced in size during the Rodwell administration.

After receiving the reports and intelligence assessments, Ramsey ordered a DEFCON 1 Alert. The Air Force would be responsible for bringing down enemy surveillance satellites upon notice. Ballistic missile submarines would launch against Chinese targets if war came. U. S. Naval Forces would open immediate hostilities against North Korean naval vessels at sea. North Korean military planes flying over international waters would be shot down.

An emergency Session of the United Nations was convened. That evening President Ramsey would issue a public statement.

The President sat alone in the Oval Office. Lost in thought, he ignored the phone. He grimly remembered his own combat experience. Talking to himself, Ramsey weighed the crisis at hand as he tried to justify his life. "Better men than me died there. Right now I'd trade places with any of them. Hundreds of millions could die? Why me? Why did I come back?"

Memories from 1969 haunted him. He arrived home from Okinawa. Donna was standing there in the airport waiting. Stuart was on crutches as she came up to him. Her manner was subdued. "Don't cry," he told her. "The doctors said my recovery will be complete. Where's our son, Bobby?"

Donna answered slowly. There was something she had to say first. She had met another man. Donna wanted a divorce. Both were silent when they arrived home in Winnemucca. Inside the small apartment, Stuart embraced his two year old son, Bobby. All he could feel was revulsion for Donna. She had been his girlfriend since high school. They separated and divorced soon afterward.

After the divorce, he worked in construction. Later, Stuart met and married Sharon. They had one daughter; a lovely girl, Karen. He hired out for Newmont near Winnemucca. It was a large gold mining corporation and he became a foreman. In her senior year, Karen and three other girls were killed by a drunk driver. His son Bobby died of a drug overdose one year before that. He was only in his twenties. Stuart sank into heavy drinking. A year later, he and Sharon divorced.

Stuart silently reminisced. I would have died, but my own dad wouldn't give up on his son. He was an old cowboy who worked on a big ranch outside of Elko. Dad never made much money. He never owned any property. But no man ever had a stronger work ethic. No matter how cold it was outside, Dad would be in the saddle. Eighteen hours a day, even more, it made no difference. My brother and I were raised in a two-bedroom house on that ranch. Dad taught us how to hunt and fish. And he taught me to work. When I wanted money, I had to earn it. I brought in the hay crop and took whatever job I could get in Elko.

Then when I almost fell apart, he took me under his wing again. Dad told me it took courage to live. He made me brace up and be a man. I pulled myself together, and even got my job back. It was one year later when I took that old Harley on the Sturgis Run. If not for that damn ticket, I wouldn't be here.

My son Bobby, Karen, Mom and Dad are all gone. But I'm not alone; I have Nancy. I wish she was with me now.

There was a knock the door. "Come in," he shouted.

Nancy entered wearing a gray women's suit. Unsmiling, she tossed her briefcase into a chair before walking to his side. She leaned forward, pulled his head next to her lips; kissed him on the forehead and said, "Hi, cowboy."

"Nancy! You're here."

"I came as quick as I could. You wouldn't answer the damn phone."

"I'm low in spirit, Nancy. I'm afraid. America is on the brink of disaster. What have I done? This job is too big for me."

"Relax, cowboy! You've been Gary Cooper ever since you came to Washington. You're not going to change now."

"Nancy, you're not making any sense. This is serious."

"I know, my love. Turn that chair around and I'll explain."

As he did she slid into his lap. Taking his head between her palms, she kissed him on the nose. "Tomorrow is your High Noon, Gary Cooper. The bad guys are waiting for you."

"Where are you going with this, Nancy?"

"These damned Chinese already think you're a cowboy. The whole world does. And that includes me. And I don't want you to disappoint them, or me. You'll play the part."

"What's going on in that pretty, blonde head?"

"Nobody really wants to start shooting, least of all the Chinese. Before they push the button, they'll want to talk first. I have a plan. It has a deuzy of a plot and you're the star."

"Tell me more!"

"You're going to act a little crazy, almost irrational; then you and I are going to play good-cop, bad-cop with them. Are you ready to hear more?"

"After the press conference, Nancy. We have an hour till then. I want you this minute more than I ever did before."

"What are you going to do about it, cowboy?"

"This!" He lifted her slightly and they fell to the floor. They were desperately clawing at each other's clothes when the Press Secretary walked in. "Not now, Grace," Ramsey said.

Blushing, she left the room with a smile on her face.

———

It was 7:00 P.M. Eastern Standard Time. All cameras were on President Ramsey in the Press Room. His broadcast was televised around the world. Laying out the entire background of this crisis, he began with the history of the oil shipments. These were set up by the Clinton Administration. They were a payoff to the North Koreans so they would not develop nuclear weapons. But they cheated and tested a nuclear device in 2007. Then came the treaty engineered by the Bush administration. Again, North Korea promised to give up its nukes in exchange for aid. This aid was increased by the Rodwell Administration. But the North Koreans weren't monitored for compliance. Now in 2011, flexing his muscles in a new show of strength, Kim Jong-il openly tested a hydrogen bomb just last month. Yesterday, he ordered an unprovoked attack on our ship in international waters.

"My fellow Americans, at 6:00 P.M. Eastern Standard Time this evening, I sent an ultimatum to the Democratic People's Republic of Korea, demanding the immediate return of our ship and release of its crew by twelve noon, Eastern Standard Time tomorrow. If the North Koreans fail to comply by the appointed time, I will ask Congress for a Declaration of War. I have already authorized our combined armed forces to commence hostilities upon any North Korean naval ship or military aircraft operating over the open seas. Fellow Americans, this was an overt act of war against United States territory, no different in character than the attack on Pearl Harbor in 1941. Throughout my brief tenure in office I have stated that I have no desire for international adventurism. I am not declaring war on North Korea; I don't have the power to do that. I am responding to an attack on sovereign U.S. territory on the high sea. As a deterrent, we must assume that any North Korean military presence over international waters is a prelude to another such attack. Kim Jong-il is one of the most dangerous men in history. He is threatening an America that he perceives as timid and indecisive. This is understandable in light of my predecessors' actions. But for him, this is a colossal mistake. This is not 1952; my name is not Truman. It is not 1968; my name is not Johnson. And it is not 1979 and my name is certainly not Carter! Please pray for our country; there will be no questions taken at this time."

Through the night and into the next morning, international calls flew between major international capitals. At 9:00 A.M. the Chinese Ambassador requested a conference with Ramsey. At 9:20 A.M., a North Korean missile battery aimed a nuclear tipped rocket toward Seoul. Intelligence sources verified this and the locations of all other North Korean nuclear weapons. At 9:43 A.M. Ramsey issued the order, "Take these positions out." Complete details proving the inevitability of the North Korean attack were sent to both the Chinese and Russian governments. Ramsey agreed to meet with the Chinese in the Oval Office at 11:30 A.M.

Before the Chinese Ambassador arrived, Ramsey briefed the Secret Service men present. They were tactically situated in various locations prior to the ambassador's arrival. A .44 magnum revolver, a bottle of whiskey, and two glasses lay on the President's desk. He began briefing the Secret Service men. "Gentlemen!"

"Yes, Mr. President?" was their combined response.

"In a few minutes, I'm going to be playing a high stakes poker game with these Chinese. You're all going to hear strange things. I may talk a little crazy. None of you must act surprised at anything I say."

"Yes, Mr. President," they answered.

Tapping his left hand on the desk, "Does everyone see this casual gesture?"

They responded positively to the question.

"This is your cue to laugh. Do you all understand?"

Again, they acknowledged.

The Chinese Ambassador and his aids were admitted. Sitting at his desk, Ramsey bit off the end of a cigar. He casually spit the tip away and lit it. He ordered the Secret Service to frisk them. The diplomats objected; but Ramsey insisted. Calmly leaning back, he propped his feet on the corner of the desk. "What do you gentlemen have on your minds?"

The Chinese were shocked by his laid back attitude. Pouring himself two fingers of whiskey, Ramsey angled the forty-four toward the Chinese Ambassador. With a casual gesture, he motioned for the man to speak.

The Ambassador stressed the gravity of the situation. If Ramsey did not immediately alter course, the U.S. and China would be involved in a nuclear conflagration.

Ramsey raised his hand. Their jaws dropped as he spoke.

"I know, and I really appreciate it. I never thought I would get this opportunity."

"What do you mean opportunity, President Ramsey?" asked the Chinese Ambassador.

Stuart pretended surprise. "To wipe out communism, what else? I still carry some Chinese steel in my body from that mortar shell in Vietnam. I always wanted a chance to pay you bastards back."

It was an Oscar class performance. The Chinese were aghast. "Mr. President, we need to talk to our people."

"Ramsey pointed to the phone in front of the Chinese. "An open line is waiting there just for you. Pick it up, Mr. Ambassador. Give my regards to Charlie!"

Immediately, the Chinese Ambassador began a heated exchange with his bosses in Beijing. After receiving instructions, the ambassador paused and spoke resolutely. "Mr. President, I am directed to inform you that every major American City will be incinerated in a nuclear holocaust if you don't stop this action immediately."

"I know; I'm counting on it." With his left hand, Ramsey tapped the signal. The Secret Service Men laughed.

"This is not funny, Mr. President. Two hundred million Americans will die."

"You'll be doing us a favor, something I could never accomplish on my own. A lot of blue states are going to become red overnight. And don't think I'm not grateful for it. By the way, our first strike is going to put 1,250 submarine launched warheads down your throats. What do you think about them apples?" He smiled at the Chinese ambassador, emptied his glass with one swallow and refilled it with whiskey.

The Ambassador was beginning to crack as he talked to his superiors in Beijing. Almost pallid, he put his phone down. "They say you are bluffing, President Ramsey. I think so too."

Ramsey shoved the other glass toward the Ambassador. "Have a drink, Charlie; it's going to be your last." Then, lightly fingering the trigger on the forty-four, he said, "Know what, Charlie?"

"What is that, President Ramsey?"

"You and I aren't ever going leave this room. I'll be sitting in this chair when your missiles hit. But you'll be lying in a pool of your own blood. As soon as those Chinese missiles are launched I'm going to blow your goddamn brains out. Right here with this pistol!" Again, he signaled. The Secret Service Men laughed.

The Chinese Ambassador's hand was shaking as he lifted the drink to his lips. "President Ramsey, I am sure we can work out this disagreement."

This was the moment Ramsey was waiting for; the Chinese wanted a deal. "Hey, Charlie; you don't like me; I don't like you. Maybe somebody's still going to be alive a few years from now. If people can still read, I'll go down in history as the guy who wiped out communism. And I owe it all to that pig son-of-a-bitch in Pyongyang. And to you guys too!" He pressed a button under his desk.

Suddenly, Nancy Colton burst into the office. She appeared to be in a high state of anxiety as she played her part perfectly. "President Ramsey, did you make the offer?"

"Yes! They turned it down. You shouldn't be here, Nancy. I told you to go into the hills in West Virginia. The country is going to need you soon."

The Chinese Ambassador burst out with his eyes wide open, "What offer?"

Nancy Colton stared down at Ramsey with her mouth open. "You didn't make him the offer!"

"Nancy, he would have turned it down anyway. These people don't like losing face." Ramsey stood up and yelled, "Nancy, I want you to leave this office. Now!"

"I will not, President Ramsey. You gave your word. The Joint Chiefs won't let you launch an attack if the Chinese accept the deal. You're not getting away with this!"

"What deal?" the Chinese Ambassador screamed!

Maintaining eye contact with the President, she answered. "North Korea is to be incorporated into South Korea. Kim Jong-il goes into exile and their military surrenders to the South Koreans. We also agree to withdraw all U.S. Forces from Korea. And we will promote, but not promise the reunification of Taiwan with China. This will depend upon you resolving your differences with them."

"You're wasting your time, Nancy; I'm giving the order to attack in eleven minutes."

The carrot and stick trick worked. The Chinese Ambassador ranted over the phone to Beijing. He began nodding, and then he lowered the phone. "My government will accept those terms."

———

The crisis was averted. Everyone shared a laugh after the Ambassador departed. That afternoon, the Chinese informed Kim Jong-il they wouldn't support him. He vowed to fight to the last man. He meant every last man excluding himself. Never since the beginning of the Cold War had any communist regime been so hopelessly alone and isolated. By order of the Commander-in-Chief, President Stuart Ramsey, all technological advantages were used. That first day, two North Korean Divisions ceased to exist as U.S. Forces exercised the nuclear option. The North Korean Air Force and Navy were destroyed piecemeal. Kim Jong-il, "The Beloved Leader," crossed the Yalu River that night into Manchuria. With the destruction of its armed forces, the Democratic People's Republic of Korea collapsed like a house of cards. A united Korea was free!

The surveillance ship and its crew were repatriated. The liberal press congratulated the ship's captain for exercising wise judgment. Expecting him to receive a medal, they were shocked by Ramsey's answer.

"He'll be court martialed for cowardice," the President replied.

THE CURTAIN FALLS

After the Korean crisis an emergency assembly of Bilderbergers convened in Brussels; this maverick American President was the topic. This elite, clandestine collection of industrialists, bankers and world leaders from all countries met to consider this Ramsey phenomenon. They were styled by some as a secret world government. Was it true? No one outside of their group really knew. Maybe, not even the Bilderbergers themselves. But they were always heavily guarded wherever they assembled, usually by the host country's own military.

The U.N. was paralyzed by the new American Ambassador. The global gun confiscation bill was on hold. The U.N. plan for world domination was threatened by this new American nationalism. Third world countries weren't getting their payoffs. The American ambassador vetoed everything. Droves of Palestinians were moving into other Arab countries in order to find sustenance. Third world nations were taking out their frustration on the international corporations.

The Bilderbergers were in agreement. Ramsey must go. Whether by legal means or assassination, it didn't matter. The Americans led by Senator Shrecker of New York would handle those details within the United States.

By December of 2011, American industry was making a comeback. The trade deficit was slashed to levels reminiscent of twenty years ago. Orders for machine tools, durable and non-durable goods were increasing. With the shrinking supply of cheap, illegal labor, manufacturers were forced to pay higher wages as the number of new jobs increased.

Internationalists cried foul, what about the NAFTA Treaty? They weren't happy with Ramsey's answer.

The NAFTA Treaty was never ratified in the Senate. Therefore, in Ramsey's own words, "It had no legal status."

Wal-Mart set up a special $350 million dollar fund to fight government tariffs in the courts. Local businesses were now able to compete with them.

The President worked hard promoting ethanol as an alternative to gasoline using Brazil as an example. By 2006, Brazil achieved energy independence. The carburetion systems in Brazilian cars contained sensors permitting their engines to use gasoline, ethanol or a mixture of both. Those carburetors adjusted to the fuel type. Farmers favored this proposal. Thousands of them stood to become very wealthy as alcohol could be readily distilled from grain and sugar right on the farm.

Democrats blocked this legislation out of hatred for Ramsey. They were supported by most of the Neocon Republicans who were in the pockets of the oil companies. Nevertheless, fuel prices dropped below $2.50 per gallon. The Arabs wanted to disarm this issue. They had previously threatened to raise the price of oil. Ramsey made it clear they would be eating raghead stew if they did.

———

The number of illegal aliens plummeted daily. Hispanics no longer rioted over the immigration issue. The liberal intelligentsia seethed with hatred as their activists inflamed racial hatred. ACLU lawsuits abounded in the courts. Legal Hispanic citizens slowly became supportive of the President. Crime in their neighborhoods dropped drastically. The increased number of high paid production jobs benefited them too. Illegal aliens were afraid to burden the hospitals or welfare systems. Communities began recovering from the financial burden imposed by illegal immigration. Many illegals sent their families home while they worked as secretly as possible. Talks with the Mexican Government over a guest worker program resumed. The Mexican government was becoming desperate. The border freeze had also crippled the drug trade.

It was the Christmas Season. Stuart never said happy holidays, only Merry Christmas. He allowed local churches to erect a giant Nativity Scene on the White House lawn.

The ACLU must have proved heaven existed. Their scream was so loud it could be heard up there. Their challenge was immediately taken up by the Supreme Court. The morning after, nine Supreme Court justices paraded into their chambers as the marshal announced their arrival with the words: "God save the United States and the Supreme Court." They accepted numerous last minute amicus briefs filed by the ACLU, lawmakers and other friends of the court. Their ruling by a 6 to 3 margin was not long in coming. Separation of church and state forbade President Ramsey to allow this Nativity Scene.

In a hastily televised interview, he replied, "The White House is my legal residence, and the Constitution guarantees me freedom of religion. If the Supreme Court, ACLU or anybody else doesn't like it, they'll have to live with hurt feelings."

Jewish groups asked if they could display a Menorah for Hanukkah; Ramsey agreed.

Desperately lashing back, the Supreme Court instructed U.S. marshals to remove the display. Ramsey stationed armed Marine guards with fixed bayonets to protect it. Directly under his command, their orders were to use force if anyone attempted to dislodge the Nativity scene.

The press flew into a frenzy in a self-righteous display of political piety. All liberal pundits, whether writers, editors or college administrators, universally denounced the tyranny of this redneck Ramsey.

———

Retaliation would not be long in coming. In New York City, CEOs of oil companies and financial institutions met with their Republican supplicants, the Neocons.

Representative Barton began, "Gentlemen, this situation is out of hand. I have regretted a thousand times that day in the House when we offered up Ramsey for Speaker. Better to have a Democrat any day!"

Senator McCann could hardly wait to speak. "We've had talks with the Democrats. They agree. New impeachment proceedings must be brought against Ramsey. This last act of defiance against the Supreme Court will completely undermine that institution if we let him get away with it. Senator Shrecker is compiling a new list of charges. We're going to take this bastard Ramsey down."

Senator DeWine spoke. "Gentlemen, the time isn't right. This is going to be problematical. Even with Ramsey gone, these damn Constitutionalists now make up 33% of registered voters. This is a little bit like closing the barn door after the horse gets away."

"Enough of your folksy humor, Senator DeWine," replied a CEO. "We've lost billions; Ramsey goes."

"What do you mean, Jeff? Your quarterly report shows a healthy figure. Your company is in the green."

"Senator DeWine, our profits are twenty billion below

expectations. These Arabs want a higher percentage to make up for their losses. Ramsey must go!"

DeWine looked glum. He spoke in his soft Southern accent. "Gentlemen, if we go along with this, it could go very badly for us at the polls this coming November. Ramsey is popular. We better get it right with the people."

"I don't care how popular he is, DeWine. If Ramsey doesn't go, this little love-in we've had with you people for many years is over."

Barton added, "Nancy Colton will follow in his footsteps."

"Get rid of that bitch too."

"But the will of the people," DeWine began to say.

"Screw them! We'll decide what's good for America. You people work out your differences with the Democrats. Give them whatever social issues they want. I don't care if they turn 2012 into a social circus. We want business as usual. These damn tariffs and Ramsey's energy independence plan must go. We'll do our part and shrink the economy. The press will blame Ramsey. Together, we'll get rid of this nationalistic bastard. The year 2012 will be remembered as a pandemonium if that's what it takes."

DeWine could not restrain himself. "Pandemonium in 2012! What about us? Don't you think this could break us too? Do you think we're just a bunch of puppets doing your will?"

"Really! I thought that was just what you were! Barton?"

"Yes!"

"See that Shrecker has those charges ready soon."

The grapevine delivered its ominous message. Impeachment lay in Ramsey's future. It would begin on January 3rd.

On the eave of impeachment, Stuart called his friends together. "I appreciate everyone standing by me." He smiled at Nancy. "From now on it's up to you."

"We'll fight them," she answered.

"The lions are hungry. I'm the main course."

"The majority of Americans are still behind you!"

"Have you seen the most recent poll, Nancy? Fear mongering has taken its toll. Corporations are making uncalled for layoffs. Gasoline prices are rising without cause. Banks are making loans hard to get. The stock market is plummeting. Congress won't act. It's obvious; they want to discredit our economic gains. Everything we've tried to accomplish is unraveling around us. These people are shrinking the economy. The fear mongers are magnifying our losses tenfold. Americans are worried about their jobs. We can't blame them."

A phone call came in from Senator Mallard. "Mr. President?"

"Yes, Senator; what news from the Senate?"

"I'm trying to coordinate our efforts, Mr. President. I'm afraid they're going to do it this time. There are only twenty-five of us opposing them. It's not just a case of removal from office. The talk is that you'll get ten to twenty years in Federal prison. I'm sorry, President Ramsey."

"You did all you could, Senator. Please convey my thanks to the gallant twenty-five who are standing up for me. It's been a pleasure working with you."

"We'll filibuster as long as we can, President Ramsey. But Canaday will be able to force a cloture vote by tomorrow afternoon."

"Talk to you later, Senator Mallard."

"Goodbye, President Ramsey."

Ramsey turned his attention to the Attorney General. "Well Carl, bring me that list of prospective pardons. Maybe I can still do something useful as your president. It's going to be up to you and Nancy to carry the torch."

"What did Mallard tell you?" asked Remini.

"Ten to twenty, Carl."

"Maybe I can still work a deal in exchange for your resignation. I'm going to try."

"No, you're not. I know you're a friend and trying to help. But I forbid it. I chose the path I was going to follow when I landed in this office. I'm not going to skulk and ask forgiveness now. Canaday, Feinberg and the others will have their day. You've got to admit, the list of charges against me is so long, I'm going to have my permanent spot in the Guinness Book of World Records."

"Mr. President, about the only thing missing on that charge sheet was a claim that you stole the White House silverware. They have you charged with ordering the murder of illegal aliens, violating the rule of law, contempt of Congress, usurpation of authority. There are over 100 charges in all."

"There must be something we can do!" Nancy said.

Ramsey chuckled. "All we have left now, Nancy, is prayer. I wonder if I have any calling cards with the man upstairs."

"Well, I can do something, Stuart," replied Nancy. "These bums still have to contend with me. I'll issue a pardon as soon as they swear me in."

"Be careful, Nancy! As President, you can hold the line. If you take a fall for me, all may be lost."

As the cabinet meeting broke up, the Attorney General lingered. "Goodbye President Ramsey."

"Goodbye, Carl!"

Remini's eyes clouded as he left the Oval Office.

———

Sixty kilometers outside of Cartagena, Bashan reclined on the sun deck of his mansion as the call came in. It was a familiar voice; he smiled. Osama!

Bashan was silent as he rode in the passenger seat of his SUV. They had already crossed the border into Venezuela. The border guards automatically waved them through upon seeing the license plate. It was a short ride to Caracas. Hugo Chavez, the President of Venezuela had carefully courted Ahmadinejad since they had established their mutual bond of hatred against the United States during the Bush debacle. Through the Iranian embassy, Bashan was able to maintain contact with radical Islamic elements throughout the world. In the coded voice message, Osama bin Laden had told him to meet a courier there.

Fleeing from the long arm of Interpol in Europe in the 1990s, Bashan had reinvented himself in Colombia. With his command of many languages, his Middle Eastern contacts and drug sources, he found his niche in a cartel based in Cartagena. Through murder, intrigue and absolute ruthlessness he propelled himself and became its boss. To his Colombian colleagues, Bashan was known as *Culebra*. His followers wore a distinctive cobra tattoo on the back of their necks. Having no desire to converse with his driver, he pretended sleep. With his eyes closed, Bashan remembered that fateful day in 1979. His thoughts often strayed back there, when his future was molded. Vividly they came to mind as he relived that afternoon.

The surrounding hills appeared in diverse shades of orange, red and brown. To the west they cast longer shadows in the late afternoon sun. A sullen breeze from the distant eastern sea tantalized the parched ground with its first waft of relief. Sounds outside the surrounding wall slowly died down as the Imams called the faithful to prayer. The prostrate young man was anonymous as his form faded into the mass of boys at devotion within the mosque. Such was a typical working day in this Wahhabi school in Sana'a in 1979.

After prayer, Bashan was lost in thought as he idled by the door longing for the cool hills of his home near Develi in central Turkey. His distant homeland was like another planet by comparison to the rigor of this Wahhabi School. Uncommonly strong for his age, well-connected and of cruel disposition, Bashan was accustomed to pressing his will upon others. Startled, he involuntarily flinched as a strong hand firmly grasped his left shoulder. The Imam's form grew larger as he came into the boy's side vision.

"My son?" said the Imam.

"Sheik bin Baz!" replied Bashan.

"I have watched you closely this last year. A vision came to me. Allah has a plan for you."

Bashan's curiosity blazed with intensity. Secretly he detested this Imam who publicly declared that the Earth was flat and the Sun revolved around the Earth. Sheik Aboulaziz bin Baz was a serous embarrassment to his colleagues in the Islamic world. Until now Bashan's life did not extend beyond his own selfish interests. His presence in this sun-baked land was sole testament to a stern and pious maternal grandfather who raised him after his father's death. "How can that be, Great Imam? I am a stranger in a strange land. The other boys hate and despise me. They call me, The Turk."

"You have greatness, Bashan, and learn rapidly. Already, you have mastered Arabic without accent though only fifteen. When first coming to us last year, you knew not one word. And you also speak many of Kafir tongues of the West. Someday, you will be a mighty sword of Islam. The infidel will bend his knee at your will to the greater glory of Allah as you bring them under Sharia law."

"Why me, Great Imam?"

"You are a leader; yet disdain to lead and remain aloof from the other boys. You understand weakness in others and use it to your own whim. I have seen this in you, and was troubled until the answer came to me. In my dream you deceived the infidel. They accepted you as their own. And I saw you exploit their weaknesses."

"I am a Turk, Great Imam. How is it they will accept me as one of their own?"

"Your skin is light, Bashan. You will gain the hearts and minds of the Kafirs. I have seen this in my dream. It must be so; it will be so."

Bashan felt this too, though he did not admit it. The Imam's revelation inflamed his passion as he coolly listened to the old man. The Imam's words echoed over and over in his brain—"the infidel will bend his knee at thy will to the greater glory of Allah." Yes, Bashan thought. I was born to greatness. Yet it must be through a mysterious, yet unrevealed path. Pledging to earn acceptance among the infidels, he would live the Imam's great dream.

After the Imam departed, Bashan rubbed the silver ring on his finger to a shiny luster and placed it to his lips. It was given to him as a child. His father died under mysterious circumstances, but not before telling Bashan it had been found in one of the ancient caves near Develi. Pulling the ring away from his lips, he carefully studied the engraving of the cobra on its broad surface. It seemed to call out to him; and he answered aloud. "Yes! I will obey. I will be the great sword of Allah and this serpent will be my personal symbol."

This memory of the Imam called to Bashan's mind the other martyrs of Islam. He mumbled *"Allahrahamahun"* (God rested them in peace) before he slowly dozed off.

OSAMA

Nancy stayed until midnight. Ramsey tossed and turned until troubled slumber finally overtook him. His dream faded back to Vietnam. It was 1968 again, the Tet offensive. This dream was familiar, even if the years had passed. Ramsey vividly relived it.

He was back in the hospital in Danang. The effects of the morphine had not quite dulled his mind with blissful release. White shrouded surgeons were standing around him. They were talking; his leg must come off. Mustering enough breath, he spoke. "Let me go; I don't want to live like that."

The surgeons were joined by a woman wearing a surgical smock. She had the face of an angel with rosy cheeks and tuffs of blonde hair poking beneath her cap. "Oh, I don't think we'll let you go, corporal. Maybe God has a plan for you," she answered.

"Who are you? Are you an angel?"

She smiled. "I'm Major Gabriela Rakowski."

Another surgeon insisted that the corporal go into immediate surgery.

She examined his shattered leg bone. "I'll take this one. I can save his leg."

This vision from the past woke him up. Drenched in sweat, Ramsey sat up in bed. He took off his pajama top. "That beautiful angel, how I could use her! Remember, Stuart! Remember what happened to her." He shuddered from the recollection. It was during his recovery on Okinawa, he mentioned her name to a newly arrived surgeon from Vietnam. Stuart was devastated by the doctor's reply. The blonde haired major had been burned to death in a c-141. It was hit by a VC mortar round on the runway during the last days of Tet. Making one more attempt at sleep, he lay back down and closed his eyes.

Secretly rejoicing as the phone rang at 3:32 a.m., he sat on the edge of his bed, listening intently to the Director of the CIA. After this; he made several more calls. There would be an emergency meeting of the Joint Chiefs and CIA at 8:00 A.M. EST.

Excited, he stood up. "Well, Ramsey, you have another chance. This play has one last act."

It was 7:40 A.M. Eastern Standard Time as President Ramsey entered the room. The Joint Chiefs meeting was already in progress. The President listened as General Bosley gave his report. Al Qaeda and Iranian Officials would meet in the small port city of Chabahar on the Arabian Sea in Eastern Iran. Bin Laden himself would attend. The transfer of nuclear weapons to Al Qaeda would be discussed there. It was now 5:40 P.M. in Tehran. The meeting would be at ten A.M. tomorrow in their time zone. The Joint Chiefs wanted to make a massive air strike to coincide with the event.

Ramsey spoke slowly with careful deliberation, hoping each word would exact its maximum effect on the audience. "Gentlemen, these strikes have never worked before. The only way to be sure of taking him out is to go in and get him. Do these intelligence reports point to his exact location within that town?"

"We believe we have identified the structure he will occupy, Mr. President," said an aide. "Satellite photos show a heavy concentration of guards around it. But it's no slam dunk for American intelligence. We have been wrong before."

"True enough," Ramsey replied. "But too many were in the information loop. What's said in this room will not leave it."

General Bosley replied, "There will be hundreds of Al Qaeda and Iranians there, Mr. President. We don't have time to organize an effective ground strike. We would take too many casualties. The first troops going in would probably be lost."

"We're going to make a helicopter borne assault supported by Apache gun ships and backed up by carrier planes. I'll lead the attack myself."

The officers stared in disbelief. Admiral Cullen replied, "You can't do that, Mr. President. This is a job for professionals."

"I am still your Commander-in-Chief, Admiral Cullen. I carried an M-16 in another war and I command the Armed Forces of the United States now. I will personally lead this attack. One thing I will make clear to all of you here. No one outside of this room is to be informed of this. Air Force One is waiting for me as we speak. You, General Connor will personally call the Marine Commander and let him know I'm taking personal command upon my arrival. But don't send the message until just before I get there. We have a razor thin timetable."

"What do you propose, Mr. President?"

"I'll be in the lead strike helicopter. Apache gun ships will flank our attack. We don't have time to soften the area up. The Blackhawk will take me right to the front door of bin Laden's residence. Other Blackhawks will discharge their troops around us and these will fan out and occupy the other terrorists. They'll cause chaos among his followers. My team will take out bin Laden's headquarters. This day has been too long in coming. I intend to see that America collects a long overdue debt. I also have unfinished business from 1968."

"President Ramsey, you can't do this. You'll be killed," said Cullen.

"I've lived almost sixty-four years, Admiral. How many hundreds of thousands will never see their first birthday if bin Laden gets those bombs?"

"I must still protest," said General Bosley.

"Thank you, General Bosley; but we'll do it my way. What forces are within striking distance now, Admiral Cullen?"

"The *Ronald Reagan* is in the Indian Ocean, Mr. President.

And there is a small Marine Amphibious Strike Force with the squadron."

"Do they have the right kind of helicopters for this job?"

"They do, Mr. President."

"Arrange for them to be on the deck of the *Ronald Reagan* waiting for me."

"Yes, Mr. President."

The small jet landed on the deck of the massive aircraft carrier. Ramsey arrived in Diego Garcia and boarded the small plane only minutes before. He was met by Marine Colonel Hamiter on the *Ronald Reagan*. "Mr. President, I was instructed to meet you and facilitate an operation at your direct command. I am confused about this, Sir. Is this a show of force?"

"Something like that, Colonel! We're taking out bin Laden. Today is his big day."

A shocked Marine Colonel stuttered as he tried to reply. "You don't mean that you personally are going to lead this attack, President Ramsey?"

"I am! Are the things I ordered here?"

"They are, President Ramsey. We had trouble finding a machete on short notice. One of our Marines bought one as a souvenir in the Philippines and he let us borrow it. You forgot to order body armor! But I have some waiting for you."

"Thank you, Colonel; I won't need it. I'll change clothes in the Blackhawk on the way. We're going to hit them at first light. It's coming soon. Let's go." The colonel protested. Carrier launched jets would take off later. Their appearance over the target would coincide with the arrival of the ground force.

Skillful Marine Pilots flew just above the surface over water and land, their intricate computers and GPS guidance systems showing the way. ECW aircraft flying high overhead provided electronic countermeasures to confuse Iranian armed forces. Surprise would be everything. If the Iranians were alerted, this would be lost. Their movement was picked up by Russian and Chinese satellites. Puzzled by the maneuver, they delayed informing the Iranian Government until first light came over the horizon near the small town lying ahead.

Hugging the ground, the force circled a range of hills and approached the target from the opposite side.

Al Qaeda guards standing by the door saw the aircraft approaching only seconds away. Alarmed, a guard knocked on the door and was admitted. The tall, swarthy man with the long beard sat in the center of the room sipping tea, surrounded by his lieutenants. The guard told him helicopters were coming from the north. Their shock was electric. The Iranian delegation was coming by car. Bin Laden grabbed his AK-47. The others ran for the windows brandishing their automatic rifles.

Ramsey ordered the helicopter's nose down right at the front door, even though it would be lost. Cracks from a hundred AK-47s erupted throughout the town. The Apache gun ships returned fire. Marines poured out of the Blackhawk. The guards outside of bin Laden's quarters were quickly dispatched.

Ramsey and a dozen Marines hugged the wall of the building as Al Qaeda fighters inside returned fire.

The Marine pilot and co-pilot were wounded as the Blackhawk was severely shot up. Hand grenades were tossed through the windows. Seconds later a series of explosions erupted inside the building. The front door burst open from the explosion. Ramsey was the first to race through the door. The tall bloodied figure of bin Laden tried to rise from the floor. He bent forward reaching for his AK-47.

A burst from Ramsey's M-16 poured several rounds into bin Laden's gun arm. It went limp as his body fell backward. Other well-placed rounds penetrated his other arm. Though unable to move either limb, bin Laden was still alive. He glowered back at Ramsey. Dropping his rifle, Ramsey reached down and grabbed the monster's beard, pulling him to his knees. Slow and deliberate, he drew out the machete. Whether or not bin Laden understood the words, it was certain he understood the meaning. Osama stared in terror as the last words he would hear quickly followed. "Here's the justice you deserve, you son of a bitch." With one stroke, Ramsey cut off his head. Bin Laden's body collapsed limp to the floor. The few remaining wounded terrorists were dispatched by other Marines. Ramsey walked outside with the monster's head dangling from his left hand.

The battle was short lived. Realizing their leader was dead, the remaining Al Qaeda fighters tried to break out. Most were cut down by the carrier born jets whose arrival corresponded to the ground attack. Occasional sporadic firing continued as the area was secured.

A Marine photographer raised his camera and captured the moment. Holding up the grotesque head of bin Laden in his left hand, the monster's blood dripped down his beard onto Ramsey's arm. The President still clutched the machete in his right. Another Marine later said the scene reminded him of Perseus holding the head of Medusa.

Ramsey cast Osama's head to ground. Marines gleefully took turns kicking it like a soccer ball. It was all on film. Colonel Hamiter ordered them to stop. Ramsey overruled him. "Let them have their fun, Colonel. This is payback for thousands of American dead."

"But, Mr. President; this is a gross violation of the Geneva Convention, maybe even a war crime."

"What do these people care for treaties? We'll terrorize the terrorists."

American casualties were light, two dead, fourteen wounded including the pilot and co-pilot of Ramsey's wrecked helicopter. The strike force consolidated. The Americans would be airborne within minutes, before Iranian forces could respond.

Over the horizon another set of American helicopters came into view. "Who is that, Colonel Hamiter? Did someone order a second strike?" Ramsey asked.

"I don't know, Sir," he answered.

Both stood waiting as the helicopters touched down. A Marine General, flanked by an armed guard approached them. "Mr. Ramsey!" he said.

"Yes, General?"

"I have been ordered to arrest and take you into custody. You have been impeached, charged with felonies and removed from office."

PANDEMONIUM

Seldom had both parties been so adamant about removing an official. Nancy Colton was grudgingly sworn in as president. She and Carl Remini worked tirelessly to broker a deal. Most of the charges would be dropped. Ramsey would only face removal from office and suspended felony charges. There would be no time behind bars.

This was President Colton's trap. She knew if her pardon were circumvented, he would not go to prison. After the deal, she pardoned Stuart and set his conviction aside. Though removed from office, his civil rights were restored. Congress was livid. She was named as an accomplice and most of the same charges were now leveled against her. After a quick impeachment, Nancy was sentenced to prison. No one was there to pardon her. She had not been permitted to appoint a new Vice President. After her removal, the current Speaker of the House, ultra-liberal Democrat, Gordie Muller of California, was sworn in as President.

Democrats, Neocons and liberal pundits across the country were mortified by the newfound folk hero status of ex-President Ramsey. An enterprising bartender at the Red Head Piano Bar in Chicago invented a new drink—the Ramsey. It had a knock-out punch and was only recommended for those who had a ride home. Its popularity spread across the country from nightclubs of Harlem to college beach parties in the People's Republic of California.

Ramsey was able to visit Nancy Colton only once at Alderson Federal Women's prison in West Virginia. He sat across from her in grim silence. "You shouldn't have taken the hit, Nancy."

"Shut up, Stuart! They would have taken me down anyway. Darling, you know what?"

"What, my dear Nancy?"

"I miss you more than I dared guess."

"Eric and Carl are working hard for us, Nancy. The big boys still want me. Maybe I can work a deal to spring you."

"No; my darling. You'll do nothing of the kind. They are terrified of you. Please hide! You must; you're in danger. Without you, there is no Constitution Party and America has no hope. Before you, there was no one to rally behind. I couldn't do it. You have the charisma."

"So you think they'll try to kill me?"

"I worry, Stuart. America only had a slim chance after you took over. Without you, it has none."

"You give me too much credit, Nancy."

"You still need protection!"

"I've got a couple good friends, a Mr. Smith and Mr. Wesson, and they tell me I don't have to live in fear of anybody."

Nancy shook her head. "Take it serious, Stuart; that's all they need to put you in jail. I'm surprised they let you visit me. Hide your guns and develop amnesia if they question you about them. They will use that new U.N. Gun Mandate that Muller and the Supreme Court are shoving down our throats. They're scared, Stuart. You started something big. Now they have to go for the whole enchilada before the election in November."

"OK, Nancy, I'll get more security. It's my fault you're in here. I'll spend every dime I've got to get you out."

"My darling, you can't help me unless you take care of yourself first. Please go into hiding. Half of America would shield you. You must be there for them. But Lord! I'll be thankful when you do get around to me. This place is horrible. These people delight in mentally torturing me. If I only had one of those new drinks everybody is talking about, the Ramsey, and at bedtime. Then maybe I could escape this place for twelve hours."

"Nancy, I'll get you out. And we will win!"

"I know we will, darling."

The guard signaled their time was up. She gave him that

come hither smile as their fingertips touched. The guard protested this physical contact. With quick goodbye, Ramsey
was gone.

———•———

Muller rescinded Ramsey's pardon. Re-arrested and taken
into custody, he was placed under house arrest in his condominium in Arlington. The Supreme Court would review his
case and determine if the original pardon was legal.

———•———

An International Human Rights Commission met in
The Hague. It was decided Ramsey must go on trial for
crimes against humanity. The Islamic world screamed for
his blood. Those videotapes of bin Laden's head being
kicked around were shown throughout the world. The
power brokers in Washington stalled. They had seriously
miscalculated his popularity. Fear of increased voter wrath
delayed their decision. Turning him over to the international court could be political suicide. The unnatural alliance in Congress was further disheartened by Ramsey's
approval rate. It shot back up to a hefty 64% nationwide
after bin Laden's demise.

Washington was swept clean of Ramsey's appointments.
Trepidation replaced optimism as both major parties now
feared the upcoming presidential election. The newly formed
Constitution Party had already drained the traditional base
of the Republican Party. Organized labor and its families

deserted the Democrats in record numbers as did Social Security recipients and veterans who had benefited under the Ramsey administration. This took on the proportions of a flood in the weeks following his impeachment.

In an effort to nullify his future influence, a specially convened electoral commission deemed that it would be impossible for Ramsey to be on the presidential ticket in November pending charges by the International Human Rights Commission. Democrats and Republicans alike faced massive voter dissatisfaction with the likelihood of the House being lost to the Constitution Party and with major losses for both parties in the Senate among Class I members, those whose terms expired in 2012.

Chairmen from each major party met in a series of secret strategy meetings. They agreed to cooperate in the coming election. The existing seats would be divided between them. In districts where the Republican candidate was strongest, the Dems would support him. Where the Democrat looked stronger, the Republicans would recip-rocate in like manner. It was hoped this would minimize their mutual losses. A joint action committee came out of this newly formed cabal.

The front page of *The New York Times* was half-covered with a cartoon. It depicted a bare foot, buck toothed Ramsey in overalls saying, "I can't wait to get back to my farm and go fishin'." The headlines read:

NIGHTMARE IS OVER, RAMSEY DUMPED

Washington, D.C.

Disgraced former President Ramsey is back in custody as President Muller rescinds his pardon. Senator Shrecker of New York says, "The rule of law has been restored." Six Supreme Court Justices are rumored to have attended a cocktail party in celebration. Nancy Colton will begin her forty year prison sentence on Monday. Her counsel vows to appeal the conviction. President Muller orders all military units on the border to stand down. They will return to their respective bases immediately.

———

Muller appointed all positions and cabinet jobs with men and women who were members of the Council of Foreign Relations, Trilateral Commission or both. He asked Senator Shrecker of New York to accept the Vice Presidency. Unknown to him, Shrecker had already been instructed to do this by his Bilderberger colleagues. He accepted the nomination.

———

The NBC helicopter hovered over the lonely stretch of desert separating the U.S. from Mexico. For three days, illegal aliens had poured into the U.S. by the tens of thousands. This area below was one of the heaviest concentrations. Border Patrol Agents stood helplessly watching. Yesterday three agents had been arrested and charged with felonies at this same location. They had used force which resulted in injury to an illegal.

The lawyer and spokesman for this man announced a lawsuit on his behalf.

TV images from this helicopter suddenly shifted to a camera in Mexico City. The image of the Mexican President came into view. "We will never tolerate a man like Ramsey again," he said.

Liberals staged street rallies. Effigies of Ramsey were burnt. Crowds roamed the streets of all major cities brandishing the Mexican Flag, overturning cars and shouting: "*Muerte a Ramsey!*"

At Harvard, Berkeley, Columbia and other major colleges, effigies of Nancy Colton were hung as radical students sang, "Ding, dong, the witch is gone, the wicked witch is gone."

The Neocons and liberals put their differences aside. In return for business as usual they would support Muller's social programs. This strange alliance was deemed critical; too many from each party had defected and reregistered in the Constitution Party. The traditional balance of power and status quo of American politics was under threat of extinction. All tariffs on imports were dropped.

The California Senate and Assembly agreed on the final version of the Public Employee and School Language Bill. It would go to the governor's desk. He was expected to sign it. All new state, county or municipal employees hired in the future would be expected to know Spanish or another language as well as English before they could apply for a government job.

Part two of this California bill authorized designated public schools in overwhelmingly Hispanic areas to teach the children in Spanish. Non-Spanish speaking children of both Hispanic and non-Hispanic backgrounds living in those districts would attend remedial language courses. Black civil right's groups were in arms over this law. Blacks, along with conservative groups filed numerous discrimination suits in Federal Court.

The ACLU vowed to fight these racist inspired lawsuits, citing: "Government employees should be able to competently respond to the needs of all of California's citizens. Pre-existing culture and language barriers must be eliminated."

—————

During the first week of February, Muller announced that the United Nations proviso forbidding the private ownership of guns was in effect. Certain Islamic Nations refused to participate in this. The Senate would not ratify the treaty with the required two-thirds vote. Muller stated that as far as he was concerned it was law. Five Supreme Court Judges openly declared that in ruling on individual rights, U.N. Law would supersede the Bill of Rights. Most Federal Firearms Licenses were rescinded by executive order. Lists of registered firearms were examined by the FBI pending confiscation. A voluntary period of compliance would be allowed before mandatory prosecution began. The mood in the country turned ugly. Muller was going too far.

Local militias organized throughout the country.

Thousands of gun dealers destroyed the registration applications in their possession. Shelves in the gun stores emptied overnight of firearms and ammunition on the eve of Muller's formal declaration.

———

It was mid-February; President Muller signed the Slavery Reparations Act. This compromise bill was designed to assuage the most radical of the Black activists. They had demanded individual reparations ranging from 100,000 to 500,000 dollars per descendant of any black slave. This was adjusted to $20,000 each, to be paid over a period of ten years. The money was non-taxable. The preamble to the bill apologized to Black Americans for four hundred years of slavery and repression with the promise to address all past grievances.

In exchange for the reduced amount of the payment, Blacks would receive free college educations. Top colleges were required to lower academic admission scores because these alleged tests were biased toward White students. States were required to create voting districts based upon ethnic population that favored the election of Blacks to Congress. This bill produced a hue and cry around America. The heartland was enraged. Hispanic groups cried it discriminated against them too.

The young, popular Caribbean-style singer, Larry Fontaine, called the bill "Not enough." He said it was "The mastah's way of buying off the niggahs cheap." Millions of Black people disapproved and would ultimately refuse to take advantage of it. Recent immigrants from the Caribbean and Africa along with tens of thousands of Whites who manufactured false genealogies attempted to scam it.

———•———

It was late February; OPEC announced a radical increase in the cost of oil. Overnight, the price of gasoline shot up to $9.66 per gallon. The Arabs were recovering with interest their perceived loss from the Ramsey presidency. The oil companies cried out they were not to blame, claiming they were trying to keep prices down.

———•———

At the beginning of March, President Muller signed the Marriage Equality Act into law. This guaranteed that gay couples could marry and their unions would have to be recognized in every state.

———•———

President Muller reinstituted Kipper Rodwell's plan to resettle Palestinians in the U.S. By mid-March, the first contingent of Palestinians arrived for resettlement. These would be settled in the more rural areas of the West that had less racial diversity. Large camps of FEMA trailers were being prepared for them in the Western States. The Palestinians cried discrimination. They complained of lower living standards compared to Americans. A U.N. commission was formed to investigate this charge of racism.

Two Mormon missionaries entered their community near Billings, Montana and were murdered. The Palestinians claimed that Islam was under attack. The State Department quashed the investigation into the missionaries' death.

———

It was early March in 2012. Richard Taylor now lived in Reno. He started up a catering business there after leaving New York. Rick had prospered under President Ramsey's economic revitalization plan. Now he could no longer compete. Muller's new Opportunity Enhancement Act made interest free loans to illegal immigrants and other minorities. Catered affairs using minority companies would receive a tax credit. Rick's livelihood was again in the toilet.

———

It was in mid-March. At 7:35 A.M. Illyana was driving Natasha to school in Reno. The girl was picking up English with amazing ease with the aid of a tutor. It was gently raining as the pregnant Illyana stopped at the intersection. Fernando Garcia approached in his boss' pickup from the cross street. Neither he, nor the other man, Emilio, sitting by him could speak English. Fernando had only been in the U.S. two weeks and was now working for a landscaper. He had no driver's license. Illyana drove forward after making her stop. As the pickup approached, Fernando failed to see the stop sign. At the last minute, Emilio shouted, "*Nando, mira!*" Natasha died instantly as her body was crushed into her mother's. The passenger door caved in three feet. Both the mother and child's bodies intermingled with blood, flesh and bone. Illyana would never recover consciousness.

Officer George Scales was the first policeman to arrive at the scene. He handcuffed the injured Fernando Garcia and placed him in the squad car. Emilio ran away. He would never be found. Officer Scales took Fernando to the Renown Medical Facility before booking him. The unconscious Illyana was taken to the emergency room. The ER physicians desperately tried to save her life.

I was working on a job site south of Carson City when the call came. Abandoning my equipment, I drove at breakneck speed to Reno. I rushed by a police officer in the hallway and begged for admittance to the emergency room. He turned and watched as I spoke to the nurse. I learned later that this was Officer Scales. She told me I couldn't enter. I became louder. The nurse called for security. The officer walked over to me.

"Sir, you need to calm yourself. You can't help your wife by going in there. You would only be in the doctor's way."

I stopped talking and nodded. Security arrived and escorted me to the emergency waiting room. A short time later, I was called into the hallway. The surgeon was standing there waiting. He said a few words as I hung my head. I walked into the emergency room and took Illyana's blood-stained hand into mine. I kissed it and looked at my wife's lifeless body. I said goodbye, and then crumpled by her side and cried uncontrollably.

The illegal was treated for his injuries and was booked at three that afternoon. After getting off, George went home. It had been a rotten day. That ugly accident wouldn't leave his mind. Inside his apartment, he took off his Sam Browne at the door and draped it on the hat rack. Going to his kitchen, he took down a bottle of bourbon. Scales poured two inches of whiskey into a glass. He gloried in its warm glow, downing it in one swallow. Looking forward to retirement soon, George mused, "I'm not going to miss this job."

The phone rang. George answered. It was his old buddy, a California Highway Patrol Officer. "Ray. What are you up to, old man?"

"I should have left California when you did. Believe me; you didn't lose anything when you gave up those three years with the CHP."

"So they're screwing you again!"

"Three hundred of us are being forced to retire early. They want to hire more women and minorities. We don't have any choice."

"Ray, take your pension. Move to Reno. An ex-lieutenant in the California Highway Patrol can land a job easy. Hell, you can run security in any casino in town. You'll make good money."

"Is this what it comes down to, George? Everybody's equal but some people are more equal than others?"

"I know it stinks."

"George, Yoneko and I bought this house in 1972. Why should we have to leave? I've never believed in White flight.

But I am coming to Reno next week. I want to show her a good time. I'll call you?"

"I look forward to it."

"Goodbye, George."

"See you next week, Ray."

———————

The following morning, Scales and his fellow officers received their job briefing. He was detailed to the escort of a special gay rights parade celebrating Muller's Marriage Equality Act. Grimly he said to another officer, "Why the hell can't this strange species of *Californicus perverticus* stay in California and do their marching there.

The watch sergeant overheard this. She was wide in the hips, with short hair barely covering her scalp, and she was gay. She then filed a complaint against George. Because of his good record, he escaped being fired for sexual harassment. George was allowed to return following a two week's suspension without pay.

During that first week, George visited his daughter's family in Sacramento. He was there as his grandson came home from school. He was alarmed at the boy's appearance. As George hugged him, he asked, "Jimmy, what's this strange outfit you have on?"

"It's Diversity Day, Grandpa. My assignment was to dress and act like an Arab, so I would understand their culture."

George was mortified. "Did the Islamic children have to pretend to be Christians, Jimmie?"

"No, Grandpa. They said it would profane Islam. Everyone had to pretend to be some other race or religion, except White and Christian."

The Cabinet meeting was one of doom and gloom. Vice President Shrecker was present too. Ramsey's appeal was greater than ever. Forty-four per cent of registered voters nationwide had embraced the new Constitution Party. Harvard educated Muller couldn't understand this.

He declared his deeply wounded feelings to those present. "All I want is to create a society guided by principles of social justice for males and females of all races. It must be free and safe from gun violence, prejudice and pollution. Our children must receive the very best education the Department of Education can provide, where such medieval anachronisms as religion will not stunt their development. Why can't Americans see this? After all, aren't Democrats the party of Roosevelt, Kennedy, Clinton and Kipper Rodwell? So the news is a little discouraging. This crisis will go away."

The Attorney General was the first to comment. "We should have left the guns alone. We tried too much, too fast."

Muller shook his head. "The America that has lived with this cowboy mentality for so long has to go. America must evolve into a kinder, gentler place. Our people have to end this reign of hunting terrorism against animals and recognize that our fellow creatures have a right to live also."

The Secretary of the Interior offered unexpectedly. "Moving

troops off the border is enormously unpopular, Mr. President. Even some native and naturalized Hispanics are joining this new Constitution Party. This issue is at least as big with the American people as guns are."

"If I can get my naturalization bill through in time we can add twenty million new voters to the Democratic Party," replied Muller.

Vice President Shrecker added, "Mr. President, have you given more thought about the upcoming appointments for those three retiring conservative dinosaurs on the Supreme Court?"

"Yes; all are Federal Judges and ACLU members. There will finally be a gay man on the court and a Black woman too. They will overwhelmingly tip the balance of the court in our favor for over a generation."

Shrecker excused himself, returning to his office. He dialed his Bilderberger contact in Brussels. Unavailable at first, the man returned his call later. Shrecker was still in his office when the man called back. Shrecker answered, "Henri, this is going badly. Muller has screwed up so horribly, Ramsey would be a shoo-in for the next election. We've got that covered, he can't run. But we're going to take a bath in the House and Senate. Everything is going to hell!"

"We are aware of that too. The matter has been discussed. If there is any resurgence of American Nationalism it must be dealt with forcefully. We will have an emergency meeting in Brussels next week. You must be there." He passed further instructions to Shrecker before their conversation ended.

The housekeeper answered the door and admitted Eric Llewellyn into Ramsey's Arlington condo. Tall and gangly, sporting a mop of tussled hair, the forty-year old attorney could pass for a much younger man. In casual attire, Stuart warmly greeted and led him into the living room. "Did you see Nancy?"

Eric smiled and nodded. "I smuggled out a letter from her." He reached into his inner coat pocket and drew out several sheets of paper. "Here!" he said, passing it to Stuart. "Serving as legal counsel for two ex-presidents has its advantages. They didn't search me."

Eagerly, Stuart took the paper from Eric's hand. Without speaking he sat on the edge of the couch and devoured every one of Nancy's words. The attorney sat down silently and waited respectfully for him to finish.

"My darling Stuart, you must have heard what the American people are saying. It dominates the news. They want you back. Everyone is fed up with this race crap. I still think you should run and hide. Muller is stupid. He doesn't realize he's playing the races against each other. It's not the same with other liberal Democrats. They know exactly what they're doing. Just like Hitler, their task is not to make men better but to make use of their weaknesses. That's what Hitler said in his own words. The left is losing numbers. Homosexuals, baby-killers and northeastern liberals don't reproduce very well. They plan to garner ninety-eight per cent of illegal immigrant vote in the November election. That's why Muller is pushing so hard for his amnesty-citizenship bill. The Neocons are the worst of all. They've sold out America to fatten their pocketbooks. They don't understand this marriage of convenience will end when the liberals don't need them any longer ..."From here it became personal. "She thinks I should escape and hide."

"A colossal mistake, Mr. President! They would use that as an excuse to kill you and discredit our movement. You have clout as long as you live. Nancy did tell me some of the letter's content. She's right about one thing; they're terrified of you. This country is fed up with both parties. It wouldn't surprise me if an insurrection broke out against this government. Americans are at the breaking point."

Unknown to them, the condo had been bugged. All conversations in every room were being taped by the FBI.

————

It was late afternoon; Vice President Shrecker's limousine neared the Brussels Airport. Air Force One waited to bring him home. The Bilderberger meeting had convened earlier that morning. President Muller dispatched him at the request of some members of the European Union to iron out a trade issue. Muller accepted the fact that only Bilderbergers could attend. Hoping to become a member himself, he concealed his resentment at not being invited.

The consensus of the meeting was grim for Muller. The American political scene was chaotic. Muller had so polarized himself from mainstream America that a Constitution Party victory in November was assured. Even if Ramsey didn't return to office, the loss of the House and Senate would jeopardize over six decades of progress.

Muller's fate was sealed; he would die. Shrecker would become president and pretend to take the country back to the center. Many far-reaching social programs would be put on hold. The Bilderberger's long range plans to achieve a new world order dominated by their own global plutocracy would take priority. If the current crisis continued, Shrecker would declare martial law as a public safety measure. If needed, under the U.N. Charter he could request U.N. troops to quell domestic disturbances. Ramsey would be eliminated for good and the November elections postponed. It was strong medicine, but global democracy had to be preserved.

In the remote mountains of Eastern Iran, Abdullah Laden concluded the deal with Iranian agents. After his father's death by Ramsey's own hand, the Iranians were in shock and avoided all contact with Al Qaeda. Now, sensing the impotence of the Muller administration, those radical clerics running the country became bolder. Abdullah took possession of two thermonuclear weapons. Each had the power of three hundred and fifty kilotons, twenty times the force of the Hiroshima bomb. Iranian agents also planted a false trail back to a disgruntled Russian General. Abdullah would use one against Tel Aviv and the other against a large American city. The infidels would soon feel the wrath of Allah and

Satan America would be ultimately destroyed unless it converted to Islam. Abdullah's father would be avenged.

The bomb destined for Israel would go by ship to the Mediterranean. There, thirty miles off the Israeli coast, it would be transferred to a large motorboat. Palestinians would use this boat in a suicide plunge into Tel Aviv. The martyrs would detonate the bomb just fifty meters from shore.

The other would go to Mexico. There it would be remanded to the custody of Bashan the Turk. Eighty million dollars were promised to a Mexican drug ring. They would smuggle him and the bomb into the United States. Al Qaeda's target was a large city having the highest possible percentage of Whites and Christians in proportion to its total population. Salt Lake City, which was over eighty per cent White was chosen. This location would be readily accessible from Mexico. It was calculated this would cause the cowardly Americans to beg for an accord with Al Qaeda and abandon Israel. Abdullah would only accompany these bombs as far as the port of Chabahar. Both attacks would take place simultaneously. One bomb would not serve as a warning for the other.

———

President and Mrs. Muller arrived at George Tauros' party. It was a grand affair, ostensibly touted as a fundraiser for upcoming Democratic candidates in November. Tauros pledged millions of his own money and illegally channeled millions more through clandestine Swiss bank accounts into the campaign. Hollywood celebrities galore were there along with leftist media muscle and liberal writers. Everyone was having a good time. Earlier that evening, Shrecker called. Tauros confided in him.

"George, is everything set for tonight?" asked Shrecker.

"Get your suit cleaned, Mr. President. You'll be the man before long."

"What are you going to do, George?"

"Shrecker, I don't play in your backyard; you stay out of mine. Agree?"

"I guess so, but this is scary."

"Relax my friend; Tauros takes care of everything. Just make sure your friends remember George Tauros' name two months from now."

"I will. Goodbye."

Tauros warmly greeted President Muller and complimented the First Lady. Putting his arm around Muller's shoulders he led him away from the throng. "Gordie, I brought you something. I save it for special occasions."

"How nice of you, George! What is it?"

"Wine from my own vineyards. Special vintage. I don't share it with just anyone." Tauros winked at a waiter who advanced on signal with a tray of glasses. Tauros reached for a specific one and handed it to the President. Then he took another for himself. "Mr. President, let's drink this Greek style. Down the hatch!" Tauros emptied his and threw the wine glass into the fireplace.

Muller finished his glass and frowned.

"Ah, Gordie, Greek wine is sometimes hard to get used to. It's the resin from the barrels; makes the mouth pucker. Go ahead; throw it in the fireplace."

Miller smiled at this offer to destroy the vessel that held that horrid liquid. "I will."

The men laughed together and shared a man hug. They shook hands before Muller excused himself.

That evening, Gordie gave a rousing speech to the packed audience. He was warmly applauded by everyone. George Tauros appeared to be his biggest fan. The food was superb; Muller was pleased. Everyone present was confident in the future of the Democratic Party. When he left Tauros' party, Muller felt fine. The fundraiser uplifted his dour spirit. Gordie Muller was no longer dreading November.

The Awakening

The squad car was parked across the street near Ryan's Bar. Stopping to check an expired tag, Officer Scales watched as the drunk staggered outside. He recognized this man. Not waiting for him to drive away, Scales turned on his light and pulled into the parking lot next to him. With a quick, short blast of his siren Scales gained his attention. The drunk stopped. Scales swung the squad car door open and got out. Then, he walked up to the man. "You shouldn't be driving tonight, sir?"

My words slurred as I replied. "Why don't you leave me alone? I wasn't doing anything wrong."

"It's not what you did, sir. It's what you might do."

"I know you."

"Yes, I was the officer that took the report the day you're wife died. And I remember seeing you in court last week as the judge handed you a DUI. Do you think you can bring her back by drinking yourself to death?"

"I don't care what happens anymore; I just want to be left alone."

"Well, I'm not going to leave you alone. But I'll do this; I won't arrest you if you'll go for a ride with me. We'll stop and get some coffee and have a talk."

"I got nothin' to lose."

"Get in the front; we'll go to Denny's down the street." Scales was taking a chance. Patronizing a drunk would get him fired. He volunteered to work an extra shift tonight after taking the previous day off to attend the funeral of Ray's wife. She was murdered, the victim of a home invasion robbery. Forensics experts identified an illegal Hispanic male. The man disappeared in Mexico. Ray was alone, they had no surviving children.

Scales ordered bacon and eggs for me. We drank several cups of coffee. I regained some sobriety.

"Life's not very sweet right now for you; is it, Mr. Raggio?"

"I wish I were dead."

"Keep drinking like this; you may get your wish. Do you think that's what she would have wanted?"

"I killed her. I brought her over here and I killed her."

"You didn't kill anybody, Mr. Raggio. You shouldn't blame yourself. What's your first name?"

"Marty."

"Marty, finish your coffee. I'll take you back to your car. You get in the back seat and take a nap. I'll keep your keys. When I get off this morning, I'll come back. And Marty?"

"Yeah?"

"I'll check on you before I get off. If I see you driving, or that car gone, you're going to jail."

"You got my keys."

"I'm telling you this in case I don't have them all."

At 7:30 A.M. George Scales went off duty. Parking next to my car, he pounded on the window, waking me up. As I lowered it, he made a face. The smell of alcohol was overpowering. But I was OK to drive. George took down my phone number and returned my keys.

"Marty, I'll call you."

————

Stooping at his front door, George picked up the bundled copy of the *Reno Gazette Journal*, and carried it inside with him. He made a pot of coffee. He would have the next two days off. He poured himself a cup, sat down at the kitchen table and opened the paper.

The newspaper headlines read:

ACLU WINS SCHOOL CASE IN MASSACHUSETTS
Boston, MA.

In a landmark decision, the ACLU won a controversial lawsuit in Federal Court which will affect the future of

millions of the nation's school age children. Citing the
need to maintain the separation of church and state, the
ACLU filed a suit arguing that children were being sub-
jected to religious influence on school buses as they were
forced to view churches while riding along prescribed
routes. This, according to the spokesman for the ACLU,
constituted a violation of the separation of church and
state. Muller commented that this may be taking the
issue to extremes, but the President also stated that
the rule of law must be obeyed. Major Protestant and
Catholic religious leaders object. Conservative groups
vow to carry the issue to the Supreme Court.

In the editorial section Scales read an article written by a man
named Richard Taylor. This man had lost his job and marriage after his white collar job in New York was outsourced to
India. Taylor described moving to Reno for a new start. But
now he couldn't compete. Government policies favored illegal
aliens. Taylor stated, "I have nothing more to lose. I'm tired of
starting over." George was particularly interested in Taylor's
final statement: "America is ripe for a revolution."

The following day George took his two dogs for a walk
along the Truckee River. He paused by the river bank and
picked up a stone, skipping it across the water. He watched
it skim along the surface and finally sink. Troubled thoughts
would not go away. Sitting on a large rock, he threw a stick
into the shallows. His two dogs happily chased it. They ran
back to him for approval as the lead one carried it in his mouth.

George took the stick and softly stroked both dogs. He knew what he had to do.

That evening George contacted Richard Taylor. He also called me and his friend Ray Morrison in Modesto. He persuaded us to meet at his apartment in northwest Reno at 1:00 PM tomorrow on Sunday afternoon. Taylor was curious; he decided to attend. I agreed and Morrison was eager to oblige his old friend.

The following afternoon was heavily overcast. Rain gently poured on the Truckee Meadows as we three arrived at George Scales' apartment. A round of introductions took place and we shared his fresh brewed coffee. Without much fanfare he called us to attention and began to speak. We all fell silent as Scales became serious.

"I thank you all for coming. What I have to say is controversial. No; that word is too mild. It's radical! We're mainstream Americans. You all love this country just as much as I do. These last few years, we've watched it slowly die. The country we live in is not the same one we were born in. I can barely recognize it. Briefly, we got it back when Ramsey was President. But that ended when a cabal took control of the government. They placed restrictions on free speech. They're trying to disarm us through a U.N. treaty. Their ethnic pandering and open border policies are unraveling this country. They're trying to eradicate religion. I'll retire in a few weeks. What can I look forward to? New federal restrictions have

almost put an end to hunting. I was divorced eleven years ago.
My children are grown and my grandkids are being brain-
washed by the Department of Education. The ACLU has
been victorious in its war against American culture, freedom
and religion."

Listening to George, I was confused. "But, George; I
always thought the ACLU promoted freedoms and helped
those who couldn't help themselves."

"You're not alone, Marty. Their big rise to popularity came
when they picked the winning side in the Civil Rights Struggle.
The ACLU was founded by a communist lawyer, Roger
Baldwin, who said, 'Civil Liberties, like democracy, are useful
only as tools for social change.' He even wrote a book called
Liberty Under the Soviets which attacked religion. In that book
he said: 'I was not a liberal. I wanted what the Communists
wanted.' The organization became a magnet for other communists. It was joined by Soviet agents. They always patronize
those groups who are attacking America. They supported the
Nazis marching in Skokie, Illinois, many years ago. This victory
enabled them to numb American minds for other attacks to
come. In 1986 they created their Gay and Lesbian Project. In
1997 the ACLU convinced the Supreme Court to protect the
rights of pornographers on the internet, including showing the
images to children. In order for them to tear down barriers to
governmental power, they must end America's belief in God.
They successfully prevented a San Francisco school teacher, a
Mr. Williams, from handing out copies of the Declaration of
Independence to his students; because it refers to God. They

have supported the right of AIDS patients to keep their diseases confidential. And the ACLU always takes up the fight to deny the freedom of worship in public places. They have even represented the Ku Klux Klan."

My eyes were beginning to open as I digested George's words. "But didn't they support equality and women's rights?"

"Marty, to a Communist, truth is always relative. They don't have a set of absolute values coming from God which I'm sure you do. Remember, these people derive their philosophy from Karl Marx. When he commented on the Mexican War, Marx said: 'Is it a misfortune that magnificent California was seized from the lazy Mexicans who did not know what to do with it?' I wonder if Fidel Castro ever studied that episode of history before he became a Marxist! In a letter to Engels in 1862, Marx described a competitor: 'it is now completely clear to me that he, as is proved by his cranial formation and his hair, descends from the Negroes of Egypt, assuming that his mother or grandmother had not interbred with a nigger . . . the obtrusiveness of this fellow is also niggerlike.' What do you suppose that Marxist singer, Larry Fontaine, would say about that?"

I was flabbergasted at these revelations. "Why haven't American leaders done more to expose these people?"

"You don't know the half of it. When Carter was President, he even awarded the Presidential Medal of Freedom to Roger Baldwin, calling him a champion of human rights."

"I never thought Carter was very smart; but who could have thought he was that stupid?" I answered.

"Marty, if this were the middle ages, Carter would have been referred to *Jimmy the Simple*. Liberal American politicians jump in bed with the ACLU whenever they can. It helps them get elected. These ACLU people thrive on ignorance and feed on slogans. They can make or break candidates in Democratic dominated enclaves."

Rick maintained a perplexed look as he took in George's words, until finally speaking. "But didn't they fight for freedom of speech during the McCarthy era?" he asked.

"I'm glad you brought that up, Rick. The Venona Papers were released in 1995 under the Freedom of Information Act. They proved that everyone McCarthy accused of being a communist or a Russian spy was just that. And a great many more besides! All during the McCarthy hearings the U.S. Army was reading the Soviet diplomatic code. To have come forth in his defense would have compromised this program. These files were verified by information released by the Russians in the 1990s. When this information came to light it was vaguely mentioned in a short paragraph buried deep inside *The New York Times*. Leftist educators, Hollywood liberals, and political activists don't dare speak about the Venona Papers. To them, McCarthyism is the Holy Grail of Liberalism. If you mentioned this to a liberal, he would duck the issue. He might not even know what you were talking about. Their sources of information are selective. And if it didn't pass over his head, he would use a device known as Talkaround to dodge the topic. McCarthy was a patriot. He saved America!"

All of us were in awe of George by now. I learned more that afternoon than I had in a half dozen classes when I was still in school.

George continued, "Let's hear your stories; how about you, Ray?"

"My wife was murdered last month. It was a home invasion robbery. Our only son died many years ago. I was one of several senior officers forced into an early retirement. We were told it was to make room for minorities. Like George, I don't like what's going on."

Richard Taylor spoke. "My name is Rick Taylor. My world fell apart earlier this year when my job was outsourced to India. My wife divorced me. We had no children. I was making a comeback here in Reno. I actually rebuilt my bank account to five digits when I became the victim of illegal immigration. Then it became impossible to compete."

It was my turn. "My name is Martin Raggio." I told them of Illyana, and how I had brought her to America. I choked up as I described how she was killed by an illegal.

"Marty?" said George.

"Yes?"

"What became of that illegal alien?"

"Under the new guidelines, he was able to make bail. But he jumped and made his way to Mexico. The government down there won't even look for him. What can we do? The four of us!"

"Well said! How about it, men?" asked George. "If we could do something, would you stand with me?"

At first, uncertain of his words, we searched each other's faces for an answer. Then, nodding in assent, all of us softly answered. "Yes!"

"How?" Taylor quickly added.

"A fair question!" continued George, "This country as it now exists is unworkable. We can apply pressure; so much pressure that this government collapses under its own weight. We can't do it alone. But we can light the fire. God willing; it will grow."

"But George," said Ray, "Ramsey might get re-elected this coming fall. Isn't it better to wait until then and see what happens? Are you proposing revolution?"

"We might as well wait for Santa Claus, Ray. Look what both parties did to Ramsey. These people in office are terrorists. They're not going to let him run, let alone get re-elected. Unrest is springing up everywhere. There is a seething tension under wraps that's begging to be released. Now is the time; we can strike before this cabal understands the nature of its enemy. We can siphon off hundreds of FBI and ATF agents, men who would otherwise be out there enforcing that U.N. gun confiscation scheme."

"George, don't forget the Federal Courts, ACLU, media and liberal colleges. They are supporting this terrorist government too," said Taylor.

"That's right, Rick. They're part of the problem. We'll have to deal with them too."

"Our lives will be over if we do," added Ray. "We'll be criminals!"

"That's the only thing I can guarantee," replied George.

"We're all going to die. The moment we enter into a pact, our fate is sealed. We'll be trading our lives to save our nation. If any man doesn't see it that way, let him leave now. If these evil men who govern want to call us criminals, I say let them."

"Is this about race; you know my wife was Japanese?" asked Ray.

"No; it's about freedom," replied George. "This government is pandering to fringe issues and illegal immigration in order to build up its political base. Let's pledge ourselves to restore the Republic and remove these terrorists from office. Who will join me?"

"I will!" we all replied enthusiastically.

Ray spoke again, "Thousands like us are out there. None of my friends are willing to give up their guns."

"I know, but we have to be careful who we pull in," replied George. "Some men will be less reliable. They must put their families first. I chose you men, because like me, no one is closely dependent on us."

"Let's seal it in blood," I said.

"What do you consider sacred, Marty?"

"What else; the Holy Bible!" I replied.

"Wait here." George returned with his old Bible and a Bowie Knife. He laid the Bible on the table. Opening it, he pricked his right forefinger with the knife and said, "I, George Scales, promise to give my life to restore the Republic of the United States of America." He pressed his finger into the page, then, passed the knife to me.

I eagerly took it from him and slit my own forefinger; then pressed it down. My blood ran together with his as I spoke. "I, Martin Raggio, swear revenge and promise to give my life to restore our country, the United States of America." I passed the knife to Ray.

Taking it, Ray also cut and pressed his finger beside our blood. "In memory of my wife, Yoneko, I, Raymond Morrison, dedicate my life to restore the United States of America." He passed the knife to Rick.

Rick sliced his finger, pressing his blood beside ours. "I give thanks for this moment. I, Richard Taylor, devote myself to restore the Republic of the United States of America and destroy its domestic enemies."

"Let's review our strengths," said George. Ray and I, as law enforcement officers, know how the system works. I don't have to retire. I can stay active with Reno P.D. From my position I can be forewarned of government moves and investigations. Ray and I can use our uniforms and badges to get in places you men can't. We understand investigation techniques; we know how to get into police records. How about you guys?"

Richard Taylor spoke first. "I was well placed in the banking industry, right in its heartland, New York City. I already have an idea that may work."

I was the last. "I was a railroad man. For nineteen years I ran trains. But I also know how easy they are to sabotage and derail. Now I make my living operating heavy equipment. This may be useful too."

"Good; here's how I think we should proceed. We'll set goals, targets if you will. From my position, I can check out police files. There we might find others useful to the struggle. Each one of us brings special skills to our own little group. We can even train men and spin them off into new squadrons. We will keep no written or computer records. As we die, these squadrons become isolated, unable to be identified. As our movement progresses, we will become a many headed beast that continually grows new heads as its old ones are cut off."

"How long do we have before the FBI cracks us?" asked Ray.

"Not long; that's why we have to hit hard and make our remaining time here on Earth count. That's why each squadron must be independent of all others. When the four of us are dead, we must have an infrastructure that keeps growing."

That evening, we each set our immediate goals. Checking police files, George would prospect for potential members. Ray would re-enter law enforcement. With his background, that would not be difficult. This would place him in an opportune spot to receive inside information. I would utilize my operating skills as they were needed. And Rick had the grandest scheme of all. He would plan and coordinate attacks against the financial infrastructure of the U.S. Government.

Before going our separate ways, George poured each of us a shot of bourbon. He raised his glass. We followed his example. "For the Republic," he said. We emptied our glasses.

"Before anyone leaves, I wish to add my toast!" I said.

They looked at me with curiosity. George answered, "OK."
He poured us another round.

As I raised my glass, the others followed my lead. "To
President Stuart Ramsey!"

"Hear, Hear!"

THE PATRIOTS

Officer Scales was looking through old police files as his supervisor approached. The man had a quizzical expression. He knew Scales was spending his days off poring over old records. "Researching old cases, George?"

Expecting this question, a well rehearsed and pat answer flowed from his lips. "I'm coming up on retirement, Jake. Sitting in front of the TV is not my idea of retirement. I want to write a book. I'm looking for some of the department's more interesting cases."

"Great idea! Let me know if you need my help."

"Will do, Jake; thanks!"

"When are you going to pull the plug on us?"

"I'm building up to it! Not really in a rush, but it's coming soon."

"When do you go back to work?"

"Tomorrow."

"Good luck, George. You know where to find me!"

This encounter went as expected. Scales quickly put his boss out of mind as he delved further into the files. He wasn't looking for ordinary criminals. Only one type of man would fit his profile, those involved in politically related offenses. Men who had never harmed anyone, stolen anything and under all ordinary conditions would be considered law abiding citizens. Primarily, these men would have been convicted as felons for violating gun laws. Scales found two in this category. One, David Blevins, was a physician. He had also been a Major in the Nevada National Guard. Blevins received a bad conduct discharge and five years in Federal prison after he was discovered in possession of an unregistered, fully automatic AK-47. The other man, Harold Wiser, was a chemist who had worked in the mining industry. His crime against society was being illegally in possession of dynamite, which he used to remove trees from his property on Mount Rose. For this he served time in a Federal prison. Both men still lived locally, and worked at jobs beneath their educational background. Neither had family ties. Both had expressed regret for violating these dubious crimes against society. Both looked like patriots.

Ray Morrison took a supervisor's job with an armored

car company in Sacramento. We needed financing. From his trusted position, Ray would know when and where to strike. This had been Rick Taylor's idea. It would require a lot of money to finance any serious enterprise.

I dried myself out. Until George saved me, I hadn't worked since Illyana's death. I sold my business and equipment. I was able to repay Aunt Irene and have some cash left over.

We put David Blevins and Harold Wiser through a series of interviews. After being accepted into our circle, they too took the blood oath upon the Bible. We were now six men. These new men, along with Rick Taylor and me would soon devote our full time to our cause. We pooled our money and resources.

On May 1st the headlines of the *Reno Gazette Journal* read:

Refugee Camp Planned in Fernley

Washington, D.C.

The Muller administration has approved final plans to set up a refugee camp on the outskirts of Fernley, Nevada. It will be placed on BLM land, where two thousand Palestinians are scheduled to arrive soon after the placement of FEMA trailers. State and local governments complain of this influx. They claim there is not enough funding for school, social and medical services. Widespread local demonstrations protesting this are planned throughout communities in Northern Nevada. Hispanics are complaining about preferential treatment given to the Palestinians, maintaining they should receive hemisphere priority.

George called a meeting. We were all there except Ray. He confronted us with the new reality of this Palestinian Camp. "Men, do any of you see an opportunity in this?"

I spoke first. "Once they get here, it's going to be impossible to get them out. If we can destroy those trailers before they arrive, Fernley won't become a dumping ground for these people."

"That's good, Marty! Great idea; but we couldn't torch them fast enough. The police and fire departments would show up before we got the job done. That would be the end of us."

Harold Wiser spoke. "I believe I have the answer, gentlemen."

All of our eyes were on Harold. "Tell us!" said George.

"You know I'm a trained chemist. Lately, I've taken work as a janitor, but I haven't forgotten my profession. This is easier than you think. I can prepare delayed action, incendiary devices. We'll burn up these tin shacks. We can place them all and be gone before the first one explodes."

"There's going to be at least one guard on duty," replied George.

"You can disarm and handcuff him. That's your specialty, George. Using surprise is how we handle him."

"There are four hundred trailers there. How can you set up that many devices in a short time?"

"We don't set up anything. We just lay one under each trailer and move on. When these bombs detonate, each trailer will be torched. There are six of us. If it takes us fifteen seconds per unit, we can have all of them in place in less than forty minutes. I'll prepare delay fuses. We'll be miles away before the first one blows."

"Do you need special ingredients, Harold?"

"All I need is gasoline, sulfuric acid, safety matches, glue and capped bottles. I'll need to run a few tests to determine the timing sequence."

"Those trailers begin arriving tomorrow. By Friday, they'll all be there. The rough-in plumbing, sewer and power lines are already in. By Monday, contractors will be hooking these tin shacks up. The Palestinians will arrive before the month is out. Can you have these bombs ready before Monday?"

"Try me! It's a piece of cake," replied Harold. "We can take them all out this weekend."

"OK, Harold; Marty, Rick and Dave will work with you. I'll get details of the camp's layout and plan a schedule. Is everyone agreed?"

We all nodded. Harold assigned each of us a different task. "Dave, you buy forty cases of quart-size bottles. Make sure they have screw off caps, and are made of glass. Empty, and dry them out. That's 480 bottles. We need 400 bombs. That will leave some for me to experiment with."

"Why do we need quart bottles with screw off caps? And why not plastic bottles?" asked Dave.

"The bigger the bottle; the bigger the bang! Pop tops won't work; we need a better seal. And the acid must be stored in glass. We'll combine gasoline and sulfuric acid inside the bottles. The mix will remain stable as long as the bottle is vertical. But when turned on its side, the acid will eat through the cap."

"For what purpose?" asked Dave.

"We'll grind match heads into small particles. Then, sprinkle them on a thin layer of glue lining the outside of the caps. The acid will burn through these caps and make contact with the match heads. Matches contain potassium chlorate. This substance burns when coming into contact with sulfuric acid. The fire will ignite the gasoline. Then all hell breaks loose. You guys understand this so far?"

"I do," I replied! "But how long does it take that acid to eat through the caps?"

"I'll have to experiment, Marty. The fuses of those first bombs need to burn through in forty minutes, the last ones we put down, in only fifteen. Some caps may have to be thinned, others thickened. I'll handle this."

"So, you work the caps first?" asked Rick.

"Right! But it won't take long. Get me these ingredients; I should be able to figure this timing sequence out by Thursday. Dave, when you buy these bottles, use cash. Pay a street person to buy them for you. Every store has security cameras. It won't take a genius to look for a large purchase of quart sized bottles once they find all that burnt glass. Don't get all ten cases in one place or buy a single brand. Disguise yourself so even the street person can't give a good description of you. Shop in neighborhoods where you're not known."

"Marty?"

"Yo!" I replied.

"Buy about fifty gallons of gasoline and some funnels for filling the bottles. And like David, don't buy it all in one place. But don't fill any of these until I tell you. Understand?"

"Got it!" I replied.

"Rick, you buy the matches and glue. Only safety matches! Grind the match heads down. Use a pocket knife. Don't try it with sand paper. The pieces can be coarse; they don't have to be fine." Rick nodded. "I'll get the sulfuric acid. I won't buy it pure; that will arouse too much curiosity. I'll buy battery acid and concentrate it with dry ice."

After Harold paused, George broke the silence. "Let's plan this for 2:00 A.M. Sunday morning. There's no moon that night. Later this week, we'll iron out the details. Questions?"

There were none.

George secured a drawing of the camp and studied its security details. Taking six thousand dollars out of his credit union, he purchased two older pickup trucks separately from private owners. Introducing himself under a false name, he declined to sign the pink slips as he paid cash, telling each seller it was for his son.

Later that week we finalized our plans. We would strike at 4:00 A.M. next Sunday morning. This would be the optimum time, when a tired security guard could easily be surprised. Those four hundred fire bombs were ready by Saturday afternoon. Ray arrived from California that same day. We turned in early but were up and ready by eleven. At 2:00 A.M. we drove toward Fernley in the two trucks. All of us wore gloves, caps, dark clothing and used false mustaches, wigs and makeup.

Parking behind a row of trees about a mile from the encampment, we waited as George went ahead on foot. He approached out of sight, slowly, walking parallel in the desert beside the access road. He came up behind the watchman's shanty. Then, casting a quick glance through a side window, he saw the elderly security guard. The man was reading, unaware he was being watched. George walked around the shack trying the door. It was unlocked. The guard jerked to his feet as George entered, pistol in hand. "Who are—?" the guard began saying as he reached for his firearm.

George pointed his pistol at the man's middle. "I wouldn't do that."

"What do you want? There ain't nothing here worth stealin'. This is Federal property. You can't come in here like that."

"Relax and you won't get hurt. Turn around; put your hands on the wall." The guard complied. "Now spread your feet far apart." After the man did, George reached around him. Holding his pistol in the small of the man's back, he unfastened the guard's gun belt which fell to the floor. George stepped back and called us by cell phone.

Within minutes, we drove up to the gate. We chained the

guard's hands and feet behind his back, securing them with padlocks. It was deemed too risky to use handcuffs. He was blindfolded; his cell phone was smashed, and the telephone inside the guard shack ripped out. Care was taken to insure he would be clear of the coming firestorm. George took the keys and unlocked the gate. Both vehicles entered the chain-link compound. George closed it behind us, donning the guard's shirt and badge.

From a pre-designated point, we set about our task. I drove the lead truck; Ray followed closely behind in his. With only our parking lights on, Harold passed fire bombs to Rick and David from the bed of my truck. One was placed underneath every trailer on each side. We turned and drove down every lane until the entire camp was completed. Care was taken to insure that no bottle broke unexpectedly. When my truck was empty, the unloading crew moved to Ray's. All firebombs were down within forty minutes.

Back at the main gate, George let us out. He closed, locked it behind us, and threw the key into the brush. We drove south on 95, careful not to exceed the speed limit. At the junction of Highway 50 we turned west. In Carson City, we parked the trucks on side streets near the Nugget. In the casino's parking lot our cars waited. Separately, we drove north on 395 back to Reno.

The first bombs exploded ten minutes after our getaway. The fuses functioned perfectly, all within a fifteen minute interval. The entire camp was ablaze before firefighters could respond.

Tuning to AM 780, George was south of Reno near the 341 turn-off when the news was announced. Firefighters were trying to put out a mysterious conflagration engulfing the refugee camp in Fernley.

He listened to the report with satisfaction. The Feds would have to make other plans. Those Palestinians wouldn't be moving to Fernley after all. This first action was a total success; and there were no casualties. George smiled.

The headlines in *The New York Times* next morning read:

Refugee Camp in Nevada Destroyed

Washington, D. C.

President Muller pledges to find the thugs who torched the new Palestinian Refugee Camp at Fernley, Nevada. The full resources of the FBI will be utilized in wake of $10 million in damages to Federal property there. ATF is dispatching a special team to Nevada. Muller's Press Secretary announces that arrests are anticipated within twenty-four hours.

The following morning, the headlines of *The New York Times* read:

Vigilante Murders in Texas

Washington, D. C.

President Muller ordered National Guard units to protect refugee camps in the wake of the shooting deaths of twenty Palestinians after an altercation yesterday, near Plano, Texas. Palestinian leaders vow to take this racist attack to the United Nations General Assembly. FBI says arrests are imminent. Leaders of all Islamic nations protest; they demand adequate protection for Muslims.

———

Officer Scales was at work as he read the security guard's report. The man described the action as being carried out with rehearsed precision. He believed the assailants had professional military backgrounds. Scales grew alarmed as he continued reading; a BOLO (be on the lookout out) was put out for Harold Wiser. With his background, he was considered a person of interest. George knew he must contact Harold before his police colleagues did. Hoping he was still at Marty's place, he called there first. Except for Ray, the other four were indeed there, still engaged in a hearty celebration of the previous night's raid. Told he could never return to his apartment or be publicly seen in Reno, Harold was secretly moved that evening into hiding at Ray's house in Modesto.

———

It was on Thursday following the raid. We were gathered at Ray's place in Modesto. Numerous ideas were being discussed. He was giving us a pitch for a personal friend.

"There's a man in Montana," said Ray. "I've known him a long time. I usually spend a couple weeks every year at his place. We hunt and fish together. He's a man we can trust. I know how old Joshua thinks; he doesn't like what's going on any more than we do. He formed a militia up there over thirty years ago. I don't know exactly what they do. For several years running he tried to get me to join up with them. Joshua always believed the country would come to this. He said this to me, 'Someday we're gonna have to fight for our freedoms.' And I always shined him on. Like most Americans, I lived in blissful ignorance. But ol' Josh, he read. He always knew it was coming. He told me this cancer would take over the government someday. I think we can bring him in."

"If you take him in confidence, he'll have us in his power," replied George.

"It's not so risky as you think. I don't have to tell him everything. He can help us, no matter what. I know he has a source of dynamite; caps too, and I'm sure I can get some. But I won't act alone and try to bring him in unless you men agree to it."

We discussed the matter of Joshua in detail. It was a gamble; but we had become high stakes gamblers. Ray was right about one thing. We needed a source of dynamite, caps and weapons. The matter was put to a vote. It was favorable. Ray should contact his old friend."

"Don't leave a phone trail," said George.

"I'll call Joshua from a pay phone downtown," Ray replied.

From the top of a low hill, Joshua scanned his 800 acre ranch while sitting astride his trusted Appaloosa. The ranch house lay visible to his left near the base of the Rocky Mountains. Western Montana had been good to him. Chill still hung in the air though the last of winter's snow was now melted in the valley below. This was his daily ritual, up before dawn, riding the fence's perimeter. Eagerly anticipating the waiting coffee and rubbing circulation back into his hands from the cold, it was still early as he turned his horse toward the ranch house. His home was lonely. Sarah, his wife, died three years before. In the twilight of his life, with failing health, the seventy-eight year old Korean War Veteran avidly clung to life. He still had the ranch and his boys. They were the inspiration that kept him going.

An unknown pick-up was parked in front of his house. As he rode closer, it was apparent the vehicle was empty. Whoever drove it up was in the house. Opening a saddlebag, Joshua drew out a long barrel, .357 magnum revolver. Opening the cylinder, he spun it around. Five rounds lay within. That would be four more than he needed if this was an intrusion. Slowly riding up to the porch he watched the windows for signs of activity. Detecting no movement from within, he slid out of the saddle and tied his horse to a column. Walking up to the front door, he made deliberate noise as he opened and entered. "I'm home! Make yourself known!"

"Joshua, you old son of a gun, come over here and drink a cup of your own coffee!"

He recognized his old friend and smiled. "Ray, you no good for nothin' cop, what brings you up here to God's country?"

Ray and Joshua had been friends for over thirty years. They had met at the Calgary Stampede when both followed the rodeo circuit. They had been contenders in their youth.

An injured disk after being thrown by a Brahma bull had settled Joshua down. Grateful that he could still work his ranch, he prospered. Ray became a policeman. Every year, they hunted and fished together. They reminisced a long time before coming to the point.

"Bring your tackle box?"

"Not this time, old friend. I need a favor!"

"Name it!"

"You still have a supply of dynamite on hand?"

"Yeah, I'll give you a couple pounds. What you need it for?"

"I want a little more than that."

"Sure. What do you plan on mining out there? Gonna blast some sand and gravel? Not gold is it?"

"Josh, I had in mind several hundred pounds."

"Whew! Hey, what're you doin' out there, buddy?"

"A business partner wants to reopen a slate mine. It's hard to get the necessary permits to buy dynamite. New government regs, you know; this damned Muller administration."

"Uh huh! You never were a very good liar, Ray! What's Mr. Law Enforcement got on his mind? You gonna start a damn war?"

"And if I said yes, what would you say to that?"

"I'd say bring it on. This country's only got two years left at most; it ain't gonna go on much longer. I quit the militia five years ago and handed it over to a friend. This damned arthritis gets me down so. But lately, I been meetin' with the boys and sharpenin' up my shootin' eye."

"I suppose you heard about Fernley?" Ray asked.

"Ha, ha, ha. I sat up late and polished off half a bottle of bourbon after hearing about that little caper. So that was you!"

"I didn't say that, Joshua."

"This is ol' Josh you're talkin' to. You always wore your feelings on your sleeve. Don't try to bullshit this old cowboy!"

"I don't know if you should be involved, Josh. When we took the blood oath to restore the Republic—"

"Whoa," interrupted Joshua. "You boys took a blood oath to restore the Republic!"

"Let me finish. Yes, we did. We set down a rule; only those men with little or nothing to lose could join our squadron. You have four fine sons. We mean for them to live and have fine sons and daughters of their own in a free America. All of us are going to die. And probably be remembered as terrorists."

"If my boys knew you wanted to keep them out of this fight, they'd whup you good! They make me look like a damn liberal. They were raised to believe in four things: the Bible, our country, hard work; and a trustworthy rifle. Ray! This is word from heaven. We got the makins' of an army already up here."

"Then you're in?"

"I was in before you boys got started. Bring the damn war on!"

"We need hundreds of pounds of dynamite."

"We got it! Now you tell me more about this little group you boys started up down there in the lower forty-seven!"

FINANCING REVOLUTION

Ray's house became our headquarters. He returned from Montana with upbeat spirits. His report was positive, Joshua was in. He would activate the militia. Care had to be taken. Not all of them could be trusted. We eagerly questioned Ray.

"Tell us more about him," asked Rick.

"Well, he's a real America First type guy. Josh organized this militia of eighty men or so back in the mid-70s. He has four grown sons; three of them are prominent on the rodeo circuit. Won't take a dime from anybody, raises cattle and horses."

Frowning, Rick interrupted. "What makes you think we can trust him?"

"I considered that. I wasn't sure if he even could be approached. Joshua is a pretty honest man and a loyal

American. I wondered how he would react. But remember our plans to spin off other squadrons? Well, here was an opportunity. I probed his mind and his heart. I even hesitated at first, because we decided to bring in men who have little to lose. He has four sons. But in his own words: 'They make him look like a damn liberal.' Joshua's no slacker. He's in, his boys too. He's screening men from that militia as I'm speaking here now."

This information was music to us. We six might become sixty or more. We shifted our conversation to more pressing matters.

"Our immediate concern is money!" announced George. "Someone said, 'An army marches on its stomach.' Who? I don't remember; but we're no different. Only Ray and I still have an income. It takes money to live. And we need the means to wage war: operating and travel expenses, weapons, ammunition, safe houses, vehicles, and special equipment. We can't be part-time revolutionaries; that would be a waste of time. We need a lot of money; and we need it now!"

Ray smiled as George spoke, waiting for him to finish. Then he announced a surprise. "Loomis is sending a large shipment soon. The details are under wraps but as a supervisor, I'm in the information loop. The Loomis people were impressed with my prior service as a CHP Lieutenant. My background put me in the right position. We must be ready soon."

"They'll be on to you right away. You're the newest high-level employee. They'll know information came from the inside," said Rick.

"No doubt about it; you're right! I'll have to disappear immediately afterward."

"I have an idea," I said.

"What's that, Marty?" asked George.

"I'll rent a place where we can keep Ray and Harold out of sight."

"So, after an honorable life of public service, I'm going to hide!" replied Ray.

Until now, David Blevins seldom spoke. "Gentlemen, I may have something to offer. Before I went to prison, I was a doctor. My specialty was dermatology. After I was released, I couldn't go back to my profession. I took whatever work I could, but sometimes I picked up a little extra cash altering faces for guys who wanted to disappear. It might not have been the most honorable thing to do. But I wouldn't work on any real bad apple. These were mostly men hiding from ex-wives or creditors. You could say I got some on-the-job training as a plastic surgeon. I can do the same for Ray and Harold."

"What do you think, Ray?" asked George.

"I'll time my disappearance to coincide with this first job. I can get a quick equity loan on my house and liquidate everything else."

———

We focused on immediate goals. No one would be looking for me. In my own name, Martin Raggio, I rented a country house on four acres between Grass Valley and Nevada City. If need be, it offered an escape route into the forested Sierra

Nevada Range behind. There was quick access to I-80 and other roads. Another plus, we had no close neighbors. Soon after we relocated, Doc Blevins changed Harold's appearance. The plan matured rapidly. Ray acquired details of the three million dollar shipment. The armored car would pass along a lonely stretch of Highway 70 after leaving Quincy. Constantly tracked by GPS, it would have a driver and two guards. They were well armed and in constant contact with their dispatcher.

George carefully choreographed our efforts. We chose an ambush site, and did time studies. In those few days available for us, we drilled, and memorized our parts. We needed Caltrans flagman's equipment; this part was easy. Two trucks were needed, painted orange with Caltrans markings; several radio handsets; a bulldozer with low-boy trailer and semi to pull it; a Highway Patrol Cruiser and an ambulance. We had sufficient start-up money from Ray's refinance. He bought a scrap highway patrol cruiser and found a convincing set of strobe lights for it. He already had the uniform and badge.

I picked up a decrepit D-6 dozer and a rig to haul it on, at a used equipment auction in Sacramento. Two pickup trucks were bought individually from newspaper ads. Harold manufactured a shaped thermite charge explosive device. Though crude, it could easily penetrate the rear door of an armored car. We would hijack an ambulance on the morning of the strike.

Ray rented an isolated cabin with a large barn in Graeagle. It was hidden by forest, near the Middle Fork of the Feather River, one mile from Highway 70. We concealed our equipment inside the barn where it was painted and stenciled with Caltrans markings.

The moment came soon enough. The ambush would be one mile west of the 89 turnoff on Highway 70. This was conveniently located just over two miles from our cabin. The chosen ambush site was protected from view by terrain, trees and curves on each end.

Fifty-four minutes before show time, David made an emergency call. An ambulance was dispatched from nearby Portola. David guided it from Highway 89 into the trees concealing the cabin. With lights flashing, the ambulance stopped at the door. David ushered them inside. "My wife is lying where she fell in the bedroom. Please hurry; she's in pain!" he said.

The paramedics entered the room. They were greeted by four pistols aimed at their mid-sections. David pulled another from behind. They were handcuffed together, back to back. Forced to sit in the middle of the room, a chain was wrapped around their waists and secured with a padlock. Other chains encircling their ankles were anchored to bolts embedded in opposite walls.

False alarms were sent to the Sheriff's Department and Highway Patrol. With luck, these calls would draw them away from the ambush. We had rehearsed this operation to perfection. Success or failure would be determined in less than ten minutes.

George and I left the cabin first, pre-positioning the bull-dozer at the ambush site. After lowering the tail ramps, we released the chain binders securing the dozer. George guided the movement as I slowly backed it off the low-boy. While I began setting up traffic cones, George drove the tractor-trailer back to the barn. He joined Harold in the ambulance, and together they waited for the call.

The armored car was now less than ten minutes away. Rick and Dave took flagging positions beyond the east and west curves, protecting both sides of the ambush site. Ray drove up and parked his cruiser by my dozer, blocking the armored car's lane of approach. After the Loomis vehicle passed Rick, he used his flagging tools and stopped all further traffic coming from that direction. He also alerted Dave who halted all traffic from the opposite end. The Loomis armored car was isolated. Ray laid down a series of flares, while I sat on the idling dozer.

As the armored car came to a stop, Ray spoke to the driver. "The road's out ahead; there's going to be a short delay."

The Loomis guards followed protocol. One called the dispatcher, informing him of the delay. Told to standby, they waited while the dispatcher logged the event. Ray called George and Harold waiting in the ambulance.

This was my signal. I shoved the dozer in gear and drove it parallel to the armored car, stopping as I came alongside it. Then I made a sudden ninety degree turn and hooked the blade under its frame. I pulled the lever and flipped the Loomis vehicle on its side. It rattled with a loud thump as I backed the dozer away. Ray approached and placed Harold's thermite shaped charge over the door lock. Stepping back, he pulled a cord. It worked perfectly. The door blew open.

Ray yelled to the guards inside. "Come out hands first or I'll throw in a grenade." The bluff worked. Confused, the guards only had time to activate the alarm. Their dispatcher immediately sent their coordinates to the CHP. Two guards emerged from the rear as the driver climbed vertically out of the door. Ray and I escorted these three men down the ravine on the opposite side of the road. There, concealed by bushes and trees, we handcuffed them together in a circle around a tree. They were blindfolded. We walked back to the road as the ambulance pulled up.

We were only five minutes into the operation. The ambulance was stopped next to the overturned armored car. The four of us formed a human chain, passing sacks of money from the overturned vehicle to the ambulance. We finished in minutes, though it seemed like hours. Turning the ambulance, George and Harold sped back to the cabin. Rick acknowledged as they passed him heading toward Highway 89. Patient motorists barely gave them a casual glance. The ambulance turned into the driveway leading to the cabin and disappeared from view. Here they waited for the rest of us.

Ray yelled to me, "Now, Marty." I climbed back on the dozer. Putting it in gear, I shoved the armored car over the cliff. It fell and disappeared into the woods below. I jumped from the dozer and it followed the armored car, both concealed from view in the abyss below. We hastily swept the slide marks away.

Then Ray told me to recall the flagmen as we drove away in the cruiser. Receiving the all clear, Rick and Dave released the restless motorists before they rendezvoused with us at the cabin. Reunited, we stashed the remaining bogus equipment in the barn. All six of us piled in the ambulance and sped toward Truckee. From there we headed west on I-80 toward Sacramento. After several miles, we took the Gold Run exit and drove the ambulance to a remote clearing where three parked cars waited.

Unable to converse with the armored car, the Loomis dispatcher alerted all local authorities. In addition to the Highway Patrol, deputy sheriffs from Plumas and Sierra Counties converged on the ambush site. Arriving at the scene, they drove past it several times before stopping to check the ravine. When the Loomis guards were located, they reported the bandits had used Caltrans equipment and a Highway Patrol cruiser. They had not seen the ambulance. It was an hour later, when the Highway Patrol located our bogus equipment in the barn, after receiving a call from the hospital. With guns drawn they entered the cabin and found the paramedics bound together inside. By then, our three cars were nearing Grass Valley.

Our mood was jovial. That evening we celebrated in our hideout near Grass Valley. We watched the evening news as a Loomis' official was being interviewed. He announced that an in-house investigation was taking place.

"All hell has broken loose," Ray said.

"Ray?" asked George. "It looks pretty certain they already suspect you?"

"They do! I'm sure of it. They're looking for me now. Ray Morrison has disappeared forever. David?"

"Yes, Ray?"

"Can you begin working on my face tomorrow?"

"I need to get a few things first. It won't take long. Maybe late tomorrow; maybe the next day."

"That's soon enough! George?"

"Yeah?"

"It won't take them long to figure out who my friends are? You'll have to go in hiding soon too."

"I realize that. By the end of this week I'll tie up some loose ends in Reno; then resign. I'll tell the Chief I'm moving to Florida. That may slow them down a bit. I won't look like a man on the run, for a while anyway."

A burning question entered my head. "George?"

"Yeah, Marty?"

"This windfall of money?" I asked. "What are we going to do with it?"

George held his palms opened upward as his eyes scanned each of us. "Any ideas, men? I know the numbers on these bills are recorded; we can't spend it outright."

We were silent until Rick spoke. "Don't worry about that. I had a lot of useful banking connections in New York. These included legitimate businessmen, foreigners and even some with mob connections. We might only get fifty cents to the dollar; but I know how to launder it. I've been thinking. I have an idea so outrageous, so improbable that it belongs in the realm of insanity. But if we could do it, down comes this government and a few others around the world too."

"Go on, Rick, you have the floor," replied George.

"The Federal Reserve Bank in New York contains over 300 billion dollars in gold. Twenty-five per cent of the free world's entire supply lies in a vault eighty feet below the surface. Suppose we try to remove a portion of that bullion? If we can pull this off, financial markets will collapse and bring down several governments with them. I doubt the U.S. Government could survive either. What I propose is an impossible task, but worth the risk."

"Rick, I hate to say this," replied George. "But you're out of your goddamn mind. We couldn't get close to that gold."

"George, you lit this fire. Hundreds of little actions like we carried out today and like the one at Fernley won't amount to much in the long run. If you want to bring down this government, we have to aim big. It's impossible. Sure! I know that. It was impossible for thirteen small colonies to take on the greatest power on Earth in 1776 too. But, just think, George; if this works, it can do the job!"

David was the first to ask the obvious question. "Assuming we can break into the vault, it would be physically impossible to remove more than a small fraction of that gold. Have you considered that?"

"Yes; but we might get a couple billion. Then, we can flood the vault with water diverted from an underground main. That would make the rest inaccessible for a long time. It should achieve the desired effect."

"Well, you certainly aim big," said George. "What makes you think it would bring down the government?"

"Even though all nations have allegedly gone off the gold standard, this myth would be destroyed if we pulled this off. Why do you think they spend so much time and effort securing it? Because secretly, gold really does underscore the financial soundness of the international banking system! The Federal Reserve System is actually owned by ten giant domestic and foreign banks. Did you know that President Kennedy had a plan to return control of the money system to the U.S. Government? He was assassinated three weeks after announcing it."

We were stunned by Rick's statement. It sounded crazy. I don't think any of us, even Rick, believed it could be done. But it was tantalizing. If Rick was right, this one monster blow could bring down this despicable regime.

George returned to Reno. The rest of us stayed awake most of the night discussing Rick's idea. Before turning in, we had convinced ourselves to go for it. Expenses for such an undertaking would be in the stratosphere. Rick would have to take the bulk of the money for operating costs and head for New York. We waited for George's return tomorrow morning. His approval was needed.

FIRST BLOOD

Sleep would not occupy us for long. Our excitement was electric. The morning after the armored car job; five of us sipped coffee and watched the world news from our hideout near Grass Valley. Commentators, experts and pseudo-experts were hashing around theories about the great armored car robbery in Northern California. Some of these tried to link it with the fire-bombing of the Palestinian camp in Fernley. The more authoritative and respected among them pooh-poohed this theory. The latter was obviously for monetary gain, and we were labeled the Caltrans Bandits.

The majority consensus over the attack in Fernley concluded it was pure thuggery, with racial implications engineered by demented minds. An FBI expert detailed the search for these culprits centered on one man—Harold Wiser. An old photo of him filled the screen as reporters interviewed his brother in Carson City. It was believed the man had been tipped off. He had not returned to his apartment, though the BOLO on him was not public information. It was unknown how Wiser could have warned in advance. His apartment had the appearance of a man who had just gone out for a walk.

"They haven't mentioned you, Ray," I said.

"You can bet I'm foremost in their minds, Marty. If they named me now, it might turn out I was innocent. They want to be sure, and avoid the possibility of being sued for defamation. As soon as they show those armored car guards my picture, they'll know."

The pick-up truck drove into our driveway. George emerged, his briefcase under an arm. Rick, on guard at the front window, saw him first. "The boss is here!" We others had casually adopted this term of respect for George.

Before he could knock on the door, Harold leaped to his feet and held it open. "Hurry in, boss! You don't want to miss the saga of the Caltrans Bandits and the demented thugs."

"Yeah, we're big news," George said. "I'm going make a quick turnaround to Reno. We have a lot of things to talk over before I do. Come to the table where I can spread this stuff out." We seated ourselves in the kitchen as George remained standing. "Before I get started, what's the final count on the armored car job?"

"Just shy of three million," answered Ray. "We left the bags of coins behind. The bills are all boxed up nice and neat in a bedroom."

Opening his briefcase, George distributed identical copies of his report to each of us. "Very soon, we're going to earn our place in the history books, though I doubt if they will speak well of us. You men take a look at this first page."

Rick answered first. "This looks like a twelve month wish list of goals for the ACLU."

"You're right on target as usual, Rick! Follow along as I read them aloud. I'll paraphrase each item:

1. Removal of the phrase *In God We Trust* from all currency.
2. Removal of the phrase *Under God* from the Pledge of Allegiance.
3. Allowing students to substitute the phrase *To The World Community* in place of to *The United States of America* in the Pledge of Allegiance.
4. Removal of all engraved Christian or religious symbols adorning any public buildings.
5. Abolishing Christmas as a legal holiday in favor of The Winter Holiday.
6. Forbidding any mention of the Christian Faith in public schools except in the context as a generalization of history. Restrictions will not apply to Muslims who will be allowed to bring prayer rugs and use them; or to Sikh males who will be allowed to wear the curved daggers sacred to their religion within their belts.

7. Removing all military chaplains. Removal of all crosses and other religious symbols from national cemeteries or transferring these properties to private corporations set up for their administration and care.

8. Denying tax-exempt status for churches.

9. Creating a Hate Speech Act. Core to this is a provision which would provide a penalty for publicly defaming Islam. Christian ministers who preached that Islam and other religions were false or described negative aspects of these beliefs would be guilty of using hate speech and subject to strict penalties. They would be encouraged to submit copies of future sermons to lawyers for clearance. Also forbidden would be the public display of the Confederate Flag, which will be interpreted as advocating racism and violent attacks upon minorities. These provisions would become felonies.

10. Removal of the phrase, 'endowed by the Creator with certain inalienable rights' from the Declaration of Independence.

11. Forbidding Americans to sing Christmas carols on public property.

12. End of surveillance against sex predators over the internet, which is high-lighted as a privacy and First Amendment issue.

13. Providing Federal funds for trans-gender types to have sex change operations.

14. Enabling the Man—Boy association to allow verbal contact with minors as a free speech issue.

15. Immediate review of all minority capital crime sentences with emphasis on racial justice by transferring blame to society's intolerance and historical persecution of non-whites.

16. Expansion of the Marriage Equality Act which would allow homosexual couples to adopt children in any state they inhabit.

17. Bring legal action against the Boy Scouts by labeling their policy of discrimination against gays as a hate crime.

18. Declaring the entire U.S. a sanctuary zone, where no law enforcement officer or court can inquire about the legal status of an alien even after arrest for a felony.

19. Declaring that any individual in possession of a valid driver's license can register to vote, in any state, which is to prevent racial profiling.

20. Establishing a new Constitutional Convention to lay the groundwork for a new document superceding the Constitution with a modern version streamlined for the needs of the 21st century. It will remove archaic provisions for the possession of firearms even beyond that which the Rodwell and Muller administrations had already achieved. And it would provide for the elimination of the Electoral College. This is meant to overcome any barrier whereby native-born Americans can out vote the influx of illegals that the Democratic Party intends to enlist and control.

21. Redistribution of wealth, and new taxes with major reductions in capital gains. Some exceptions would apply. A social achievement provision would apply exempting certain artists, performers, professors and writers who had already put social values foremost in their working careers, having thereby possibly reduced their earning potential.

22. Elimination of the death penalty as cruel and unjust punishment."

"Whew! They really mean to go for all of it," said Rick.

"If they were just another crackpot left-wing group it would be laughable," added George. "But the liberal media has been brain-washing this country since the end of World War II. A high percentage of Congressmen actively support them; and worse, many more are intimidated. This is on all levels of government, even state and local. For generations, persons of their ilk have gone to law school, have become judges and been in position to put into effect their anti-American agendas. They mean to destroy this country and shape what's left into a humanistic society totally submerged within a one world community. They have the full support of many tax exempt institutions, originally founded for humanitarian purposes, whose boards of directors are composed of these very same types of people. With deep pockets from such men as George Tauros and other billionaires, they can outspend the traditionalists. Now go to page two of these papers."

Everyone turned to the next page. In bold headlines, it read:

"ANNUAL AMERICAN CIVIL LIBERTY UNION CONVENTION"

Beverly Hills Hotel, Beverly Hills, CA

"Is this going where I think it is?" I asked.

"What do think I'm leading up to, Marty?" responded George.

"I think you want to hit the bastards!"

"Do you think it can be done? Well, men; what about it?"

"Let's blow up these son-of-a-bitches in one stroke," yelled Harold. "We'll never get a bigger or better concentration."

"But how can we concentrate enough explosive in the right place. Where exactly should we hit them?" asked Rick.

"I'm not sure; but most likely at a general business meeting or dinner," answered George. "We only have a short time to put this together. Harold, what would you use for an explosive?"

"A fertilizer based bomb, ammonium nitrate and oil, like the one used in Oklahoma City would be easy to make. I would concentrate 3,000 pounds of it."

"How can we buy that much nitrate without attracting attention?" I asked.

"Don't forget, Marty; I'm a chemist! We buy ordinary fertilizer mix in smaller quantities. I can separate and concentrate the nitrate out of it. The ammonium nitrate is the part we need. It's the oxidizer."

"I have an easier way," said Ray. "Don't forget Joshua in Montana. He has access to dynamite. How much? I don't know. But his head's in the right place. He's one of us."

Interested, George pursued the subject. "Can you set up a meeting for me with him soon?"

"I'll get on it right away."

George turned his attention back to Harold. "After we get this much explosive; how can we concentrate it at the right moment and place? A truck bomb probably won't work. It might blow up all the wrong people."

After a period of silence, Harold replied, "I'll work something out!"

"I don't see how we could do that," added Ray. "Assuming we could, I mean, you know, blow them up. A lot of innocent people would get hurt. Just think; wives, maybe children, waiters, onlookers, passers by. Do you realize what you're leading up to?"

"Yeah; I know, Ray," replied George. "Remember Mogadishu; our troops hesitated to return fire because terrorists and thugs stood behind the women and children. And could our forces separate the bad guys from the good ones when German and Japanese cities were firebombed in World War II? I don't think so. This is war, Ray! Innocents are going to be hurt. I don't like it any better than you do. But you know, as well as any man here; Harold is right. This can be a paralyzing blow to this group if we can pull it off."

"I know you're right, George," replied Ray.

"We have a lot of details to work out. And we have to join with Joshua's people and work out a coordinated plan of action. I have to make some sense out of Rick's plan too. Ray, you set up that meeting for me with Joshua! Did you say he has a supply of dynamite?"

"I will; and he does."

———

Reluctantly, George gave Rick's project his blessing. Rick and Harold would leave for New York, taking over 2.8 million dollars with them. They were delayed waiting for Doc Blevins to give Rick a new face. He needed time to heal. Rick was well known among the financial elite of New York. But unless Rick's team could be reinforced with sufficient manpower from Montana, this plan would just be a hopeless dream.

———

Thirty vehicles, mostly pick-up trucks and SUVs were parked around Joshua's ranch house. Most of the men milled outside; a few smoked. Scarcely a bare head was to be seen, most were covered with a medley of baseball caps and western hats. A few sported side arms. Anxiously, George waited as Joshua delayed the meeting long enough for a few stragglers to arrive. Finally, he called the men to order and they filed inside.

He and George headed the table at one end of the room, flanked by Joshua's sons: Matthew, Mark, Luke and John. Their audience occupied folding chairs throughout the center of the room. Joshua simply introduced George as, our speaker, without naming him. This part was dangerous. The assemblage had already been trimmed to forty candidates. Among so many men, some would react negatively and report this meeting to authorities. It was hoped a window of opportunity existed before this happened. Only the general goals of the freedom movement would be discussed. Skepticism from a few attendees proved this was true. But many eagerly embraced the movement. These men were the real audience. There was another bonus; the militiamen had a 3,500 pound supply of dynamite and ample blasting caps. This saved time. Harold would not have to manufacture the explosive charge.

After the meeting broke up, the men separated into numerous groups. Individually, these patriots had to determine if their fate should be linked to the movement. This was not an easy decision. They stood to lose everything. The clock was now ticking. Joshua knew they had to be far away before the FBI was tipped off. His sons worked among the receptive militiamen establishing a network for future contact.

Before leaving, Joshua introduced George to Rusty Morgan. Rusty was an 87 year old veteran of World War II, a B-25 pilot. With incurable prostate cancer, Rusty had less than three months to live. "Rusty here is gonna deliver your little present to them ACLU fellers."

Mildly interested, George replied. "Even if we had a B-25, there's no way to deliver that load of explosives accurately. These planes were used for saturation bombing. We have to pinpoint a concealed target in the dark of the evening when these communists are concentrated in one small location. The dynamite would fall out randomly; at most taking out a lamp post or house here and there and probably hurting the wrong people. I know you mean well, Joshua. But we have to come up with better plan."

"Now just listen. You didn't hear me out. We ain't gonna drop nothin'. Remember them ragheads that took out the World Trade Center?"

George's senses sharpened as his attention focused on this last statement. "Yes!"

"They showed us how! Rusty here wants to fly the damn thing right into their soup bowls."

George studied Rusty's expression. The old man nodded slowly and cracked a slight smile before speaking. "We didn't make all those sacrifices back in the war to see our country come to this. I don't have much time left. I can make what remains of it on this Earth count for something."

"Do you have a B-25?" asked George.

Joshua answered for him. "No! But we know where to git one. There's one at the Chino Airport, not far from Los Angeles. Security there ain't gonna be much. We take it at the last minute; load it up; and before anybody realizes it; we're in the air. A few more minutes and we're over Beverly Hills.

Then Rusty here makes a swan dive outta the wild blue and sends all them atheists to someplace that ain't called heaven. They'd probably like it better there anyway."

"I don't think we can pull it off, Joshua. How could Rusty, in only a few seconds, make the right decision, pick out the right set of lights in Beverly Hills from thousands or at least hundreds of feet high? What makes Rusty think he can still fly one of those birds? I'm sorry; it can't be done."

"Easy, partner! We done gone over the details. My boy, Mark, pulled it off the computer. This shitteree is gonna take place in the International Ballroom there in the Beverly Hills Hotel. It overlooks the pool. All we gotta do is set up some guide markers. Rusty will line up on 'em and finish his glory ride. Ain't that right, Rusty?"

The other man nodded. "Until five years ago, I still flew my own plane, a two engine, high performance craft. Don't worry about the B-25. I can spruce up my skills on it too. The owner of that crate in Chino takes up passengers on joy rides for about five hundred bucks. It helps pay for his toy. When he hears my background, he'll probably let me take the stick."

"What are these guide markers you're talking about?" asked George.

"That ain't a problem. One of our boys out in the street shoots off a flare gun; even several times if needed. Rusty can see it from up there. Then, he knows where to look. Two more of us get in by the pool. They light five-gallon cans of gasoline

at ground level below opposite corners of that ballroom. Rusty
lines up his dive into the building between them. The light
from that gas will high-light the floors. Maybe he can even hit
'em on the nose. Maybe not! But he's gonna get close enough
to git the job done."

"I'm amazed!"

In less than an hour, Joshua's ranch was abandoned. Their
waiting vehicles were already loaded. Miles away, they substi-
tuted new license plates for the old ones. A new network of
communication with those militiamen who joined the movement was put in operation.

It was just after 6:00 A.M. twelve hours after they departed
Joshua's ranch. The small caravan of vehicles pulled into a
station off I-80 inside California. Mark worked the gas nozzle
while Joshua went inside the building. Returning, he handed
George the newspaper.

The headlines from the *Sacramento Bee* read:

SUICIDE IN MALL PARKING LOT

Sacramento:

Retired California Highway Patrol Lieutenant Ray
Morrison, using his service pistol, committed suicide
inside his truck while parked at the Arden Fair Mall
in Sacramento yesterday evening. Recently, Officer
Morrison came under suspicion for possible complic-
ity in the Caltrans armored car robbery occurring early

this month on Highway 70 near Graeagle. An arrest warrant had been issued for him. Recently hiring on for the Loomis Company, investigators say Morrison was well positioned from inside to retrieve confidential information. Subsequent search shows Morrison recently destroyed all of his records and sold his home before disappearing.

Morrison, who apparently had plastic surgery, was located by tracing his cell phone to this mall where he frequently came to call his only sister. He was identified by a former colleague there who recognized Morrison's voice and his familiar style of walking. The undercover officer alerted his team and Morrison was surprised by authorities as he attempted to leave the parking lot. Failing to respond when ordered to surrender, Morrison turned his pistol upon himself. No leads were found for the missing money—

George sighed and shook his head. "I told Ray to quit using that damned cell phone. He killed himself to slow them down and protect us. But we're still only one step ahead."

Our house near Grass Valley was the assembly point. Over the next few days, militiamen arrived in small groups. This concentration could not last for long. Except for a few of us, the others would soon be gone. We reorganized into three major and several small strike groups. George, Rusty, Joshua and his son Mark, along with six militiamen would go south. They would assault the ACLU convention.

I was appointed captain of the second group. Four of the militiamen and David Blevins were assigned to me. I was chosen to lead over David because of my experience. Our strike group would concentrate on railroad sabotage.

The largest group, including three of Joshua's sons and Harold Wiser were assigned to Rick Taylor. He became their captain. Numbering twenty-two, this contingent would head for New York City.

The independent commands of militiamen were divided into two man strike teams. These would concentrate on attacking the power grids and assaulting ACLU offices throughout the west.

———

That first two-man team struck after dark on the evening they left Grass Valley. The pair had chosen their target carefully. It was outside of San Francisco. As they stood near the transmission line hanging between two towers, String Bean notched the arrow into his longbow. Attached to the rear of its shaft was a thin thread of brass wire which trailed down to a large spool lying on the ground.

"You're goin' to get fried, String Bean," announced his companion.

"I don't reckon so. Watch this!" The lean country boy unleashed his arrow. Followed by his companion, he ran with his bow for the cover of a nearby live oak tree. From here, they watched its effect. The arrow arched over the elevated power lines a hundred feet above. As it came down the thin

wire completed a live connection between numerous lines. A
lightning eruption followed as the lines exploded. Tens of thousands of homes and businesses in the Bay area went dark.

Rick and his group drove east in groups of two. In the ensuing
days Rick was able to launder the money. This imposed a
special burden as the 2.8 million dollars was reduced by over
half. He set up a dummy company with its own bank account.
Homeland security measures made this difficult. By making
illegal payoffs and breaking a few other laws, Rick was able
to set up a chain of business references from foreign sources
giving the operation cover as an import company. This was
a temporary solution at best. It would only take IRS a few
months to poke holes in their cover. And it would have been
impossible without the false I.D. and paperwork supplied to
him by George Scales. These had been secreted from stored
evidence boxes in Reno where George had been granted access
to research his book.

Rick was able to negotiate a line of credit based upon the
initial deposit. This was enhanced by financial tricks learned
from his banking career. The strike team's purchasing power
rose above three million.

But the project only became viable after he leased the
basement of a large building on Maiden Lane, just a few
hundred feet from the Fed. The building was recently purchased by a Japanese business man, who had every intention
of rapidly recovering his investment. Rick was able to beat

out competition for this basement facility by leasing it for the obscene sum of $368,000 per month, well in excess of the going monthly rate of $80 for each of its 2,500 square feet. This imposed a serious timetable upon the Patriots—get the job done or give up the premises.

The swat team burst through the door of George's apartment. As expected, it was empty and they assumed he went to Florida. An FBI investigation revealed a long standing friendship between him and Ray Morrison. A check of phone records showed activity between these two men prior and subsequent to the armored car hold-up. No incriminating documents were found in the apartment.

The FBI interviewed his daughter in Sacramento. They established that George left his dogs with her along with money for their care. They also found boxes of his personal goods in her garage. In one of these they found the Bible. Investigators thumbed through its pages looking for hidden evidence. The blood stain was located. Forensic evidence showed this blood contained the DNA of six men. Three of them were identified: George Scales, Ray Morrison and Harold Wiser. Three remained unknown. The FBI now linked Fernley with the Caltrans holdup. Information volunteered by a former militiaman in Western Montana added to the mix. These were no ordinary criminals. Revolution was taking place.

That evening, George listened to his description over the TV news. An impassioned plea came from his daughter as she begged her father to turn himself in. Watching glumly, the Patriots knew life's journey was coming to an end. Tomorrow they would strike the ACLU.

———·——

It was a stellar night. The Hollywood luminaries pranced and strutted before the adoring crowd in the International Ballroom of the Beverly Hills Hotel. Tonight Hanoi Hattie would be presented with a special lifetime achievement award before flying to Washington for her meeting with President Muller. There, he would present her with a gold medal, the Presidential Medal of Freedom. Accolade followed accolade as the ACLU speaker gave his vision for a new America. The cream of the Hollywood elites, actors, directors, and writers mingled with the most successful left-wing lawyers. Numerous rising stars of the liberal intelligentsia cozied up to them. High profile media magnates and billionaire donors were in attendance. George Tauros himself only canceled at the last moment for a business related matter.

The fire alarm brought the festivities to a screeching halt. The windows on the pool side became brightly illuminated. The microphone was taken from the speaker by a security man. "Ladies and gentlemen, we have a problem. It will be necessary to evacuate this building until further notice. There is no immediate danger; this is only a precaution. Please file out orderly through the exits. The fire department will arrive momentarily."

At first, they reacted calmly. At the sound of gunfire by

the pool, the crowd panicked. Exit doors became choked from bodies pushing and shoving through them.

By the pool below, Mark's dead body lay next to an employee who had tried to use a fire extinguisher. Security guards and policemen exchanged fire with militiamen. The flames grew ever higher adding to the melee in the ballroom. Just minutes before, Joshua's son, Mark, received a call. "The baby is in the sky," said his Dad.

The warm-up flight earlier that day was successful. The plane's owner indeed offered Rusty the chance to handle its controls.

That evening, a handful of militiamen overpowered the watchmen. Strong hands rapidly transferred the dynamite into the plane. George followed Rusty inside the cockpit. The veteran pilot paused. "This is as far as you go, George. This is a one man ride."

George answered. "I'm going along. Because of me, hundreds will die tonight. I'm going to die with them. I'm not proud of this. That's my decision."

"You can't do that," said Rusty. "The boys need your leadership."

"I'm no more use. They authorities know I'm involved. It will only make it harder on the rest. I would only draw attention to them."

"There ain't no turning back."

"I'm going."

Joshua had been silent. "I'm going too. Make room!"

Pursuing police could only watch as the plane lifted off the runway. Calls were made and jets were scrambled from Edwards Air Force Base in the high desert to the north.

From the cockpit of the B-25, these men watched their destiny unfold. By cell phone, they acknowledged the flares. Mark's crew placed and set off the beacon lights, their skyward flames marking the target. Rusty reset his course on an imaginary bearing between them. He turned the vintage bomber's nose into a dive. As the plane plunged into the ballroom, its charge exploded, killing everyone on several floors instantly. Almost everyone else died in the fire as the building collapsed.

The country was in a state of shock as proclaimed in next morning's Sunday edition of *The New York Times*:

Domestic Terrorism Hits Los Angeles

Los Angeles, California:

Americans are devastated in the aftermath of the second most scathing terrorist attack in history. Right wing terrorists fly vintage WWII bomber into the Beverly Hills Hotel with the obvious intent of annihilating the attendees of the annual ACLU convention there. No survivors have been found as of this writing. The ACLU has been foremost in fighting for the rights of America's beleaguered and has become one of her most cherished institutions. Numerous Congressmen are known to have been in attendance along with high profile members of the ACLU and Hollywood personalities. A national veterans group proclaimed that Hanoi Hattie finally received justice. President Muller has declared Monday a national day of mourning; vows to mop up this right wing criminal element. Preliminary investigation points to a radical cabal formed by law enforcement officers, George Scales of Reno and Ray Morrison of California. They have known ties to a militia founded in the 1970s by rancher Joshua Rollins of Montana. Numerous arrests have been made in connection with that militia.

Muller was furious as he lambasted the head of homeland security. Key supporters had died in that bombing.

On Tuesday morning following the attack, two masked militiamen entered the ACLU offices in Denver, Colorado. Using shotguns they killed an even dozen. Fleeing to a nearby building they escaped via a makeshift tunnel leading into the main sewer. Leaving the building behind them on fire, the police were unable to immediately pursue. Their method of escape was not determined until six hours after the fact.

Other militia groups across the U.S. were motivated by these successes. ACLU offices were attacked in Cincinnati and Baltimore. Several known ACLU lawyers were gunned down in random drive-by shootings.

Throughout the West, the power grid of the country was systemically attacked by the same silent method used near San Francisco. As this simple technique was adopted by other groups across the land, America was grinding to a halt. Reacting from these devastating results, President Muller declared martial law. Rewards of Fifty Million Dollars were placed on each of two men: George Scales, who was believed to be still at large and Harold Wiser. Other rewards of up to twenty million were offered for information leading to the interdiction of any act of terrorism related to this group.

———

Enacting full implementation of the U.N. gun ban, thousands of road blocks were set up. From these, all vehicles were thoroughly searched for guns.

The first neighborhood sweep for firearms was scheduled to take place in Pine Bluff. The Arkansas National Guard was mobilized to make a house by house search there. Most of these officers and men mutinied or deserted; a few reorganized as an independent command. These troops later fixed bayonets as they faced off regular Army troops brought in to salvage the crisis. The Governor persuaded them to surrender and the Guardsmen were disarmed and taken into custody. An already polarized America quickly lined up under different banners. President Muller declared the country was in a state of insurrection.

Violence escalated as most Americans refused to turn

their guns in. Under Article Forty-Seven of the U.N. Charter, Muller asked for U.N. troops. His request was quickly granted by the Security Council. A large Norwegian contingent would land in New England. Ukrainians and Bulgarians would be stationed in the Midwest. Nigerians, Moroccans and Portuguese troops were stationed in the Mid-Atlantic States and the South. In all, troops from twenty-six different countries would be sent to the U.S. The Northwest would receive a large number of Indonesians.

THE TRAIN

J im Scott was one of numerous agents temporarily transferred to the West Coast following the attack on the ACLU convention. One by one, from the most recent working backward, he carefully studied the files lying on his desk. All were cases handled by George Scales over the last two years. After examining the report of Illyana Raggio's death, he paused. Here was something, a profile. A quick check proved this was what he was looking for. Martin Raggio had no gainful employment since Illyana's accident. Running a credit check, he discovered the man had recently rented a rural house near Grass Valley, in California. Excusing himself for the afternoon, Jim left the office.

Sullen U.S. Airmen stood by silently staring at the blue hel-
meted Indonesian troops and their equipment disembarking
from the c-5a Galaxies and c-141s on the tarmac at Travis
Air Force Base. The Indonesians were arranging their vehicles
into a convoy for transport to their new staging camp near
Oroville. Waiting Military Police from the Army National
Guard and Highway Patrol units would be guiding them.

Under the direct command of President Muller, these and
other foreign troops would help stabilize the domestic crisis.
Though U.N. troops had been used hundreds of times since
the Korean War, this was the first time they ever set foot
on U.S. soil. The U.N. mandated gun confiscation law only
received lukewarm support from domestic law enforcement
agencies. With a new wave of violence, many ATF officers had
already been shot. These Indonesian troops were assigned to
the Northwest. One division landed at Travis, another was
destined for Fort Lewis, Washington. The troops in Oroville
would be dispatched in battalion sized units to points
throughout a four state area. They would make selective
sweeps through cities and rural areas searching for firearms.
Already a troop train was scheduled to transport one these
battalions from Oroville up the Feather River Valley route
into Northern Nevada.

David and I sipped coffee as we watched the arrival of these
blue-helmeted troops on TV. The program was frequently
interrupted by news alerts from other parts of the country.

Some were protests by patriotic groups; others were stories of random attacks against Federal authorities. Later that morning Muller spoke to the nation in a televised broadcast from Washington. He said some personal freedom had to be sacrificed for order and security but emphasized that this crisis would pass. He further stated that this was for the common good, so that all Americans could live in peace and security without the threat of gun violence.

The film clip switched to newly elected head of the ACLU in New York City. Screaming, he denounced President Muller for not doing more to uproot the ring-wing Fascists who blew up the convention in Los Angeles.

I laughed at David's next statement.

"It seems like we hurt their feelings, Marty. Should we mail them a get-well card?"

"Why not a letter bomb instead!" I answered. We both laughed at this. "David, I'm going to town; we're running short on food." I paused. "Goddamn it! I've got an idea. I was a railroad engineer. I know how to stop that trainload of Indonesians!"

"How do you mean?" asked David.

"That line along the Feather River was tailor made for an ambush. In a thousand different places! When I get back, I'll work out the details."

Minutes later, our shopping list was completed. David would remain behind. I walked outside. My truck was parked by the side of the house. Taking the door handle in my left hand, I pushed the fob to unlock the vehicle with the other.

The door lock clicked as a hard thrust jabbed me in the back. I froze.

"Don't move! Put your hands behind your head. Is the front door of the house locked?"

"I don't know," I lied.

"Just hang on to the keys and walk over there."

I complied. My hands were still elevated when we reached it. I waited for him to speak. He ordered me to lower them and open the door. As it opened slightly, he suddenly shoved me through it from behind.

"Forget something, Marty?" asked David.

Once inside, I threw myself to the floor reaching for a .25 automatic in my boot. Jim Scott followed. With a hip shot refined from years of practice, he nicked the bicep of my gun arm. I dropped the pistol.

In less than a blink, he aimed at David. "Don't try it!" David relaxed his hand. "Maybe you shouldn't be so quick on the trigger," said Jim Scott. "You should have heard me out first." He pulled his coat to the side, revealing the badge attached to his belt. "FBI," he announced.

"I'm a physician. May I look at his arm?" asked David.

"Go for it! But if either of you gets squirrelly, you're going to feel the bite of this .40 automatic. Before you touch him, kick that handgun away from his boot." David complied.

"Where are the rest of you?" I asked.

"What makes you think there's more than me?" replied Jim.

"You wouldn't come out here alone. There's probably a

goddamn army out there in woods. Why haven't you called them?"

Jim ignored my question. "So you're the guys who burned down the refugee camp and took the armored car. And that little caper in L.A, all the big wigs of the ACLU down in one shot!"

Silent at first, I became defiant. "And if we did, so what! You may have us, but others will carry on the fight!"

"Shut up, Marty!" said David.

"Ha, ha, ha! Don't worry, I already know there's more than you two. As for the fight as you call it, I salute you!"

We were stunned. Speechless, we waited for the FBI man to continue.

"Anyone with half a brain knows what's going on in this country. America's days are numbered unless somebody acts now. Which one of you is Martin Raggio?"

"Me," I answered.

"And you?" he asked, looking at David.

"Dr. David Blevins. Formerly Major Blevins of the Nevada National Guard."

"And does your group have a name?"

"Sometimes we call ourselves the Patriots," I said.

"The Patriots! Nice touch. If you promise to behave yourselves, I'll lower this gun."

We both nodded.

Jim put his gun away. "Is his arm going to heal, Dr. Blevins?"

"The bullet didn't hit the bone or tear up the muscle. He's barely winged. I can patch him up."

"Good! I haven't lost my touch. I wouldn't want to hamper the Patriots in their good work. What was the significance of that blood in the Bible?"

"We all took a sacred oath to restore the Republic," I answered.

"Restore the Republic!" His eyelids rose in wonder as he paused and reflected on my statement. "DNA from six men was found in that blood stain. So six men are going to overthrow this government and restore the Republic. I'll say this; you guys have balls. Isn't that a lot for six men to tackle alone?"

"There's more than six of us now. We know we're going to die. We're all mentally prepared for it. But we lit a fire. It's growing. You can see it all around you. Muller is getting desperate! And those ACLU rats have gone into hiding."

"Yes; you men have certainly lit a fire. Anyway, I was never here. I'm not even going to tell you my name. But if I call, can I depend on you?"

"Welcome to the fight, Mr. FBI."

"It'll probably be my ruin. But somehow I feel like that crooked French policeman in that old movie *Casablanca*. Do you remember that one? At the end he joined Humphrey Bogart instead of taking him into custody. And from there, together they went south to join a Free French garrison."

Excited, I butted in. "I know how to hit the bastards. Listen to this."

"Stop; don't say anything. Everything is on 'a need to know basis only.'"

"You're right; I should know better."

"Anyway, how can I contact you?" asked Jim.

"David and I both have cell phones under other names."

"Before I leave, give me those numbers. I'll identify myself to you as J from the Big Easy. Can you remember that?"

"J from the Big Easy," we both repeated.

"Before I leave, let's talk more—"

———

UP Extra 8013 East had already cleared the last siding heading east into Portola. The engineer called out the signal over his radio. The intermediate signal beyond the bridge showed a yellow indication. The train dispatcher called back with a message. There was an unknown track indication ahead of them, but no maintenance of way work was scheduled that day. A signal maintainer had been called.

There were four men in the train's cab. Besides the usual engineer and conductor, there was a Union Pacific officer, and an Indonesian colonel. Impatient with their slow progress, the colonel inquired about the delay. The rear of the train cleared the long bridge behind as the lead engine rounded the next curve. Two men in overalls wearing maintenance of way helmets waited ahead, one holding a red flag. He gave a stop signal. Two others similarly dressed waited nearby.

"Damn," replied the UP officer. "Must be a broken rail ahead! The dispatcher was mistaken." The engine's sanders came on as the troop train ground to a stop. The UP official climbed down from the cab. When he stepped off the train, David Blevins shoved a gun in his mid-section. "Don't move!"

Defiant, the man replied, "What do you think you're doing. You can't get away with this!"

"Shut up!"

Alarmed, the man froze.

Ascending the steps, I entered the cab. "Good afternoon, gentlemen." Pulling out a P-90, I leveled it at the Indonesian officer's heart and pulled the trigger three times. Heavy droning from the four diesel engines between us and the train muffled the sound as the man collapsed. I didn't recognize either crewman, or they me. "I'm taking over this train." Motioning with my pistol, I looked at the engineer. "Get up!"

The man rose. "I'll do as you say; don't shoot!"

"You'll only get shot if you give me trouble. Now, both of you get down in the nose." I sat in the engineer's seat, grabbed the automatic brake handle and drew the trainline down to zero pounds of pressure. Then I released the handle. As it charged back up to fifty pounds, the train brakes began to release. I turned my cut-off valve, interrupting the air flow. Looking back out the window, I waved to my colleague standing by the air cut-off valve between the train and the engines. The train brakes continued releasing. He waved back and climbed on the rear engine. I reversed the power, and moved the throttle in short increments. The train backed up with increasing speed. By cell phone, I called the man waiting at the bridge. "Now!" I said, bringing the engine to full throttle. The rear car was one eighth mile east of the bridge.

The man on the bridge removed a homemade derail from

the bushes. It was composed of wood and metal scraps. He placed it upon one rail.

The Indonesian troops became visibly alarmed. My colleague riding on the rear engine pulled the pin connecting us to the train. He signaled for me to stop. The train, now separated, was moving over fifty miles per hour as it came on the bridge. Too late, panicky Indonesian soldiers tried to crank the hand brakes with less than a hundred feet to the derail.

As that first wheel climbed the derail, the inside flange holding it to the rail became elevated. Without this restraint, the wheel was diverted outward by an angled piece of iron. This channeled the car's motion outward over the edge of the bridge. As that first car derailed, the others followed it into the ravine below. Except for a few soldiers who jumped before the train came onto the bridge, all the Indonesians and their equipment perished within seconds. Conflagration followed as fire erupting from three hundred feet below consumed the bridge.

I reversed the locomotive back to where David waited with the UP officer. I made the other crewmen get off with their baggage before reversing the engine again. I pulled out the throttle before getting off. We watched it running empty back toward the burning bridge. We shot up the crew's portable handsets and cell phones before chaining them to trees. Then we melted into the woods and regrouped in our vehicles nearby. We faced one desperate hour of driving before we could disappear into Reno's traffic. Fate was with us. We ditched the cars in a mall and from there walked to the safe house we had prepared in advance.

From their newly rented basement in Manhattan, Rick Taylor read with satisfaction the headline from *The New York Times*:

TERRORIST ATTACK ON U.N. TROOPS

Portola, CA:

Terrorist attack near Portola, California, destroys troop train destined for Northern Nevada. Under the U.N. brokered agreement allowing President Muller to deploy foreign troops on U.S. soil, a battalion of Indonesian troops was annihilated west of Portola. Renegades pretending to be railroad workers set up an ambush five miles west of Portola. After overpowering the train crew, terrorists drained the air brakes dry and reversed the train's direction. A derailing device was waiting on a bridge to the train's rear. The entire train, including all Indonesian equipment and vehicles and most of the troops plunged into the gorge over three hundred feet below. Authorities maintain the operation was professionally directed, obviously with assistance from a person or persons knowledgeable about railroad procedures, equipment, technical operations, and territory.

In another section of the *Times*, Rick noted with satisfaction that other attacks had paralyzed a quarter of the nation's power supply. These resulted in blackouts, communications failure, work stoppages, and urban chaos. He stopped reading as Harold approached him.

"What's in today's paper? Any more news about our people?"

"You have to read this," answered Rick. "Marty and his crew are really kicking butt out there."

Harold took the paper. His eyes opened wide. "Jesus! If we had a thousand more like him, this would be over by tomorrow."

ALLAH'S ANGELS

Culebra inspected the large crate labeled *Maquinaria Agricultura* as it was lowered by the crane onto the dock. He handed the customs agent a thick envelope. With a slight nod, the Mexican official looked the other way. A five-ton truck backed into position, its engine remained idling after it stopped. As soon as the large forklift loaded the crate into the waiting vehicle, workers lashed it securely in place. Culebra crawled into the passenger seat as the Mexican Mafia truck driver released the parking brake. They departed Monterey. Their immediate destination, Juarez!

Upon arrival, the crate was camouflaged with boxes of newly manufactured electrical equipment. Crossing into El Paso was easy. The vehicle belonged to a trucking company licensed to operate in the U.S. under the newly relaxed standards of the Muller administration. And having all accompanying documentation and permits, only a cursory inspection took place as drug sniffing dogs cleared the load of suspicion. To further divert attention, dozens of Mexican decoys distracted Border Patrol agents as they ran through the check point.

On the outskirts of El Paso, the truck turned off the main road where it was driven into a garage. The license was replaced with a set of commercial Texas plates, and the VIN number was changed. Mexican markings were removed and new ones denoting American ownership were stenciled on the doors. A new set of papers and a change of drivers completed the disguise. Leaving El Paso, Culebra and his associates followed closely behind as the truck, now driven by an Anglo, headed northwest.

On the second day, both vehicles pulled into a large truck stop and motel near Salt Lake City. The truck driver made a long distance call to Patterson, New Jersey. Immediately afterward, he rented a room in the motel where he was joined by the others. That evening, they waited for the coded signal. It was given by Ahmadinejad in a special televised TV broadcast. The terrorist conspiracy was on time.

That evening, Ahmadinejad made peace overtures to the West while publicly disavowing terrorism. Photo images showed Iranian troops rounding up Al Qaeda terrorists from their hideouts and forcing them out of the country. This was

244 PANDEMONIUM IN 2012

the anticipated signal. Early next morning, the truck was driven into Salt Lake City. There, it was securely locked in a commercial garage owned by a Muslim businessman. The timer was set to arm twenty-four hours later.

Bashan, aka Culebra, had an international profile. He could not be seen in airports. Along with three associates, he left the city along the same route they entered. Their destination was New Orleans. From there, his Colombian colleagues with Iranian assistance would secret them out of the country.

———

Jim Scott looked out the window of the 757 as it descended through the clouds on its approach to the Louis Armstrong International Airport. Elaine would be there waiting for him. Now he was looking forward to a couple days off. During his sixty days on special assignment in Reno, he had lost or misplaced several files relating to George Scales. Afterwards, Jim reported a dead end to his research and requested reassignment back home.

Mixed emotions tortured Jim's mind as he crushed Elaine's body into his own. "Wow," she said. "After such a short absence, now I'm so popular! To what do I owe this?"

"I just realized how important you are, Elaine. You and the other things I love could all be gone so quickly. I feel like I need to live these next weeks like I never lived before."

She smiled at this revelation. "I'm glad things worked out this way in Reno. Maybe you should go there more often?"

"Uh, uh, Elaine. It wasn't like that at all. There's grave danger.

My whole world will change very soon. And, uh, yours and everyone else's."

She pursed her lips in thought, then looked at him with her big green eyes. "Let's go to my place. I made some beef stew. You can tell me all about it there. And if we both get lucky, I've got something else for you too."

He smiled, knowing that soon he could bury his thoughts in her soft embrace. Taking her by the hand, they made their way to the luggage carousel. Forty-five minutes later, Elaine pulled her Toyota into the parking garage. Jim had two full days of leave. He would stay at her place until tomorrow. All he cared about for the moment was spending some quality time with Elaine.

Israeli coastal radar picked up the fast moving boat. Its trajectory indicated it would arrive in Tel Aviv within twenty minutes. Numerous radio calls had been placed. The craft would not answer. Israeli patrol craft had been diverted to deal with other suspicious ships. Unknown to them, these decoys were sent to distract them. Now it was unlikely the Israeli Navy would intercept this strange vessel in time.

The operations officer picked up his phone and made the call. Major Laban Itzack responded as he flew over the Negev. He maneuvered his F-16 toward the coast. Followed by his wing man as he dropped altitude, Major Itzack caught sight of the large motorboat now only three kilometers from Tel Aviv. Coming from behind, he dove on it. Seeing the jet bear down on them, the terrorists tried to zig zag. Four hundred meters high and still two kilometers from the city, Major Itzack pressed the button. The twenty millimeter Vulcan spewed hundreds of rounds in less than two seconds. The motorboat disintegrated from gunfire. These cannon shells also damaged the warhead without causing it to go nuclear. The deadly cargo went to the bottom of the sea. Tel Aviv would survive. Within weeks, radiation levels in the water revealed the presence of that bomb. Only then would the people of Tel Aviv know what they had narrowly missed.

At the scheduled moment, Culebra and his escort were sitting in a coffee shop in Dallas. Intently staring at the elevated TV screen in the corner, he waited with apprehension as the minutes slipped away. Suddenly, the TV broadcast was interrupted as an emergency alert flashed across the screen. After an awkward period of time, the broadcaster, with a sudden expression of horror, stammered as she attempted to read from the teleprompter. "Ladies and gentlemen, Norad has reported a nuclear device was detonated several minutes ago in Salt Lake City. Reports are beginning to come in from multiple sources. Oh, this is dreadful! Please standby as we expect to hear from Washington any minute! I am urged to caution you all not to panic as we wait for verification of this report."

Culebra's trembling driver jumped up as he yelled "Allahu Akbar" in uncontrolled excitement. As Bashan gave him the death stare, the man shrank back into his seat. The coffee shop was silent as all eyes were upon Culebra's group. Knowing he must defuse the situation, Bashan stood up and backhanded his companion. "You vile excuse for a man! You give us all a bad name. I want nothing more to do with you." His confused companion stood up and faced him. With one rapid blow to the man's chin, Bashan knocked him out. Leaving two twenties on the table, Bashan smiled, and made numerous apologies. Then stooping, he slung his unconscious colleague over his shoulder, and the small group departed.

———

Jim and Elaine were sipping coffee after breakfast when the call came. Salt Lake City had been nuked. Jim Scott was to report to the office immediately. Before he left Elaine's place, he received another call. It was Mark Obledo. Jim answered, "Mark, I don't have time to talk. I've got to report in."

"No, Jim; you better hear me out first."

"It'll have to wait; you know what's going on!"

"That's what this call is about."

"OK; let's have it."

"I maintained informal contact with Manuel's people. They've been having a running blood feud with Culebra's gang since that briefcase and the drug shipment were lost. An informant told me he's in Louisiana. His boys plan to smuggle him out down there, someplace out of the swamps into the gulf. Jim, he's the son-of-a-bitch who blew up Salt Lake City!"

"Why tell me? Didn't you report this?"

"The informant told me that mole in the Bureau will tip Culebra's people off if the Bureau finds out. This has to be a one man job. I can't come. But I can link you up with what's left of Manuel's gang. They've taken a lot of hits; but I'm told they'll help you with all they got."

"I don't want to be a one man cavalry charge. How many am I going against?"

"Maybe up to two dozen. I don't know."

"How many of Manuel's men can I count on?"

"Three, four. Again, I don't know."

"Goddamn! Are you sure we can't call our own people?"

"I will if you want, Jim. But we may lose him. You have no idea how much political correctness we have here in Washington. Muller has almost put the agency under U.N. control."

"Yes, I know. We're in an awful spot. How do I contact Manuel's people?"

"They'll call you when they know something. I gave them your number. That's the only choice we have."

"Look, Mark! I may try to bring in some more guns."

"Get anybody you can trust. Have anyone in mind?"

"Three, I think. Joe Friou! Remember him. He's the fisherman who found Raul, the one whose daughter was murdered. He knows the swamps and waterways. And no man alive has a better motive for going after this Culebra son-of-a-bitch than him. And I have a couple more in mind."

"Who are they?"

"I'd rather not say right now, just in case this operation gets compromised. But they may be our best men."

"Well OK, buddy. I'll keep you posted from this end."

————•+•————

President Muller lay on his deathbed at Walter Reed Hospital when the news from Salt Lake City reached him. Dimly his senses came back as the full impact of the tragedy set in. He summoned his remaining consciousness. Four weeks had elapsed since the party at George Tauros' mansion. The chemical placed in his drink had worked its deadly magic. Muller's liver was totally rotted and his kidneys had failed. With its rapid onslaught, his doctors had not been able to find a tissue match in time. Muller would die that same afternoon.

During that first week following the party, President Muller felt fine. His symptoms began with fatigue. Then they rapidly progressed. Now he recalled that moment he drank George Tauros' bitter wine. Muller realized he had been poisoned. He voiced his suspicion to the Vice President who was sitting by his side. Acting surprised, Shrecker spoke. "Gordie, we have to act immediately. Do you understand what happened in Salt Lake City?"

Muller nodded.

"Will you transfer the "the football" to my custody with the codes? I need to act in your behalf now. This crisis won't wait for you to recover!"

"I understand; Call in witnesses immediately. I will resign. Carl?"

"Yes, Gordie?"

"Investigate Tauros! He did this to me. I know it now. I don't know why; but I know he used poison. Promise me?"

"I will, Gordie!"

———

Next morning, the headlines of *The New York Times* read:

SALT LAKE CITY DEVASTATED, PRESIDENT MULLER DIES

Washington, D.C.

Vice President Carl Shrecker was sworn in following the death of President Muller. Hundreds of thousands are dead and injured in terrorist attack on Salt Lake City. Abdullah Laden takes credit for Al Qaeda. Shrecker declares a national emergency. Rejoicing and street celebrations are reported in all major Islamic cities. Widespread panic is taking place in many urban areas. Grocery shelves are emptied as frightened citizens stock up on food. Sporadic attacks on Muslims have been reported.

———

From their hideout, Dave and Marty watched a terrified nation as all regular programming was suspended. The Department of Homeland Security and FEMA were issuing instructions and guidelines over the air. The camera shifted as Shrecker began giving his press conference. Both men shook their heads in mutual disbelief as they heard him speak.

"Fellow Americans, in these troubled circumstances, we must not lose our heads or stray from our path. America must remain strong, committed, and yet compassionate. We must not yield to the temptation to blame good Muslims or the peaceful faith of Islam for the actions of a few misguided fanatics. Devoted and innocent adherents of the holy Koran should not be blamed for the actions of a few. I have been assured by all Islamic States of their support. All have made gracious offers to help. And they have promised to work with our people in tracking down and arresting all persons suspected of taking part in this cowardly attack. I must further emphasize that the Government of the United States will not tolerate wanton attacks against Muslims anywhere in this country, nor violations of their civil rights. There will be no racial profiling. We will remain morally superior to those evil persons who have profaned a great religion. We will not stoop to the level of these terrorists."

The film clipped switched to newly elected head of the ACLU in New York City. Downplaying Al Qaeda's role in the attack, he suggested they were only taking credit for it. Screaming, he denounced President Shrecker for not taking stronger action against the real perpetrators, the same right-wing Fascists who attacked the convention in Los Angeles.

The scene shifted as televised clips showed millions of Americans leaving the Metropolitan areas to small towns and rural areas throughout the country. The freeways were jammed to a standstill as many took only what belongings they could in their cars. Tens of thousands had run out of gas and totally clogged the system. The impassioned head of Homeland Security was begging them to return home. The Patriots stared at the TV as Ahmadinejad spoke. The Iranian stated that neither he nor anyone closely connected to their government had a part in the attack. He would render all assistance necessary to capture the perpetrators. But if attacked or threatened, Iran would not hesitate to use its own nuclear stockpile in defense.

Then David spoke first. "Those ragheads really blew it. If Al Qaeda hadn't jumped up and taken credit right away, we would have been blamed for Salt Lake City."

"Yeah," I said. "That would have finished us and helped Shrecker hold on to power. But those simple sons-of-bitches had to take credit. The camel jockeys wanted to prove what they could do. Now, everyone is against them. Can you believe what Shrecker said?"

Shrecker moved the military back to the border. This was little more than a gesture. They had no authority to intercept illegal aliens and the Border Patrol was too intimidated by those previous prosecutions of its people to be really effective. The country was in an ugly mood; Hispanics remained quiet.

Ramsey was writing at his desk when a line of shiny vehicles pulled up. Small flags sprouting from the bumpers marked this as an important visit. Secret Service men watched anxiously as numerous top brass emerged from them. Ramsey was dressed in Levis and a blue flannel shirt when he received them at the door. A black armband and an American flag pin on his lapel completed his appearance.

They saluted, "Mr. President."

"I can't claim that great honor any more, gentlemen. What can I do for the Joint Chiefs?"

"May we speak privately?"

"Come inside." The lead Secret Service man, a Shrecker plant, attempted to follow.

"You wait outside, Robert! I want to talk to these men alone."

The band of officers followed Ramsey inside. They declined his offer of refreshment.

General Bosley got to the point. "The military will back you if you agree to return. America is unraveling at the seams, Mr. President. The attack on Salt Lake City would not have happened if you were in office. And these U.N. troops would not be on American soil. The country needs you."

"Gentlemen, I appreciate your confidence. I'm saddened by this more than I can express. But if I go along with this, I'll be participating in revolution. That's all these people need to finish our hopes for America. I'm going to trust the American people to set things right in November."

"But Mr. President, your name won't even be on the ballot!" said Bosley.

"Hundreds of Constitutional Party candidates will; and that's where it counts. If I go along with this, these people will

have an excuse to declare the whole Constitutional Party movement an act of rebellion. And then use it to ban the lot of us."

"Mr. President, Shrecker has already threatened to put us
under U.N. command," replied Bosley.

"Can he do that, General?"

"He may try. All Shrecker has to do is ask the U.N.."

The entire conversation was recorded from bugs hidden
in the ventilation ducts.

———

That evening, these same General Staff Officers were arrested
for treason. A new list of charges, including treason, was
drafted against Ramsey. Alerted to his fate by an anonymous
phone call at midnight, he was dressed and ready to go when
Federal marshals came for him in the night. Per Shrecker's
orders, he was held in Custody at Camp David.

———

The veiled woman entered her chauffeur driven limo and
departed from the newly reopened Iranian Embassy in
Washington. She had little to fear from the police. She was a
diplomat's wife. She was also aware of being closely watched
and followed. Since the bombing of Salt Lake City, all of the
Iranians were suspect. With diplomatic immunity protecting her, she moved unhurriedly to her destination. Later that
morning in a shopping mall, she casually went to the rest room.
There in a stall, she pulled out a coded message and shoved in
down into the rear of the metal wall mount holding toilet seat

covers. Playing the game further, she flushed the toilet before leaving. The message was retrieved later that morning.

From his safe house in Metairie, Bashan smiled as he received the news. It was too dangerous to extricate him immediately. He was ordered to remain safely hidden away for several weeks until a safe channel of escape could be arranged. What Bashan had not been told, was that if he could not be successfully extricated, he was to be killed. Ahmadinejad could not risk Iran's part in the bombing coming to light.

⸻

After hearing from Mark, Jim sprang into action. From a public phone he called Marty in California. Worried by the excessive number of rings, relief came when he finally heard a voice. "Mr. Raggio?" Jim asked.

I hesitantly answered. "Speaking!"

"This is J from the Big Easy. How's the arm, Mr. Raggio?"

"No worries; it's great. Just call me Marty!"

"I congratulate you on that train job," said Jim.

"Thanks J; but I know you didn't call to tell me that."

"I need you and Mr. Blevins to come to New Orleans. I have a very dangerous job for you. The Bureau cannot be trusted."

"How soon do you need us?"

"Yesterday!"

"ASAP, huh! We'll be on the road in a couple hours."

"How long will it take you to drive here?"

"We'll take turns behind the wheel and drive straight through."

"I know you have plenty of hardware."

"The usual stuff; rifles, pistols and shotguns," I answered. "I don't know how we're going to get through the U.N. checkpoints though. We'll think of something."

"I forgot about that. Better not try it. Travel light. I can arm you on this end. Make haste, Marty! Soon, we'll have to face down the most dangerous criminals you're ever going to meet."

"What makes you think they're so tough?"

"They're the ragheads responsible for Salt Lake City."

"Thanks, J. I'm going to take this one real personal."

"No, you're not. This is deadly serious business. You've acted like a professional so far. Stay that way. And uh, you can call me Jim from now on. Now pay attention and write this down."

Finding Joe Friou had not been hard. Jim walked into Frank's Bar on the main highway a couple miles south of Des Allemands. It was not yet ten that morning. Disheveled with an unwashed look, he was sitting alone at the bar. As Jim walked up he could see an empty shot glass and half empty beer bottle in front of the man. Joe turned his head up at the sound of Jim's approach. "You," he said with glazed eyes.

"Mr. Friou, buy you a drink?"

Joe nodded and waved to the bartender. The man walked over, wiping his hands with a bar towel. "Yeah, Joe," he answered.

"A round for me and this gentleman here."

"No more credit, Joe! I'm sorry, you owe too much."

"It's on me," answered Jim as he laid a twenty on the bar.

"Thanks," said Joe.

"You're having a rough time. How's the wife?"

"Jenny, she's gone. I try working, but it's no good. Ah can't forget. Y'all didn't come down from Nawlins to check on my welfare. What's you name; Ah forget?"

"Jim Scott, I want to talk to you. Alone! It's about Marie's murderer. I need your help."

Joe snapped to attention as new life gleamed in his eyes. "Y'all know something?"

"Yes, Mr. Friou. When you finish your drinks, or as many more as you want, I'd like you to come with me."

"We go now." As the bartender returned with the drinks, Joe waved him off. "Put 'em in the cooler."

They got in Jim's car. Over the next two hours as Jim drove aimlessly, he explained the situation. Joe sobered up quickly as he came to grips with this new reality. "So you see, Joe; this operation is off the books. I am an FBI man; but this is not a Bureau operation. I could go to jail for just talking about this, a moot point considering other things I'm involved with. Are you with me? I need help."

"Ah'm in!"

"Good! This Bashan is dangerous. He has a lot of backup. And he's going escape through these swamps if we don't stop him. Do you have a firearm?"

"A shotgun."

"I'm sure you know how to use it?"

"Ah was raised in these swamps huntin' and fishin.'"

"And you're for this?"

"Ah'll help you."

"Good; I need all the help I can get. There won't be many I can call on. Maybe a couple Columbians from a rival gang, a couple friends from out of state, you, me, that's all."

"Ah know two good men. They're brothers."

"We can't bring anyone else in. I don't know them."

"Turn right, up ahead."

"Why?"

"We're goin' into Lafourche Parish."

"Why do you want to go there?"

"Y'all gonna meet Armand Billiot."

"Who's he?"

"He's a tribal elder of the Houma Indians. He used to be a lieutenant in the Lafourche Parish Sheriff's Department."

"Damn it, Joe! We can't bring in anyone connected with law enforcement."

"He ain't law enforcement; he's Armand Billiot. The *popo* canned him long ago. He cares about justice more than law."

———

It was a short drive to the mobile home lying at the edge of the woods near the main highway. The afternoon was productive as Jim Scott came to know Armand Billiot. A medley of dogs and small brown children with doll-like faces ran about the cluttered yard. An old pickup truck was parked by the mailbox. The door was answered by a giant who weighed at least three hundred pounds. He looked at Jim with a steady, unreadable face before acknowledging them. Warmly greeting Joe, Armand Billiot welcomed them inside. Joe explained they needed to talk alone. Armand spoke to his wife in French. After a brief exchange in this language, she went outside.

Meeting Armand was an experience unto itself. What counted most, he hated drug dealers and murderers. Terrorists were murderers. And he believed in doing it his way. As far as Armand was concerned, there were no legal formalities in the swamps. Bad men he had pursued were known to have permanently disappeared. He promised both his and his brother Deon's help. Deon, who was actually a half-brother, lived on the other side on the law. Armand, with some modifications, lived mostly on its correct side.

————

First light of dawn was breaking over the bayous. Moisture hung heavy in the air, yet it was cool. The horse flies and chiggers hadn't begun their day's work. At low throttle, Deon Billiot skimmed over the reeds. It was time to check the gator traps. These were skillfully concealed out of sight from the main channel. With his checkered past, securing legal tags was impossible. Nor was legal game a steady supply of income. From countless hiding places Deon often evaded detection upon hearing the sound of the approaching game warden's high speed boat. A borderline sociopath, in another age Deon would have been a pirate; but fishing and poaching suited him best in this one. In local parlance, he was raised down de bayou, and lived near Chauvin. Shirtless except for a lightweight vest with pockets, Deon wore a sweat-stained western-style hat low over his eyes and sported a scraggly beard. Faded out jeans and ragged sneakers completed his attire.

Finally reaching a lonely finger of swampland branching off Muserat bayou near Bay Charlie, he cut the motor and left his boat unseen in the reeds. Moving lightly across a mud bank, he reached a growth of stunted trees. Papou had been spotted here recently by fishermen. Deon set the trap, then settled in and waited. Concealed by thick brush, he watched the rope dangling from the long pole. It jutted at an angle over the murky water. Tied to its end was a dead chicken. This concealed a large fish hook. Dangling at just the right height above the water, this discouraged smaller alligators from trying for it. Patient this morning, he waited for the big one.

Final reward came as the morning slowly passed. Eyes and snout suddenly became visible as the log-like, shadowy outline of the creature became faintly visible just below the surface. At least sixteen inches between its eyes and snout indicated this was the big one, a sixteen footer. Slowly but with purpose, it zeroed in on the piece of meat. The stout pole sagged as the animal's body thrust out of the water and viciously took the bait. The hook clove deep within the creature's throat as the chicken disappeared within its jaws. Immediately the water around the panicky animal churned as the gator went into a spin trying to escape. This only lodged the hook deeper into its flesh.

"Got you, Papou!" yelled Deon. He rose from his hiding place clutching a long staff. Hooking its gaff into the gator's hide, he dragged him onto the bank. As he did, Deon slowly tightened the rope, denying the gator the ability to turn its mouth. The confused animal was still preoccupied with escaping from the hook as Deon evasively maneuvered along its side. He dispatched the animal with one .22 round from a pistol in the back of its head. Though dead, parts of the animal still twitched as the primitive nerve endings in its extremities resisted the finality of death.

Drawing his skinning knife, Deon separated the animal from its hide, careful not to damage the finer parts. He noted with satisfaction its overall length. Papou was indeed a sixteen footer. Its hide would go for thirty dollars a foot. From a sack he drew handfuls of salt and sprinkled the fleshy side as he rolled the hide into a bundle.

Deon suddenly froze at the sound of the high-powered motor boat rapidly approaching. Then he sprung into rapid motion, thrusting the hide into the crook on the lower branch of a stunted cypress tree. Almost as quickly, he took the alligator carcass and drug it into the quagmire of reeds and water. Jumping in his boat, he frantically started the engine and headed for open water. The larger boat was quickly upon him. Deon breathed a sigh of relief. It was his brother Armand. Two other men were with him. He recognized Joe Friou; the other man was a stranger. As Armand and Deon maneuvered close together, Joe threw Deon a rope and drew the boats together. Cutting the engine, Armand began speaking in French to his brother.

THE FED

Rick Taylor stood at the junction of Liberty and Nassau staring up at the large building across the street. A monolith of construction, it seemed as invulnerable to the people and automobiles moving below, as if it were Mt. Everest. With Harold Wiser at his side, Rick gave the grand tour. Built in 1924, the behemoth was 223 feet high; its fourteen floors supported thousands of tons of masonry and steel. The three story high cash vault held up to 300 million dollars in cash. But the jewel of the collection lay in the deepest vault eighty feet below ground and fifty feet below sea level. There, in the holiest of financial sanctuaries in the world was the largest concentration of the world's monetary gold, totaling over 10,000 tons. It represented the confidence of almost every nation on Earth; that confidence which was expressed in this branch of the Federal Reserve Bank. Effectively located in the financial capital of the world, governments and entities could safely transact business without ever moving their gold from the basement.

The finest surveillance and guard systems in the world further insured its sanctity. A masterpiece of security completed the final touch. Entry for approach to the vault required descent through elevators five floors below. Arriving from these at the vault level, there were no doors into it. The vault could only be entered through a ten foot passageway filled by a ninety ton steel cylinder that revolved vertically in a 140-ton steel and concrete frame. It required a ninety degree turn of this steel cylinder to open the vault. This could only be opened by a series of time and combination locks, which no single employee had access to.

The Patriots had one overwhelming advantage. An undertaking of this type was deemed impossible. This gave them the element of surprise.

The entire crew ate and slept in the basement. They seldom left the premises and then only to secure supplies. Bathing was a problem. Facilities were sparse; luckily there was a lavatory. Personal sanitation relied on the use of wash basins and buckets. The logistical problems even on this small scale were enormous. The men needed food, a lot of it. Special equipment had to be procured to complete the excavation. Special vehicles had to be obtained to remove the debris from mining. Security precautions added expense.

Harold Wiser was the other key figure in making this plan work. Only his special technical expertise might enable them to pull it off. Underground blueprints of all excavations and structures including pipes, drains and subways going back one hundred years had to be procured. The technical details were daunting. Harold and Rick sat down and brainstormed the project at the very beginning.

It was Harold who spoke first. "At most we can get a couple tons of gold out of there. Maybe not even that much! Are you sure the risk is worth it?"

Rick paused. "It's not so important what we get out of there; it's what governments and the international banking world think we get away with. From our standpoint, we want to paralyze their mentality."

"So this is a mind game, a publicity stunt," replied Harold. "We're not really going to get away with the crown jewels of American banking?"

"That's the way I see it. It will accomplish our purpose if we only get a few hundred pounds of the metal, and we'll never be able to sell or trade it."

"I'm glad you said that. Because if we can pull this off, we ain't getting away with much more than that! We'll only have minutes to grab a few bars, stuff them into a couple car trunks and hope we can get out of Manhattan before the authorities recover from the shock. And personally, I think the tunnel and bridges will be blocked before we can get out of Dodge City."

"We won't be able to escape either on foot or by car."

"You mean we're not getting out of here?"

"I don't mean anything of the kind. I will get those underground schematics for you. We won't need just one tunnel; we'll need three and they must be interconnected. You can use them to locate a suitable sewer we can use to escape. We need another tunnel to a water main so we can flood the vault when we're finished. This will cover up our handy work for a while; and the powers-that-be won't know what we got away with. Also, when we make our escape you need to set a charge in the tunnel leading from this basement to the vault. That will confound and slow them down too. And also place another charge at the end of the tunnel leading to the water main. We must blow it open after we make our getaway and flood the vault. Understand?"

"Rick, you expect a lot from me. Do you still believe in Santa Claus too?"

"Can you do it?"

"I've examined the geology of Manhattan Island. The underlying layer of metamorphic schist is strong. That's what makes this place so good for building skyscrapers. You don't make it easy. There's actually a lot of stuff under Manhattan. Hundreds of miles of subways, tunnels, drains, passageways; and many of them are blocked off and sealed. The biggest excavation is right under Grand Central Terminal, an open secret itself. If I knew how tough this was going be, I'd have stayed in California with Marty and Dave."

"I didn't make it anything at all, Harold. Goddamn it! Can you do it?" Rick pleaded.

Harold looked disgusted. "I don't know! One thing I learned about this rock though. It's a mica-like schist with intermingled layers of hard and soft minerals. I have an idea. But I'm going to have to experiment first. We can't use explosives or noisy pneumatic drilling equipment. One good thing! This ground is so hard, we probably don't have to do any shoring. But I'm not certain of that yet."

This first major planning conference ended with Harold giving Rick a preliminary wish list of materials. That evening Harold left Manhattan for the solitude of a rural area in upstate New York. It was there he would conduct tests on collected samples of the Manhattan schist. Despondent from their exchange, Rick set about in his absence acquiring the underground prints, and procuring that first batch of materials.

In Harold's absence, the basement was converted to living and working quarters. The crew was restless; this was understandable. Rotting away in a basement was not their idea of fighting tyranny. Difficulties also arose when Mr. Yamata's building manager wanted to inspect the basement. Rick was able to temporarily stave him off.

When Harold returned one week later, he was upbeat. It was quickly apparent why as they reconvened. "Cheer up, Rick! I think you're gonna like this!"

"Lay it on me."

"Remember when I told you this Manhattan schist has a lot of mica in it?"

"Yeah, I remember."

"I'll explain this a little better. Manhattan schist is very hard. But! It's foliated with a lot of mica in between its layers. By applying intense heat followed by rapid cooling I was able to produce cracks in its hard surface. Follow me so far?"

"I guess so."

"Here's the beauty of it. By exposing the silicates in the mica to carbonic acid, I was able to dissolve them. Get it? This is nature's process. Over thousands of years, carbonic acid formed from carbon dioxide and water erodes the silicates in mica."

"Uh, Harold! I hope you realize; we don't have thousands of years to get this job done."

"Easy, Rick! I ain't finished. I remembered something from studying the history of Gold mining in California. This was back when I was a young man at the University of Nevada. I studied mining and chemistry there. Big operators used high pressure water to dissolve mountains of earth in open mines in California until it was outlawed generations ago. These people actually reshaped a lot of natural terrain in Northern California."

"Ok, Harold. Put it all together for me."

"First, we heat treat the rock with acetylene torches, then cool it rapidly with carbon dioxide fire extinguishers. Tiny cracks form. We coat these cracks with flux. Then we apply the torches again. The flux gets sucked into the layer of mica, making it more porous. Then we saturate the rock with a high pressure solution of cold water, carbonic acid and other chemicals which enhance the eroding rate of the acid. This accelerates the aging process in the mica. The solution hammers the rock under hundreds of pounds of water pressure. It fractures and starts to break up. Then we can easily chip it out with picks. Hell, I could have made a fortune on this back in the normal world. Then we peel it away, layer by layer. Get it? Alternate cycles of heating and cooling followed by even more intense pounding from high pressure hoses delivering the cocktail of water and chemicals."

"What do you need?"

"I made another list. I'm going have to go shopping with you. One thing we need is a large storage tank; maybe with as much as ten to twenty thousand gallons storage capacity. We can't constantly use city water. Our needs will run into tens of thousands of gallons per day. That would trigger an alarm and we'd have no place to get rid of used water. We'll have to recycle it. I'll have to build a collector to recover the bulk of the liquid so we can return it to the reservoir. And we'll have to constantly extend both sets of pipes, both output and return piping between the collector to the storage tank. We'll need several high pressure pumps capable of delivering hundreds of gallons per minute so we can work in three separate shafts. We'll need backup pumps too. Protective suits for the men are a must. Their skin cannot take that acid mix. We may run into ground water. So we're gonna need auxiliary pumps to handle that. We need cables, hoists and winches. And hundreds of cylinders of oxygen and acetylene and cutting torches with nozzles at least an inch wide. Fortunately, we don't have to excavate straight down and tunnel laterally from the bottom. We can dig this shaft on a slant. All I have to do is make sure we don't hit some cables or pipes already underground. This rock will have to go someplace. We can't get away with using a dump truck. We'll have to load sacks of it into a delivery van. This part is going to slow us down. That's just for starters. I hope you have plenty of money!"

"If I don't, I'll get more."

———

The first hurdle was breaking through a thick layer of concrete foundation in the basement to get to the underlying rock. Using jackhammers was impossible; the noise would have betrayed them. Under Harold's supervision, they acquired a concrete cutting machine which only produced long thin, shallow cuts in the masonry. But by making these cuts in a checkerboard pattern and expanding the concrete squares with heat and cold, chunks could be loosened and removed. The process had to be repeated every time a thin layer of concrete was removed. Work began at a painfully slow pace. Rick began to have doubts. But he kept the possibility of failure to himself; it was critical that he keep up the façade of confidence for the other men.

As the curiosity of the building manager increased, it generated the necessity of putting on a good show. Under the guise of being an importer, Rick bought tens of thousands of dollars worth of luxury goods and wines. False rooms were built to conceal their work and living quarters within the basement. The import-export business remained closed to walk-in traffic. But a sham office was set up to receive unwelcome visitors when this couldn't be avoided. Rick also resorted to the old fashioned but time proven method of bribery. This inventory of fine wines, along with tickets to sports events and Broadway shows interspersed with expensive dinners, kept the manager under wraps for the present. Emphasizing that he could review their progress very soon, Rick impressed the manager that he really wanted to wow him with the finished product. An unwelcome visit from the city building inspector was also imminent. Working through the building manager, Rick was able to temporarily delay this. Fortunately, leasing the basement for an excessive amount and making payments on time, endeared him to both the owner and the manager. This process was aided by the economic effects of Muller's and Shrecker's policies and the incessant guerilla raids. These raids on the nation's power grid were already crippling the business community nationwide.

By poring over the underground schematics, Harold was able to lay out an escape route. An auxiliary shaft would branch off the main tunnel and rise to the level of the sewer. Close to it there was a water main which could be easily tapped. More equipment had to be acquired for this purpose. There was not enough manpower available to do the additional work. This forced Rick to open up channels of communication with the independent teams still operating in the West. All available workers must be put to the task at hand.

Using Harold's plans, Rick finished working out details for the get away. Escape would take place through an inter-connected series of sewers converging near the East River. From there they would escape through a manhole and only need to traverse a few dozen feet over the surface to the river's edge. Transportation must be arranged by water out of Manhattan. Using their new business for a cover, he was able to purchase an old charter fishing boat. Using only a small down payment, Rick was able to finance the boat from a dealer on Long Island. It needed considerable work and there was a mooring fee. But he could keep its monthly expense to a minimum. After the operation the craft would be abandoned anyway. As he left the sales office people around him were running through the streets in a state of panic. Rick walked into a corner liquor store and asked the cashier what was going on.

"Somebody blew up Salt Lake City," the man replied.

"What?"

"Yeah, that's what I said. They blew it up with a goddamn A-Bomb. Excuse me, mister, I gotta close up. I'm getting outta here. We may be next."

This state of chaos delayed his return. After receiving the password, the curious guard let him enter the basement and asked what was going on outside. Rick told him to lock the door behind them and follow him. The transport crew just finished closing the rear door of a loaded van as he entered. He yelled out for them to stop and join him. All work halted in the tunnel as Rick called the men in the shaft below, back into the basement.

Startled and confused, the tunnel crew sat or stood around the table as Rick monitored the radio news. At first some of the men were getting angry, thinking their Western colleagues were behind the attack. Rick reassured them this was not so. And the truth wasn't long in coming. Al Qaeda was quick to take credit, threatening more attacks unless America converted to Islam and ceased supporting Israel.

Disbelief turned to anger as some of the aggressive types wanted to go hunting for ragheads. Joshua's sons, knowing these men for years, were able to calm them down.

Muller's death came as a surprise too. The new president, Carl Shrecker, had been the most vocal advocate for gun control in the Senate. His appointee for VP was a Senate colleague from the West Coast, Daphne Feinberg. This was her first term in the Senate having previously been a representative from Oregon. Rick referred to them as "Marx and Lenin."

The gun issue and the numerous random shootings of U.N. troops following the destruction of the train near Portola caused severe consternation in the Bilderberger hierarchy as well as in the United Nations. America was becoming more difficult to govern. Few Americans were turning in their guns. Private factories for the production of ammunition sprang up in thousands of garages and workshops across the land. The warning signs for November's election in 2012 were becoming ominous.

"Harold, I think we're caught in the crosshairs of time. I don't know how much longer I can stave off an inspection of this place."

Harold seemed unconcerned. "Pretty impressive all right! Those baboons in the U.N. are demanding Shrecker take harsher measures. He's acting like a fighter on the ropes. The American people are already pissed off beyond anything he can repair. If we pull this off, it'll be the final nail in his coffin. You made a believer out of me, Rick."

"How's progress going in the tunnel?"

"OK; here's where we're at. You still got plenty of that money left I hope?"

"Enough! We'll manage."

"We have to install those pumps to control ground water," said Harold. "And I have to figure out where to pump the water. The only thing I can come up with is the sewer. This means opening up that end of the escape shaft sooner that we wanted. But there's danger. Any sewer worker might find the opening and wonder what it's doing there."

"Do what you have to; we'll just take a chance and hope they don't find it. Maybe we'll post a guard. I've fine tuned my thinking on this strike. I've decided we're only taking out six bars of gold."

"All this, for six bars of gold!"

"Right! When is the best time to blow into the vault? Midnight? What do you think?"

"I've given that matter some thought too. I'd go for three A.M. More people are going to be in bed. And another thing; one minute after we blow into that vault, the cops will be descending on that bank. Their own controls will slow them down a little, but that won't help us much. I think they can get into that vault in less than thirty-six hours."

"Won't flooding it correct that problem?"

"Not for what you want! If they send a diver into the vault, it won't take long for them to prove the bullion is still there. We need something else."

Rick raised his eyebrows. "What?"

"We blow up the building above at the same minute we blast into the vault from below. The Feds won't know if it's a robbery or a terrorist attack. That building weighs thousands of tons. When it collapses, it should cover the upper vault with a layer of twisted steel and masonry many feet thick. Maybe even collapse into it! And it should destroy the elevators too. It'll take them days to reach the bottom level eighty feet down. So if we bring down the building, it'll collapse and seal that vault for over a week. Maybe two or three! That's what you want; isn't it?"

"That will add up to a lot of innocent casualties? I can't go along with it. Think of another way," replied Rick. "Some loss of life may be inevitable, but there's going to be hundreds, maybe thousands of people in and around that building. This is revolution, not murder."

"Yeah, Rick; some people are going to die. But at 3:00 A.M. in the morning, the number of people around it will be at a minimum, and probably no kids. Remember; George and the other boys faced this same crisis in Hollywood?"

"I see what you mean. How could you bring it down? With a truck bomb?"

"Nope! Only one way it can be done with certainty!"

"How?"

"From the top. I'm working out the details now. I want you to pull Luke off the work crew. We're sending him to school."

"What school? I don't get it!"

"He already has a private pilot's license. We're going send him to helicopter school."

"We don't have money to buy a helicopter, Harold."

"We can charter one; and at the last minute hi-jack it. But not just any chopper will do. We need something like one of those big commercial jobs, like a Sky Crane."

"Are those the ones used to lift logs?"

"Yeah, but they're also used to lift heavy structural forms, like prefab sections of bridges and buildings or transmission towers where it's hard to get in with other equipment. I know they're available from an outfit in New Jersey. And there's a helicopter school there too."

"Why couldn't they bypass the rubble and drill into the vault from another angle? What's stopping them?"

"Nothing, but they'll have to drill through the same hard Manhattan schist we did. It'll be slow for them; they'll have to do it the hard way. They don't have my method. The shock effect of bringing that building down will paralyze their thinking. They'll need time to figure it out."

"How much time will we have to work in there after we blow our way through?"

"As much time as you have the balls to take. But if you want to escape with any bullion, I wouldn't stick around for more than a half hour. If we blow into that vault at 3:00 A.M. we'll only have a couple hours of dark left. I'm guessing that gives us less than an hour to get away. Everything on water is likely to be stopped and searched as soon as they collect their wits."

"What's our rate of progress below?"

"Ventilation is bad. The heat is slowing us down. The men can only work twenty minutes at a time down there. We're only progressing a few feet per day. If we could overcome these obstacles, this could become dozens instead. If you can get me some air ducting and powerful fans, I can blow fresh air into the tunnel's extremity and force the heat out on this end."

"I'll get them."

"Do you want me to go with you?"

"You're needed right here. Stay on the job, Harold. I'll handle it."

The rate of progress increased as their mastery of the experience curve grew. The acid-mix dissolved the schist better than Harold originally anticipated. And the combination of heat and high pressure streams of water made it easy for the tunnel crew to chip out the loosened rock with picks. The pace increased from a couple feet per day to over a dozen.

Summer passed into fall with only six weeks left until the big election in 2012. The Patriots extended their main tunnel under the vault. Work now began hollowing out a chamber beneath it. The auxiliary tunnels were nearing completion too. Data had been pouring into the Air Force Technical Operations Center at Patrick Air Force Base in Florida from numerous seismic warning centers throughout the Northeast and various colleges for days. Mysterious sounds were emanating from lower Manhattan Island in the vicinity of Maiden Lane. Numerous experts were consulted, who came up with a mixed review. The sound signature matched that of rushing water. While some experts recommended a follow up investigation, the general consensus concluded that an artesian stream had penetrated into the rock strata at this location and disappeared straight down into the layers below. The experts would continue to monitor these sounds. They did not deem the situation to be of significant importance to sound an immediate alarm.

The excavation continued eighteen hours per day, seven days a week. The work crew had been showing signs of fatigue for weeks. Realizing the men needed a break, Rick called a halt to the work early on Saturday and announced that Sunday would be a day of rest. That evening, leaving the basement in groups of two or three, the men looked for diversion in the Big Apple. For some this was dinner and a movie; for others sightseeing and a few drinks; for a few of the younger ones, it was total release from weeks of pent up confinement in the tunnel.

It was 4:00 A.M. when Rick was roused from a dead sleep. Two of the younger men were arrested for fighting in a bar that evening. The details quickly unfolded; they had gotten drunk and into an argument. Blows were exchanged and their opponents were hospitalized. These men were unwilling to tell the police their names, place of residence, occupations, what they were doing in New York or even how they got here. As a precaution the evening before, none of men had carried any I.D.

Rick convened an emergency council. This crisis threatened to undermine the project. A computer search of fingerprints would undoubtedly link the two young men to the militia in Montana. Though it was Sunday morning, it was certain the FBI would be called in this same day. Maybe they already had been. Rick had no ideas as they all sat sullenly in despair. One of the men ventured a theory. Maybe these two would hang tough, and refuse to talk!

The situation was becoming more hopeless until a young lawyer, Dave Mosby, suddenly rose and spoke. "Yes, they will. I represented both of them in DUI cases before. I know they can be intimidated. Federal authorities will suspect Patriot activity here, and cause them to be water-boarded. They'll be broken within twenty-four hours. Though I belong to the Montana Bar and am not licensed in New York, the police might let me in to see them."

Several men ventured the same question. "Why would you want to do this?"

His answer followed quickly, "To kill them!"

Stunned by this revelation, Rick pressed him for details.

"We've come too far to risk failure. All of our lives can probably be numbered in weeks if not days. If they talk, all is lost. We can't fail. If I can get to them, I can end their lives, mine too. It will plug this leak. Because I'm a lawyer, I just might get in there."

"You won't be able to get a firearm past their metal detectors, Dave!"

"Among our emergency supplies is a deadly poison we made by boiling down oleander leaves, for just such an emergency where firearms couldn't be used. I'll smuggle in three small vials in my shoes. One for each of them and one for me! If I'm successful, you all will have to go on without us. That will buy you time; the chain will remain unbroken."

"What happens when you swallow the oleander extract?"

"We suffer immediate cardiac arrest. The mix is concentrated and potent!"

"What makes you think they'll take the poison?"

"They have to! I can't fail! We can't fail!"

The horrible reality set in. Everyone was struck by the enormity of Dave Mosby's sacrifice. Something inside each man died that moment; something else within us turned into steel. They would go forward, a band of brothers, united in a common cause.

Next morning, the Monday edition of *The New York Times* reported the self-inflicted death of three Montana men while in police custody. A data base had linked all three to a militia in Montana. The FBI was reported seeking clues to their presence in New York.

As the chamber underneath the vault neared completion, Harold worked twenty-hour days trying to solve the penetration problem. It was obvious to him that an ordinary explosive device would not undermine the sanctity of the vault. Giving himself a crash course in modern military bomb technology, he discovered a possible solution. They would need a JDAM type bomb to puncture the foundation from below. This was the same technology that busted Saddam Hussein's many bunkers bringing his regime to an end.

He decided to use three separate charges working in sequence. First, a shaped charge would invade the outer shell creating a weak point, and loosening tons of concrete and steel. This would trigger the second explosion, a weaker propellant type charge which would slam a massive steel projectile, two feet in diameter, upward into the weakened foundation. A third charge, consisting of a shatter-type mining explosive enclosed within rear third of the projectile, would then detonate. This final explosion would complete the projectile's penetration into the vault and enlarge the fissure. Much of this was speculation on his part. There was no way to test his theory in advance. Welding crews worked around the clock to complete Harold's bomb design, while he prepared the various explosives on a rented farm in upstate New York.

Final preparations for penetrating the vault were fever-ishly completed. The final explosive charge and its detonating device were sealed within the lower third of the steel projectile. Over six feet tall and tapered into a hardened point at its apex, the bomb was placed above the propelling charge. These were buried underneath rubble from the dig, directly below the target point. Its sides were packed solidly with rock, which would secure the bomb's vertical alignment. Further guarded by inches of rock covering the projectile's tip, these final precautions protected the warhead from the initial charge suspended above it.

The shaped charge was then installed against the vault immediately above, and held there with scaffolding. If the timing sequence worked properly, this first explosion would activate sensors which would detonate the propellant below the projectile. The impact of the warhead into weakened crevasse above would in turn set off the third charge. This would have to work. If it didn't, the project would be an exercise in futility.

———

Luke attended helicopter pilot school for four weeks. Taking every opportunity to learn and operate these aircraft, his training did not come to an end after his solo flight. He continued flying and fine-tuning his tactile skills for the challenge that would soon be upon him.

The Sky Crane could lift over eight thousand pounds. Harold improvised a bomb that weighed four thousand. Its explosive force would be concentrated downward. Each successive floor would collapse from the increasing and overwhelming weight falling from above. The addition of magnesium and thermite to the explosive would produce intense heat. This would melt the collapsing steel girders into a twisted and fused conglomerate. The helicopter would lower the device onto the roof. Luke would activate its release mechanism remotely from the cockpit. This would cause the cradle to deposit the bomb on the roof and activate its timer.

Two weeks before the November election, preparations were completed. Only a dozen men would be on hand for the actual strike. For days, Rick had drilled this penetration team in their escape routine. They styled themselves as the Wrecking Crew. The other men left the basement days earlier, via normal travel routes. They would form the recovery team. The stage was set.

The Reckoning

The expressionless brunette crossed the room. As she stopped by Bashan's side, she handed him the envelope and waited. He raised his left hand and flicked his wrist. Without a word she unceremoniously left the room. The men sitting around the table waited for him to speak. He read the note silently. With a nod, he pushed it away and leaned back in his chair. Tension grew as everyone waited for him to speak.

"Gentlemen, how pleasant it is to see all of you this morning. Smoke if you like. There's coffee in the corner." Though his manner was intended to put the others at ease, everyone present feared Bashan. But these men never allowed their fear to show. Each man projected his own façade of confidence.

He waited for them to settle at ease. A few got coffee. Most of them began smoking.

When all had satisfied their whims, he spoke again. "I'm leaving this land of Kafirs at the end of this week. The submarine is nearing its position now. When everything else is right, a seaplane will take me to it. The plane will rendezvous with an Iranian submarine in the Gulf of Mexico and many of you will never see me again. Lorenzo?"

"Si, Culebra," he answered.

"This note says you will arrange the airplane? Is all in readiness?"

"I have taken care of the details myself."

"Good!"

Relieved by this news, Lorenzo continued to listen as Culebra broke off into a tirade against the infidel West. The slightest hint of a smile was visible on his lips. Soon, he would run the cartel. Colombian by birth, he had converted to Islam only to get close to the source of power and make money. He controlled the cartel's U.S. operation. Secretly he hated Culebra's crusade; it was bad for business. Tonight, he would drop a dime and tell Manuel's people of Culebra's departure. With the Turk dead, both cartels could unite under his lead and dominate the trade.

It was almost like payday many weeks later as Jim Scott received the call from Manuel's gang. It was early in the morning when a man identifying himself as Rodolfo, relayed

Lorenzo's message. Culebra would leave Louisiana just before first light tomorrow. Leaving by boat was impossible; the Coast Guard was inspecting all small craft. All airports, large and small were being observed too. A seaplane belonging to a drilling company from Morgan City would land on Boudreaux Lake before dark with some testing equipment for the large gas field there. Before dawn, Culebra and his close associates would board a yacht waiting at nearby Chauvin. The boat would rendezvous with the seaplane on the lake. From here the plane was cleared to continue its flight to an oil platform in the Gulf, ostensibly to deliver supplies before returning to base. The plane would bypass the platform and fly hundreds of miles further into the Gulf. There it would set down and Culebra's group would transfer to the submarine. Unknown to the pilot, neither he nor the plane would ever return. The fix had been expensive, but this was of no consideration to the Colombians. The company would claim its plane had been hijacked on the lake.

The downside of the message, neither Rodolfo nor any other of Manuel's remaining people would be there to assist. Jim called Marty and David in their safe house near Houma. Relieved, they had been chomping at the bit for weeks waiting for this. He then called Joe who contacted Armand. Armand passed the word to Deon.

Jim secured emergency leave from the Bureau by late morning. That afternoon, he met with the other five men and they formulated the final plan.

Armand and David were waiting in a hidden location just north of Chauvin. It was 3:00 A.M. when several speeding cars passed his truck. There was no mistaking their identity or purpose. An expensive Mercedes led, followed by several Humvees. Altogether, at least a half million dollars worth of vehicles. David alerted Jim by cell phone. Armand pulled onto the highway and raced to another hidden spot where Marty waited on the boat.

Reaching Chauvin, Culebra's caravan pulled off Highway 56 and parked next to a small yacht docked between two shrimp boats. Within twenty minutes the yacht left its mooring, plying slowly southward until it reached the nearby canal. Turning into the Boudreaux Canal, it headed west toward Lake Boudreaux.

Earlier on the previous evening, Armand, Deon and Joe determined the best place to situate their boats in relation to the waiting seaplane. These men were in their element, and Jim Scott let them work out the details. From their vantage point near Hog Point, Jim waited in Deon's boat while Joe occupied another. The other three men discreetly followed the yacht in Armand's boat as it passed through the canal and into the lake.

That previous afternoon, a vintage Mallard landed on the lake. It taxied to a point three miles from the mouth of the canal in a lonely area near the gas field. Though it was a moonlit night, Jim had supplied each of the men with infrared binoculars. Timing was crucial. They must isolate Culebra's group and finish them off before escape was possible.

The plane was in an isolated location, no solid land was anywhere near, only marshy swamp which could not be penetrated on foot. Escape was possible only by water or air. Joe and Armand determined the most opportune moment to strike was soon after the plane took on its passengers.

The tension was almost unbearable as the ambush team followed the progress of the yacht across the lake. The boat carrying the Colombians was brightly illuminated as it approached its destination. The plane's engines could be heard firing up and its lights flickered on as the yacht converged.

Their pent up anxiety was finally released as Joe gave the signal. "Now!" Joe's boat surged forward while Deon's purposely followed at a slower pace. Within minutes, Joe halved the distance to the Mallard. In the moonlight, spray from the seaplane's wake could soon be seen as it glided across the lake. Joe's boat was at full throttle as he held it on a collision course with the Mallard. He lit the cigar in his mouth as the outline of the plane grew.

Inside the plane's cockpit, the pilot realized he did not have enough speed to lift off and avoid the inevitable collision that lay ahead. He backed off the throttle and turned the plane's nose away at the last moment. "What are you doing?" demanded Bashan from the passenger compartment.

"We almost ran into a boat. Probably some damn coon-ass fisherman who doesn't have enough sense to go to bed." After saying this, he realized the boat had turned with him. "He's going to run into us!" The pilot rammed his throttle forward trying to out distance the boat.

Joe threw a bottle of gasoline on to his boat's rear deck. As it broke, the fuel quickly surrounded six five-gallon cans of gasoline lying there. Joe threw the lit cigar into the loose gas. It flamed and filled the boat with light as the horrified pilot stared in disbelief. Using a bungee cord to steady the wheel, Joe jumped over the side two seconds from impact. The boat plowed into the fuselage just behind the cockpit as flames spread across the water. The gasoline cans exploded enveloping the aircraft in flames.

Joe swam under water as a sheet of fire illuminated the surface above him. Within five yards he was able to rise to the surface. Hearing the sound of an approaching boat, he yelled. Deon slowed, and Jim dragged him up into the boat. Deon turned his boat in a wide circle to confront the approaching yacht.

Enveloped in flames, it was impossible to exit from the side hatch. Bashan lurched into the cockpit. He emptied the magazine of a Mac-10 into the windshield and then kicked away the fragments. As the plane began to sink, the pilot attempted to crawl out of the opening ahead of him. "*Tu chancho*" (pig)! yelled Bashan as he grabbed the man by his head. Twisting viciously, he broke the pilot's neck. Crawling out onto the nose of the plane, Bashan dove into the water ahead of the flames. He was the only one to escape. Dog-paddling, Bashan conserved his strength as he waited for the approaching yacht.

The yacht reacted quickly, racing toward the fiery impact only a few hundred yards away. As it did, Armand's boat pulled up parallel near it. David and Marty began shooting. They were answered by more than a dozen guns from the yacht. As Jim had guessed, the Colombians were armed only with pistols and sub-machineguns, having limited range. Armand maneuvered his boat beyond their effective reach. Only a few, wild shots hit his fast, low silhouetted speed boat. Marty and David were armed with semi-automatic assault rifles supplied by Jim. In the boat were also 12 gauge, pump shotguns for close combat. They poured hundreds of rounds into the yacht. Gunfire from that source lessened but didn't entirely cease. Once the yacht had to be brought back on course after its helmsman was hit. It was now only yards away from the burning plane where Bashan waited in the water.

The yacht received a temporary respite from gunfire as Armand and Deon had to turn their boats for another pass. Slowing to a crawl, the yacht finally heaved to by the burning wreckage. Flashlights crisscrossed the water. Bashan yelled and was acknowledged. With a few long strokes he came upon the yacht's stern and climbed up a ladder. A wounded associate met him there. All but two of the men on board were dead or dying. Gunfire resumed as Deon's boat bore down on the yacht. Armand completed his turn. Now four men were peppering the Colombians with rifle fire.

Jim yelled for Deon to put his boat between the yacht and the canal two miles distant.

Bashan yelled for the helmsman to run the boat ashore. With bullets flying around him and the yacht's structure disintegrating, Bashan dove to the deck for cover. All gunfire from the yacht ceased and it plunged pell mell into the darkness.

Looming ahead was a small spit of solid land on the south shore. The yacht came to an abrupt stop as it hit the muddy bank. Bashan jumped off the port side and groped forward blindly. He sank to his knees in the slime until reaching semi-solid ground. Another Colombian jumped off the starboard. Escape was only an illusion; only swamp lay ahead of them.

As Deon's boat pulled alongside the grounded yacht, Joe was the first to jump off. Armand came to a stop on its other side. He too leapt into the darkness. Groans could be heard on the deck of the yacht. Grabbing their shotguns, Jim and the remaining men scaled its sides. A few scattered shots met them. They answered with a barrage of buckshot until everything on deck before them went silent.

Armand caught up with a Colombian, knocking him to the ground from behind. The man jumped to his feet and drew a stiletto. Before he could balance himself into a fighting stance, Armand put three hundred pounds of weight behind a kick to the man's jaw. Then moving with speed reminiscent of a rattlesnake's strike, he scooped the man up like a rag doll and threw him backward over his shoulders. With one arm hooked around the Colombian's arm and another around his leg, Armand suddenly dropped to one knee, breaking the man's spine. After a loud snap, the man uttered a hideous screech of pain and died.

Hearing the commotion only feet away, Bashan yelled out. "*Cortador, esta alla?*" (Cutter, are you there?). He never knew what hit him as the butt of Joe's shotgun came down on his head.

Light was barely breaking night's shadow as Bashan came to. His vision was blurry. A man's form appeared squatting near him. The wrecked yacht was tilted at an angle nearby.

But what was this man doing? What was he throwing into the water? Bashan tried to move his arms. They were bound behind him with multiple layers of thick tie-wraps. His legs were tightly bound with rope. He tried to force the bonds on his wrists. With his great strength, he could have broken one or more and busted loose. But there were too many. Bashan was securely bound.

Joe spoke first, without looking up. "Afraid y'all wouldn't come around, Mr. Bashan. Don't want y'all to miss the main event. The feast is gonna start soon."

Slowly, Joe rose to his full height, picked up his shotgun and pumped out all the shells Then, slowly he began to reload it, making sure Bashan could see his every move.

"What are you doing?" asked a confused Bashan.

"Don't want y'all dyin' too quick." Setting the firearm down, he strode in front of Bashan. He lifted his foot and shoved it full into Bashan's face forcing the big man to his back. Bashan feverishly worked at the bonds behind him. Given enough time, he could skillfully wiggle his way free from them. "So that's the face of a monster!" said Joe. "Glad we gonna finish this in the light. Now y'all can see me too. Look good on this face, son of a bitch. Look well! Does it remind y'all of a young girl?"

Glowering back, Bashan's dark eyes were filled with hatred. He became defiant. "You can't kill me. My destiny is too important. Every man has his price. Name yours; I'll give you the world. I am a hard man, Cajun one; but my word is good."

"Bring back Marie," Joe said casually as he cinched tight a tie wrap on Bashan's left arm. The blood flow to that limb was cut off. "And those innocent people in Salt Lake City, too!" He drew tight another one on Bashan's right arm. Then, dragging the large man to the mud bank, he tied him to an inflated inner tube.

Bashan suddenly felt fear, a fear he had never known before. He tried to guess Joe's intentions. His desperate eyes now resembled those of so many he himself had killed. He pleaded and begged.

"Did Marie beg, you son of a bitch? Y'all ever show mercy to anyone? Ah don't think so. Just think! Y'all are goin' home. Hell's awaitin'. He shoved Bashan's body in the swamp. The murky water was already red from the bloody chum Joe had already tossed into it. Joe retrieved his shotgun lying nearby and waded in after him. He buried the muzzle into Bashan's left arm below the bond. "This is for all those poor people in Utah. Y'all need to settle up with them." Joe pulled the trigger. As he did Bashan's lower arm exploded from the blast. Joe shifted the blood stained muzzle to the man's other arm. "Look at my face. See Marie in it? This is for Marie!" Joe pulled the trigger again. With the gun's muzzle, Joe pushed him toward deep water.

Struggle was no longer possible; Bashan could not move his arms. He shrieked in terror and agony. Remembering his youth at the Wahhabi school in Sana'a, he called upon Allah. But Allah did not come. Joe backed out upon the mud bank and faced him. Log-like forms converged on the screaming man. They struck suddenly and the big man's body jerked in the water. A hideous wail came from his lips and blood flowed from his mouth. The inner tube bobbed in the murky water as his nearly dead body was ripped to shreds below the waist.

His soon to be lifeless eyes fixated on Joe. A large alligator suddenly took Bashan's body under the surface in a death roll. Joe stood silently, watching the spectacle he had created. With a hollow feeling in his stomach, he slowly turned away and walked toward Deon's boat. From the bank, the others stood silently, aghast from the scene they had just witnessed.

————

Sounds of gunfire on the lake had been reported. Soon escape would no longer be possible. But they had one more ace to play. The swamp was Deon's home. Followed by the other boat, he led them through little known bayous before law enforcement could respond.

That evening, Jim conversed with Mark Obledo. Mark suggested that he bring Marty and David to Virginia. At his home in Fairfax County, Mark could hide them. The entire country was boiling over. Shrecker was almost at the end of his options. It was likely this national crisis would soon come to a head. And if it did, their combined efforts might be needed in Washington.

————

At 2:50 a.m. the alert sounded for the New Jersey Air National Guard's 177th Fighter Wing at Atlantic City's International Airport. Within minutes two F-16s scrambled to intercept a large helicopter reported flying low over the Hudson River near the Holland tunnel. A belated report placed it previously near East Orange, New Jersey. Again the craft was spotted lifting a large object from a flatbed truck in an open area south of Passaic. The unknown craft did not respond to verbal communication from Air Traffic Control. They assumed the worst; this could be another nuclear terrorist attack. The fighter pilot's orders were clear. Shoot it down!

Luke guided the Sky Crane by the city lights below. They illuminated the grid work of streets in lower Manhattan. He had already committed these to memory. Luke had no illusions about his coming fate. He received several calls demanding identification and ordering him away from the city. After several near misses bringing him within feet of the high-rise behemoths in lower Manhattan, he located Liberty Street. Luke maneuvered low between these skyscrapers toward his destination. He raised the Sky Crane several feet as he reached the Federal Reserve Building.

Protected from view by the New York skyline, the F-16s made two passes before spotting the large helicopter. Hovering above the building, Luke repeatedly jerked the cord which would release the bomb from its cradle onto the building's roof. Minutes were lost as it would not respond. He knew there was no escape if the mission was to be successful. He shut off the power. And as the helicopter touched down, he leaped from the cockpit onto the device. The blade's still rapid rotation and uncontrolled stick caused it to bank toward one side. Barely clinging to the craft as the Sky Crane started to tilt, Luke had just enough time to hit the detonator before the spinning blades ripped into the roof as the helicopter crashed. The Air National Guard pilots watched the explosion below helplessly as they zoomed over the skyline.

The device exploded simultaneously with the fuel tank of the Sky Crane. It was 3:06 A.M. as chunks of metal hurdled through the night sky in all directions. The device directed the bulk of its blast downward. Seismographs recorded a prior explosion deep under the surface six minutes before this. Yet later these two would be identified as one. The outer wall of the building remained largely intact as the upper floors crashed to ground level. Flames from the interior shot hundreds of feet skyward as windows burst outward onto the streets below. Remarkably, there were few casualties.

John, Joshua's youngest son backed the boat away from its dock and slowly plied his way toward the East River to rendezvous with the wrecking crew. It was 2:55 A.M. as he looked at his watch. Eleven minutes later, he was looking toward lower Manhattan as the sound of the blast washed over him. A fiery conflagration could be seen between the high rises. He brought the boat into a holding pattern near the Brooklyn shore and waited for Rick's call. String Bean waited forward with the bow line, ready to toss it after they crossed the East River.

Dust and smoke choked the tunnel where the wrecking crew waited. After setting the timer, they retreated into the auxiliary tunnel leading to the sewer. Though they wore respirators and goggles, all were lost in darkness. Concrete dust covered everything. Rick wiped his goggles and plunged forward followed by the rest of the wrecking crew. At the mouth of the cavern, precious minutes were lost as they frantically removed rock and masonry blocking the entrance into it. They managed to open a crawl space. Rick leaned inward and shined his flashlight over the scene. Gold bars lay in disarray in all corners. Following the blast, the weight of the bullion helped collapse the base of the vault. He scrambled through the opening followed by several men. They had been instructed to grab six gold bars. Remaining huddled together, they picked up the six closest ingots.

Rick stopped them. "No! We must get bars from different locations within the vault. We'll have to go inside. Just take one from here."

One man climbed the shoulders of others through the jagged sections of the eight foot wide hole above them. He was quickly followed by a second man. Rick instructed them to go to five extreme points within and bring back one bar from each location. It seemed like an eternity as the men below waited for them.

So far the immediate mission was a success. The men laboriously made their way out of the cavern and along the main tunnel to the side shaft leading to the sewer. Harold was the last man out. He set timers for two charges. The first would seal the main tunnel where it connected to the basement. The second explosion would blow the water main and flood their handiwork. It could also drown them if they moved too slow. The wrecking crew was well into the sewer as the vibration from those charges was felt in the distant darkness.

Thirty minutes later, the men waited expectantly as the strongest among them climbed the bars under the cast iron sewer cover. Matthew shoved with all his might, dislodging the circular cover. A passing car hit it. The men slowly emerged amid numerous cars swerving around them.

Within minutes of the blast, the New York Metropolitan Police Department reacted. Its units concentrated upon the Fed. Liberty, Nassau, and Maiden Lane were nearly impassable. Fire crews brought their equipment as close as possible.

John answered his cell phone. It was the expected call from Rick, "Time applies!"

Gunning the engine in full throttle he pointed the fishing boat toward an empty pier on the Manhattan side of the East River.

As the wrecking crew approached their destination, a couple of security guards had to be disarmed. Fortunately for them, they didn't offer resistance. As John edged the boat by a descending ladder, each of these men dropped from it onto the deck from the pier above. Commands to stop could be heard from policemen running toward them. With the last man aboard, John gunned the throttle and the fishing boat lurched upstream into the East River.

Escape by boat was only a momentary fix. Rick assumed in advance they would confront at least one police boat. All of them put on wet suits and life jackets. The gold bars were placed in sacks and strapped to inner tubes. At a predetermined point upriver, everyone abandoned the boat and swam to the waiting shore. Other Patriots waited there for them with cars. John was the last one off. He reversed its direction and tied down the wheel. This bought the time they needed. The police followed the empty boat.

The Jubilee

Shrecker flew into a rage as details of the Federal Reserve attack began to pour into his office. Calls flooded into the Fed from all around the world as well as from domestic banking institutions. Advisors persuaded him to do a photo-op at the site of the destroyed bank. It would be reminiscent of Bush's famous speech at the fallen Trade Towers just a few years before. Here was his chance to look presidential, take charge and channel America's wrath against these revolutionaries. The Marine helicopter waiting on the grounds of the White House would fly him to New York City this same morning.

In the narrow streets beside the hollowed out building, few were allowed to approach other than media types, city officials and a few Democrat toadies. Hundreds of cameras focused on the makeshift podium set up for President Shrecker's arrival. Sound technicians scurried about their several tasks. Security was tight as hundreds of pre-positioned sharpshooters were anxiously watching every window and door. Other security men assisted by police thoroughly screened and searched each newsman before any were allowed to come close. At last, his Press Secretary signaled for them to commence as he introduced the President.

Shrecker put on his best show expressing outrage against the terrorists that had targeted America's greatest financial institution. In this nationwide telecast, he assured the country and the world of the continued soundness of the Federal Reserve System. After his speech, Shrecker allowed reporters to pound him with questions. Trying to appear calm and in control, he replied with the canned answers that were supplied to him earlier that morning.

"Fellow Americans, as all the world can see, behind me lies the remains of this Federal Reserve Bank. It was destroyed and has collapsed over the vault. But the supply of gold and currency stored beneath it is safe. These criminals could not have gained entry into the vault which safely lies eighty feet below."

Shrecker's spirits were buoyed as the photo-op wound down. Surely these damned revolutionaries had overplayed their hand this time. The country would turn against them. There was a commotion at the edge of the crowd. Shrecker noticed the arrival of a heavily escorted entourage. Security stopped them. With a distinctive German accent, their leader demanded admission. An aide whispered to Shrecker, "That's the local representative of the largest German Bank."

Shrecker signaled his security team. He sensed an opportunity. "Let him in. I'll let this man speak."

He was allowed to approach within twenty feet. In a cold, clinical voice, he asked, "Mr. President, Sir; have you recovered the rest of the gold?"

Shrecker felt confident. "We did not lose any gold, sir. All assets in that vault are more secure, even after the bombing than they were before. Even more secure than they would be in their own country."

The German answered without any display of emotion. "Then how can you explain this?" He unwrapped the bar he was holding and held it over his head. "You can all come close and look at this gold bar. It is stamped with the serial number belonging to the Deutsche Bundesbank. It was delivered to me by gun point at my residence this morning. How can it be safe in this bank if I am holding it now, here in front of you?"

This revelation was followed by a detailed search of all buildings within the radius of one mile of the Fed. The remains of the collapsed access tunnel were found in less than an hour. A major water leak was reported by the New York City Department of Environmental Protection. Inspection of the sewer revealed water was pouring out of the sewer escape route. To the consternation of much of Manhattan as it lost service, the main was located and shut off. Experts began their damage assessment.

That evening anonymous tips poured into reporters and bankers from widespread areas in the Mid-Atlantic and New England States and one from as far south as Virginia. These anonymous reports purported to have come from individuals witnessing suspicious behavior. None of these persons could be located after the calls. Police raids located five gold bars hidden in car trunks, and bus depot lockers. The identifying marks on these pieces of bullion showed they came from many different locations within the vault. The world financial market exploded over this revelation. Foreign governments and various overseas banks demanded the immediate return of their gold.

President Shrecker was unable to calm the world community. He downplayed the loss, referring to it as "that barbaric metal." And claimed it would have no effect on the economy. Most foreign currencies immediately fell in value, some to a low fraction of their previous level. The world market ceased accepting the U.S. dollar as the universal medium of exchange. The stock market collapse made its 1929 predecessor look like a boom year.

Shrecker waited anxiously as crews punched through the debris. A large rig was erected to drill an exploratory hole into the vault. Days later a camera was lowered into the chamber. The entire lower vault was covered by a layer of water. It was impossible to assess what was missing. The room would have to be drained before anything could be recovered or inventoried.

By week's end, the value of U.S. currency fell to twenty-seven cents on the dollar. Housewives were unable to buy food. The value of the dollar changed so rapidly, that premiums were demanded before paychecks could be cashed. The cost of gasoline rose to nearly twenty dollars per gallon by the end of that first week. Then the supply began to dry up altogether.

Numerous financial experts including the head of the Federal Reserve Bank spoke at length on TV. They tried to convince the American people that the dollar was not backed by gold. Its value, they said, was solely determined by public confidence and the strength of the economy. This revelation did not help Shrecker's cause. And the American people didn't buy into it. Neither did the business community or foreign markets. Food riots became commonplace. Crowds numbering in the hundreds of thousands protested in the streets. America was grinding to a halt.

It was unclear to Americans who had really attacked the Federal Reserve Bank. Accusations and counter-accusations ran rampant. With only days left before the election, one thing became certain; Shrecker's days as President were numbered. The crisis peaked when a massive crowd gathered in Times Square during a Democratic campaign sweep through the Northeast. This was considered sacred and safe liberal turf. The crowd knew President Shrecker was inside giving a news conference when someone took up the chant—Ramsey! Ramsey! Ramsey! Like a bolt of lightning it flashed through the crowd. Only a few faces displayed disgust as the tens of thousands took up the cry. Television cameras moved into the streets covering the spontaneous eruption.

The mayor went outside and begged the crowd to exercise restraint. "Please, go home before this turns ugly. Please go home."

Someone threw a bottle; a store window broke. Over the next several hours, crowds raged through the streets of Manhattan, Brooklyn, the Bronx and Queens. They smashed store fronts, attacking anyone who could pass as a Muslim. Even innocent Indians wearing turbans became unfortunate targets. The body count rose dramatically as police were unable to control the crowd. Many blue-clad officers only looked on. Others disappeared or failed to respond to dispatchers' calls.

The offices of *The New York Times* were ransacked as citizens turned their pent-up rage on the staff of life of American liberalism. Armed guards abandoned the local ACLU offices as hundreds of enraged New Yorkers trashed their premises.

A company of Nigerian soldiers was brought in to guard the United Nations building. The crowd pelted them with rocks and bottles. Their commander panicked, and ordered them to fire into the crowd. News cameras caught this and flashed it around the country before government censorship could set in. With the country being under martial law, normal protections guaranteed by the Constitution were suspended. Shrecker called for more troops in all of the major cities.

U.S. forces stationed at nearby Fort Dix were hastily brought in to augment the New York Police Department. A youthful and frightened Second Lieutenant ordered his men to fire into a crowd of rioters. They refused! When he drew his pistol and aimed it into the mob, one of his own men shot him dead.

Back at the United Nations Building, the Nigerians had retreated within it, still firing sporadically into the street. Seemingly from nowhere, hundreds of banned hunting rifles, shotguns and handguns appeared in the hands of Americans as they surged through Manhattan. This did not escape Shrecker's attention as he was removed from the top of the building by the Marine helicopter. Compounding an already bad situation with a worse decision, he contacted the Captain of the Destroyer, USS Arleigh Burke (DDG51), lying at anchor in port.

Captain Stone received the President's command. Turn his big gun against the crowd storming the U.N. He called the ship to general quarters. His personal alarm at the realization of the President's order turned into disgust. He was being ordered to fire upon Americans who had already been fired upon by Nigerian troops wearing blue U.N. helmets. His troubled mind could not accept this new reality. Stone figured it was the end of his career and his life as he gave the fateful order. The five-inch Mark 45 gun was swung, not toward the crowd, but upon the United Nations building. Unknowingly, Captain Stone ignited the spark.

Images of Americans being gunned down in the streets by U.N. forces flashed across the country, followed by images of gunfire from the USS Arleigh Burke. This was followed by more photos of the Nigerians surrendering to the crowd.

A horrified Shrecker watched this spectacle from the Pentagon as senior officers looked on in silence. In panic, he passed the order to all base and ship commanders to reaffirm their loyalty to his authority as Commander-in-Chief of the armed forces. Some of these were quick in coming; many weren't. Some never came!

Feeling its own mortality, the Supreme Court hastily met and concluded that Nancy Colton's pardon of Stuart Ramsey was indeed legal. Cheering, servicemen carried him on their shoulders at Camp David. That afternoon he was back in his condominium in Arlington.

The Senate and House jointly went into emergency session. Televised images of hundreds of thousands of Americans chanting—Ramsey! Ramsey! Ramsey! dominated every channel. The blame game was being played out in full. And most of it fell on Shrecker's shoulders.

The insider's world in the nation's capital was growing smaller as fear permeated the ranks of the House and Senate. Then it fractured as dozens, then scores of elected politicians openly disavowed Shrecker's administration. Calls for his resignation rang throughout the land from Washington to the West Coast. Over a hundred separate attacks against U.N. troops had been recorded that previous week by independent militias throughout America. Law enforcement all but refused to even investigate these incidents. Roadside check points for U.N. gun confiscation became untenable and were abandoned. Unless heavily re-enforced, they were too unsafe to maintain. The final crack came when Moroccan U.N. troops fired on rampaging citizens in Kansas City, only forty-eight hours after the Arleigh Burke incident. The Kansas National Guard engaged them in a pitched battle. Soon afterward, the entire Moroccan battalion was taken prisoner.

Vice President Feinberg begged Shrecker to resign and flee the country. In her delusional state of mind, she believed peace could be restored through reason. Shrecker resisted. He consulted his international base of support—the Bilderbergers. That's when he received a startling revelation when they informed him, "You are Shrecker who?"

His support from Base Commanders and Naval Captains began falling like dominoes. The Navy ignored the President's command to take Captain Stone into custody. Shrecker realized his race was run. Following advice from a few diehard supporters, he made hasty preparations and headed for Andrews Air Force Base. That same afternoon he flew to Sweden and asked for political asylum.

That evening Feinberg begged to be sworn in as President. She was unceremoniously shuffled to a sealed room where the party faithful grilled her for hours. Finally, upon threat of impeachment she resigned from the Vice Presidency that evening. Two days before the general election, the Speaker of the House temporarily took control. He would not allow himself to be sworn in as President.

This was the most vulnerable time in America's history. Acting independently, the U.S. Navy made it known that any attack from a foreign power against the U.S. in its weakened condition would be met with massive nuclear retaliation from its missile submarines and aircraft carriers. The rest of the world wisely sat back and watched this drama play out.

The day before the general election, die-hard Democrat politicians, with a sprinkling of ultra, left-wing college administrators and professors held a clandestine meeting under the direction of Senator Edmund Canaday. In a last ditch effort to seize power, he persuaded the assembly that Ramsey had to be killed for the good of the country. Their numbers disillusioned them into thinking they had a mandate. Several of Canaday's colleagues agreed with his assessment.

One present at the meeting kept his silence. Professor Kohn of Georgetown University had been a liberal all his life. He listened with alarm at this transaction. A vociferous firebrand in his earlier years, he realized that deep inside he was not like the rest. Excusing himself, he left the room. Chaos reigned as he considered what he should do. The government was so fragmented there was no longer a chain of command. It would be unproductive to call the FBI directly. They had been flooded with 10,000 calls about various conspiracies. Neither they, nor the CIA or military knew who was in command. Kohn knew one man in the FBI—Mark Obledo. He spent the next two hours trying to contact the agent. It was late afternoon when he finally got Mark's home phone number from a mutual acquaintance.

Mark received the call from Kohn. Frowning as he hung up, he acted like a man paralyzed until Jim spoke and brought him back. "What's going on, Mark?"

"Canaday and some others plan to kill Ramsey. They're going to the President's condo this afternoon. Get your guns; we're outta here!"

"Let's call for backup. I have the number for the Arlington Cemetery Marine Guard," said Jim.

"Do it from the car; let's go!" answered Mark.

———————

Dozens of well-wishers filled the modest sized condo in Arlington: reporters from the *Washington Post*, politicians, military officers, enlisted men, even neighbors. But nobody was armed. Stuart was happy again. Nancy was coming. He just finished speaking to her. She was released from prison that afternoon, and would soon arrive by car.

Ramsey also received a call from a repentant Canaday. He congratulated Stuart, and promised to embrace the anticipated victory tomorrow by the Constitution Party. The Senator asked if he could drop by, say hello and bury the hatchet. He added that he wouldn't be staying long. Though Stuart had no use for this man, he was not petty. The country would have to heal, and come together soon. Canaday was still influential; Ramsey agreed.

One critical element was missing—the Secret Service. No guard detail had been reassigned to him after his sudden release from Camp David. Pandemonium had left the police disorganized too. They were uninformed of his arrival. Stuart Ramsey was unguarded.

Dozens stood in front of the condo waiting for their chance to enter and greet Stuart. Three cars recklessly drove up. Mark Obledo's car was still two blocks away when they saw twelve men emerge from these vehicles. Leaving the car doors open, they advanced toward the front door.

"We're too late!" yelled Mark.

"Damn it! The front door! Hurry!" said Jim.

Mark's car went airborne as it jumped the curb. Four men armed with pistols stood guard out front. Sounds of gunfire came from within the building. Two guards jumped back to avoid the onslaught of our car. They acted unsure of themselves as our car slammed to a stop.

I was in the rear passenger seat as we poured out. Mark leveled his pistol into the nearest man's face and pulled the trigger. He fell, but his nearest companion put two shots into Mark's belly. He collapsed.

Jim came around from the passenger side and dropped a second man. Then he caught a bullet from the one who shot Mark. It entered his arm. Jim returned fire and the man fell dead.

From the rear driver's side, David dropped the fourth one, who stood there in a state of shock.

Jim was the first to reach the door. He was met with another bullet that penetrated his hip. Collapsing, he continued firing and killed his assailant.

David and I rushed inside. We were greeted with screams and a scene of horror. Dozens of bodies lay strewn about. Numerous military officers and NCOs had tried to shield the President. All of these now lay dead or dying. Throughout the room, women and men had thrown themselves to the floor or sought concealment behind furniture. The seven remaining gunmen were moving bodies aside trying to reach Ramsey. Seeing us, they turned and began firing. We pumped bullets into them as fast as we could. Fortunately, our skill with firearms prevailed. We only received minor wounds. Canaday stood closest to President Ramsey's body. My first three rounds entered near his heart. He had the strangest look of surprise. Then he took his last breath and fell. Only two gunmen survived, and though they were severely wounded, both lived to testify later. We paused for a couple seconds and waited expectantly in case more gunmen popped up. There were none.

I made my way through the tangle of blood and bodies until I reached Ramsey. I sank to my knees. Gently cradling his head, I spoke. "Mr. President?" Getting no reply, I looked to David Blevins. "Is he going to make it?"

Blevins moved as rapidly as he could, trying to staunch the flood of blood from Ramsey's chest. Blevins looked back at me silently and shook his head.

"President Ramsey?" I asked again.

He slowly opened his eyes. Not focusing on the people around him, they looked hollow as he stared toward the ceiling.

"Easy, Mr. President! You're going to be alright," I said.

"She's waiting for me."

"Who, Mr. President?"

"The same beautiful angel who came to me in Vietnam, Major Gabriela Rakowski. She came to me again. And led me to the river; she's going to take me across. They're waiting for me over there: Mom, Dad, Bobby, Karen, everybody. They're smiling and waving."

"Don't give up, Mr. President. We need you!"

"Ask Nancy. I must go; I want to go." Ramsey's face went rigid as his eyes continued staring toward Heaven.

Blevins checked his pulse and breath. Then with a single motion from his hand, he closed the President's eyelids. "He passed."

Sounds of approaching clamor on the street reached us as we waited patiently inside. Outside, newly arrived Marines in full combat dress poured out of their vehicles and charged individually toward the front door with blood thirsty screams. From his crumpled position, Jim Scott rose to his knees and held up his FBI badge for them to see. He yelled as they bypassed him at the door, "Don't shoot! They're ours." The Marines lowered their weapons as we tossed our guns aside. With his left arm hanging limp and dripping blood, Jim Scott, slowly rose to his feet and hobbled until he stood over Ramsey's body. "Is he finished?"

"Yes," I answered.

"Colton will be here soon," answered Jim. "We'll try to delay his movement for a few minutes. She will want to see him."

The President's body was shrouded as he was slowly being wheeled toward the ambulance. We waited beside Mark Obledo as a medic tended his wound. When she arrived,

Nancy Colton was still in her prison attire. She flew out of the limo and ran toward us. "Where is he?" she screamed.

We couldn't speak. Jim looked toward the gurney. With a cry more reminiscent of a banshee than a woman, she shrieked. Nancy ran to his side and ripped away the shroud. Wailing, she buried her head in his blood-stained chest.

President Ramsey's body lay in state inside the Capitol Rotunda on Election Day in 2012. Hostilities nationwide ceased as the nation mourned. A record turnout was recorded though many had no way to get to the polls. An emergency Congressional Commission was convened which delivered its demand to the U.N. It was understood that all U.N. troops would begin making an immediate departure from our shores. The President would be interred in Arlington Cemetery two days later.

The Republic

The election of 2012 was chaotic and left the country in shambles as Stuart Ramsey, deceased, was elected President as the first write-in candidate in history. In light of public hostility, the Supreme Court attempted to save itself by throwing out Nancy Colton's impeachment. The House of Representatives followed this by electing her to the presidency. With her administration began the first U.S. Government since before World War II to return to the ideals of George Washington and the founding fathers.

There were no paybacks or blood reprisals against those radical liberals who had sought destruction of the Constitution and America's enslavement by the United Nations. Radical liberalism was allowed to survive; anything less would have undermined the principles of the Republic.

But after the Pandemonium of 2012 they remained emasculated. No longer would they be allowed to indoctrinate the young or control the air waves. No longer would their judicial appointments pervert common sense and written law. They still congregated, ranting and raving, whenever they could find one of their own choirs to preach to. And they still cried that they were victims of Fascism while exercising their rights to free speech, the press and peaceful assembly. It was a curious thing though; few had ever worn the uniform of their country or done a decent day's work with their hands.

The tyranny of the Supreme Court was finally broken. With a new Amendment to the Constitution, these judges were elected for six year terms, one from each of nine national judicial districts. No longer were nine old men and women immune to removal from office. No longer were they unaccountable for their actions. No longer could they rule by decree. No longer were they permitted to rule on matters of legal principle, only on established law. Federal Judges were also elected. And no longer would these offices be mere prizes distributed in a partisan manner by the elected president of whatever party was in office.

America continued to be a nation of immigrants, legal immigrants. The Constitution was also amended to drop the anchor baby provision. Children of illegal immigrants were no longer automatically citizens if born on U.S. soil. Strict penalties were imposed and enforced upon illegal aliens from any country.

First and Second Amendment rights were reaffirmed by a stronger and newer Amendment to the Constitution.

The power of the liberal media was broken forever after unlimited licensing qualified dozens of new tele-broadcasting companies. The big three, ABC, CBS and NBC became miniscule in comparison to their former operations. No one philosophy dominated the air waves. Everyone, even liberals, could now choose their own source of information from the plethora of available networks.

Nancy Colton easily won reelection in 2016. By the last year of her second term, government revenues exceeded expenditures. America regained her ascendancy as the economic giant of the world. Life was by no means perfect. New problems always loomed ahead in the re-established Republic of the United States of America. But, slowly at first, and then with greater rapidity, the quality of life improved in the coming years. America was not paradise on Earth; it never would be. But it was infinitely better than that future the enemies of the Republic had sought.

The pall of the ACLU was finally broken until it became a term of schoolyard derision to call another kid: "ACLU."

A one strike Federal law protected women and children from child molesters and rapists after which they faced lifetime incarceration. Homosexuals retreated back into the closet where they continued doing whatever they do to each other. Muller's bill permitting them to marry was rescinded and a new law stipulated that marriage could only take place between a man and a woman. No longer did school texts and children's books push acceptance of the gay lifestyle. There was no Department of Education to promote it; this branch of the executive having been eliminated during Nancy's first term. Deterred by strict prison sentences, homosexuals seldom molested underage children, thereby losing a major source of recruitment into their lifestyle.

The races grew steadily more tolerant of each other as everyone learned to rise by his or her own abilities without using color as either a tool or a matter of privilege. Affirmative action soon joined segregation as words belonging to other, nearly forgotten eras. The foolish legislation enacted by Muller was rescinded.

An anti-ballistic defense system shielded America from nuclear annihilation. Radical Islam began to fall apart after President Colton announced that any further attack from a Muslim source would result in a nuclear strike against Mecca and Medina. This reigned in the mullahs. They knew the loss of these crucial sites would cause the entire collapse of Islam, and eliminate their hold over the masses. The second strike came when her energy policy freed the U.S. from imported oil. With its plummeting price, fundamentalist Islamic regimes began to collapse.

The American people were no longer subordinate to the interests of international corporations whose only loyalty was to profit. No longer could these corporations ignore national boundaries, escape taxes and expand their profits at the expense of working men and women.

After her second term, Nancy was elected as the Supreme Court Justice from the Northeast Judicial District. Subsequently reelected, she became and remained Chief Justice until her retirement in the early 2030s. It was often believed that she was the mysterious woman in black who placed flowers on the grave of President Stuart Ramsey.

After the great Pandemonium in 2012, the surviving Patriots made their transition back into normal society. Their fates along with other key figures in this narrative were recorded as follows:

JIM SCOTT: Nancy Colton appointed him to head the FBI, a position which he held until retirement. He married Elaine and they had three children together. He successfully suppressed further investigation of the Patriots. Many files of incriminating evidence came up missing during the reformation of the Bureau. He gathered memoirs from each of the surviving Patriots. These papers were placed in a legal trust and not released for publication until the last of them, including him, had died.

MARTIN RAGGIO: Was never identified as a member of the Patriots. He returned to private life. Four years later he died in a motorcycle accident on Highway 341 outside of Virginia City near Mt. Davidson in Nevada.

RICHARD TAYLOR: Like Marty and David, had never been identified as a member of the Patriots. This was a fact he would carry to his deathbed, where he finally confessed it to his four children. Returning to his financial roots, he quickly became the head of a major bank. During Nancy's second term, he received her appointment as head the Federal Reserve System. He remained in this capacity until retirement many years later.

DAVID BLEVINS: Received a presidential pardon for his prior gun conviction which had originally sent him to prison. Reentering his chosen profession, he retired as a respected dermatologist many years later while living in Elko, Nevada.

HAROLD WISER: Though his was the third proven set of DNA in George Scales' Bible, he was never apprehended or brought to trial. Jim Scott was able to supply him with a new identity and supporting documentation so he could work in his chosen field. Utilizing his skills, he was able to make big money in the mining industry. After retirement, he almost disappeared from view, though occasionally was reported seen in various bars throughout Costa Rica.

JOSHUA'S SURVIVING SONS: Returned to Montana. The elder, Matthew, followed in his father's footsteps and became a rancher. The youngest, John, later became Governor of the State of Montana.

MARK OBLEDO: Was despondent from the debilitating wound which left him crippled from the gunfight on the day of President Ramsey's death. He later attempted suicide. With the love and support of his wife Lupe, and guidance from Professor Kohn, he resurrected his confidence, acquired a Ph.D. in American History and became an instructor at Georgetown University.

JOE FRIOU: Dried out and resumed life as a crab fisherman. His wife Jenny, haunted with the horror of Marie's death, was institutionalized later in life. Joe visited her every week until she died many years later.

THE BILLIOU BROTHERS: Armand achieved success as head of security for a large Indian Casino in the coming years. His brother, Deon, died in Angola prison, Louisiana, many years later after killing another man in a bar room brawl.

THE DECEASED: In the years before his untimely death, Marty and other survivors erected stones over empty graves; one was placed next to Yoneko Morrison in Modesto for Ray; another for Joshua next to his wife Sarah in Montana; two more next to Joshua and Sarah for their sons, Mark and Luke; and one in the family plot belonging to his daughter, for George Scales. These simple stones were engraved with their names, vital statistics and the inscription "For the Republic."

CARL SHRECKER: Was granted political asylum in Sweden. The U.S. did not press for his extradition. There he planned to write his memoirs while living in seclusion. Years later, after contracting AIDS from numerous homosexual encounters, he committed suicide with a handgun, the like of which he had tried to ban.

GEORGE TAUROS: Retreated in seclusion to his private island near Greece. Other than occasionally being seen at European jet set parties, he was seldom heard from again. His daughter Athena inherited most of his fortune, making her the richest woman and fourth richest person in the world.

"FOR THE REPUBLIC"

About the Author

Lee Cross, a graduate of California State College, is a retired locomotive engineer for the Southern Pacific Railroad, and a historian. He lives in Sparks, Nevada with his wife and two daughters.

Other books by Lee Cross:
Twelve Dreams of Laima
A Far Place in Time

Printed in the United States
121363LV00004B/14/P